HEALING GRACE

A NOVEL

Lisa J. Lickel

Fox Ridge Publishing

Healing Grace © 2016 by Lisa J. Lickel

Fox Ridge Publishing

Edited by Anne Duguid
Copyedited by Greta Gunselman
Layout and Book Production by Lea Schizas and Lisa J Lickel

Print ISBN-13: 978-1490366647
ISBN-10: 1490366644
eBook ISBN: 978-1-77127-305-3
Production by MuseItUp Publishing
Previously published by Zumaya Publications, 2009

*For Lane, Jane, Ryan, and Matt—
family is everything.*

Acknowledgements

My thanks again to early readers, and my friends in the medical and family court and legal communities who contributed to the original story. I'm grateful to Lea Schizas for the opportunity to tell this story again in a way I can be proud of, with the help of ever-faithful Annie Duguid and Greta Gunselman. Thank you.

Chapter One

Grace Runyon paused in the doorway of the little house. She listened to the real estate agent drive away with a little zip and a crunch of the gravel drive and felt a moment's panic.

"Not buyer's remorse at this stage of the game, my good woman." She marched inside, carrying two overloaded paper bags of supplies from the convenience mart. "And stop talking to yourself."

The real estate lady had checked the lights to make sure the local electric company in tiny East Bay, Michigan had "turned her on"—her words. Grace's responding chuckle came out like a zebra snort, one that smelled lion and was trying to warn the herd.

"You'll be all right," the plump, business-like woman reassured her before she left. "It's a ways out of town, but not too far, and the neighbors are good people." She looked down at the drive and stirred some gravel with her brown patent pump. "In fact, this place used to belong to one of the brothers next door."

She pressed a card into Grace's limp hand. "Now, here's my card. You just call any time."

One of the brothers? Not information pertinent to the deed, she hoped.

Grace had merely glanced at the place before signing the papers yesterday. "The house hasn't been opened in a number of months. The last occupant was ill," the agent said. "I can give you the name of a good cleaning crew."

"A little dirt doesn't scare me. I can handle it," she'd blithely replied.

Today, in the sparse rays of early spring through fly-specked windows, she wondered if she'd been a little hasty. The dusty, braided rug did not look like an inviting place to set down the sacks she toted in from her green Subaru.

Deep, calming breaths read the story of the place: sickness and neglect hovered almost tangibly. Cobwebs, glittering dust motes. Dangerously lopsided drapes.

A lonely pile of toys, a car and some plastic figures she didn't recognize huddled beneath a cobwebby weight bench in the corner near the open stairway.

Passing through an opening across the long, narrow room, she found herself in the kitchen—a sad, neglected kitchen—and definitely not the heart of this home. She set the bags on the table and dumped her purse on a chair and turning slowly. What made her crazy enough to buy this house?

"Who paints a kitchen ice-green? And what's up with the grinning daisies? Honestly."

Her Tennessee kitchen had been painted a cheerful yellow and kept as spotless as her exam room at the clinic.

Something rustled in the cupboards. Hopefully only mice. She sighed and picked up two forks and a bent serving spoon that had been left on the kitchen table. Flotsam, napkin bits, and nut shells of some kind decorated the cracked and scorched ancient linoleum countertops.

She opened one of the packages of cheap paper towels she'd purchased and used one to gingerly swipe away attached spider webs. With a grimace she quickly thrust the wad into a trash bag and cinched it with a zip tie. *You wish it was that easy to erase your past, don't you? Created a web of a mess. Ran—right from the funeral. Who's left to clean up after you?*

Grace blinked and twisted the porcelain handle of the tap. Warm orange gunk gurgled out and spewed thickly around the stained sink bowl. At least it didn't smell bad. She cheered when it soon cleared up.

"Call me easily pleased. And, seriously, stop talking to yourself."

She pulled a pad of paper from her leather handbag and toured the one and a half story cottage, making notes of the supplies she needed. Clean first, then patch. Definitely paint. And figure out some furniture.

Something to sleep on. "Do I even have a hammer? Talk about starting from scratch."

Putting together a whole new life after everything she'd been through was risky. She wasn't exactly hiding, but neither did she care to let anyone know where to find her. Yet. In good time. When the wounds weren't so fresh and raw; when the wonder of her failure faded from their memories. Jonathan had been a good man. He hadn't deserved his fate.

Her heart ached for him, for what they'd lost, even though he'd been dying for a long time. Losing him was more of a release.

Still, they blamed her. And rightfully so. So she gave them what they wanted. Her absence.

Time for a normal life, remember?

A good night's sleep will do wonders.

By the time the sun faded, Grace had exhausted herself. Scrubbing the kitchen and a cubby of a room behind it she'd claim for her own took buckets of hot water and a pair of neon-yellow rubber gloves, but at least she'd have a clean spot to lay her mattress and sleeping bag. Too tired to eat, she'd stretched herself out and groaned. Thirty-five-year-olds should not be this out of shape.

The room seemed to whirl in a nauseating kaleidoscopic frenzy. No! She wasn't ready to think about it. Not yet. When she focused again, she stood in bright daylight, looking down into the newly dug hole. Without looking up she knew they were there, standing around her and staring, accusing.

"Your fault! You let this happen! You let him die when you should have saved him!"

"I wanted to!" God knows she wanted to save Jonathan. "He was the one—he told me not to try again." At first, she'd tried to help. Of course she did. He was all she had left. Everyone needed him. Everyone loved him. But it had hurt so much when she touched him. She hadn't complained, but after that second time when they had to revive her in the ER, shocked out of her ability to feel anything, Jonathan made her go home. Alone. She'd been more afraid of that than the pain.

She drifted into the nightmare again. Jonathan's father had his back to her. As she watched, they all, one by one, turned their backs until only Lena, her best friend, was left. "Please, Lena, not you too!"

Running away over the clipped grass of the cemetery seemed the smartest thing she could do. Run, run! Why couldn't she get anywhere? Her high heels stuck in the lawn and she couldn't pull free.

Grace reached automatically for the warmth that was no longer there anchoring the other side of the bed. She forced her eyes open against the sleep-tears that nearly welded them shut. The blackness of the room calmed her frantic breathing. She lay still a moment, stars from smacking her head against the wooden floor buzzing like angry lightning bugs. She pushed the tangled sleeping bag from her legs and got to her knees, willing her legs to hold her, her ankles to be strong. She stood. So much for sleep tonight, the first in her new home. If she had to be alone now, at least it was amongst strangers who didn't know what she'd done.

* * * *

By the third day and the fifth trip into town, Grace decided to treat herself to a side trip. She had passed often enough the sweet chalet-style building that housed the local library. Time to stop in.

"So, you've taken over the Marshall house? It's an afterthought—you know—a whad'ya call it, mother-in-law's cottage? Built on the edge of a big apple orchard," Marie Richards, the town librarian, told her when she went to apply for a card. "The Marshalls, now, they did real well. Put this town on the map, you know. Keep us alive these days through the co-op."

Grace nodded and smiled as if she knew what the woman was chatting about. The librarian went on to tell her that the property edged East Bay, and was not actually in the village limits. The apple trees had been torn out and not replanted.

Uh-huh, well, there was something Grace could do on rainy days—dig up local history. Something new to learn, instead of the almost intuitive understanding that came with being raised in Woodside, where their story was almost like an extra rib or a twenty-fifth vertebrae. "Thanks, Marie, bye now." Next errand.

The local resale shop proved to be a blessing filling in for her missing wardrobe and no one there said a thing when she went back three days in a row, modeling the former day's purchase. Casual clothes…something she'd found grimly amusing for her new life of leisure. Her beautiful suits and silk dinner dresses would be so out of place here; running away as she had might have been a blessing in disguise, if she wanted to try to fit in. She certainly had no need of her uniforms. She'd missed the nice leather recliner set she and Jonathan had purchased for the family room, though. Could she stomach buying something others had used, touched with their germy hands, mite-infiltrated clothing, infested pets? Maybe slipcovers for a sofa and some chairs would be all right. She could use some dishes instead of paper plates.

Service for one.

* * * *

On Saturday Grace was so intent on brushing cobwebs down from the high ceilings she didn't notice company coming until pounding on the front door rattled the pane. She screeched and nearly tumbled off the kitchen chair. A peek through wavy glass revealed her visitors: a delegation of two.

"One and a half," she amended as she pulled off the threadbare tee shirt covering her hair. She cautiously opened the oak front door to a man and a small boy. "Good afternoon."

The man was very tall, black-haired, and comic book gaunt. He leaned on one crutch and stared through narrowed eyes, frowning, as though he had not expected to see her. A little boy held a pillowcase with something lumpy inside and the other hand of the man. She thought she recognized them from the day at the bank when she went to sign the closing papers for the house. She had been surprised to find no one besides the real estate agent and the bank's vice president at the meeting. The former owners had not been able to stay and meet her, but everything was in order, she was told.

The man cleared his throat and spoke at last, breathlessly. "I—we—wanted to see that you were all right," he said, glancing down at the child and then back at her face.

"Yes, thank you, I'm fine. Last occupants apparently left in a hurry," she replied.

"Um, right. I guess the place is a mess. If you need help with anything…" His voice fell away. Grace guessed the "you can call me" would be meaningless, and not just to her. His sallow face paled. Perspiration trickled down his temple, even though the air was cool. His left arm and leg started to quiver. Sweat rolled past the startling white rictus of a scar, along the premature age line around his eyes, and dripped down his jaw onto his faded navy shirt labeled "Sleeping Bear Dunes."

Grace slumped against the doorframe, breathing shallowly, trying not to scream or burst into tears. God's sense of humor escaped her. Why did he insist on making her the butt of a cosmic joke? The last few days had only been a calm moment in the midst of a virtual hurricane. *This man,* screamed in her inner ear; *This is why I brought you here. For your touch.*

She willed the voice into silence and shuttered her heart. *No.*

Grace waited on the porch until the silence became uncomfortable.

"Are you all right, ma'am?"

"Yes." The word came out more clipped than she'd intended; ice instead of pleasant. "How may I help you?" As she spoke, she blinked away the thought of his eyes echoing the color of the Morning Glory pool at Yellowstone. Jonathan's eyes had been a mossy brown. Grace looked down at the child. He stood behind the man's legs, clutching the bag to his chin, and peeked back at her, anxiety creasing his forehead.

Really, God? Is it necessary to punish me this way? Grace bit the inside of her cheek so hard she tasted sweet rust. But she would not, not, *not,* let anything touch her heart. Ever again.

The man urged the child forward.

"Give Mrs., ah, Mrs. …"

"Runyon."

"…Runyon the bread."

A miniature grubby hand thrust the pillowcase in Grace's direction.

"Good job, Eds. I'm Ted Marshall," he said, apparently recalling they had not exchanged names. "And this is my son, Eddy."

Eddy stuck his head sideways from around the side of his father, eyed her solemnly, and then disappeared again.

Grace took the bundle. "Nice to meet you both. I'm Grace Runyon." She did not offer to shake hands. Although running away from Woodside more than likely lessened the strength of the gift, she wasn't taking chances. Besides, it was strictly forbidden to let strangers know what happened there. "Thank you for your thoughtfulness."

"I—can—work a bread—machine." He wobbled and reached a hand out to steady himself against the jamb.

She reached out anyway, stopping just short when he held up the same hand to ward her off. "I'm all right. Just give me a second."

"Um, thank you, Mr. Marshall, and Eddy, for the bread. Would you like to come in and sit for a minute?" The case felt cozy in her hand, warm from the fresh-baked loaf and the child's hand.

"Ted. Call me Ted. We have to get back." He straightened using the crutch. "I have an appointment, but thanks anyway. We're over there"—he indicated a hedge of tall scraggly bushes— "on the other side. At the house." They turned and clumped across the gray-green, cupped porch boards. Eddy looked back through the open door. Grace followed his gaze to the abandoned toys piled in the middle of the room. He turned and bent to grasp his father's crutch to help him manipulate down the steps.

Ah. "One of the brothers" now made sense. She watched, her mouth pursed. How old was the child? Maybe four? Too young to have to help a parent.

She looked up at the ceiling of the living room, free of webs but showing cracks in the white paint. "I will not, Lord! No! You brought me here for a reason, but not that. Please, not yet… I want to be free for a while! Away from sickness and everyone else's hurt. Let me heal myself, first." Sinking down and slapping the tee shirt against the smooth floorboards, she hunched up her knees. Staring at nothing, she let her forehead rest against her wrists and rocked. *No tears. You promised. No feelings. If you don't feel, you can't hurt.*

A long time later Grace ate dinner, butter melting on the re-warmed slice of bread. She sat at the now shiny chrome kitchen table, occupied with thoughts about her visitors. Ted was obviously the former occupant. Her medical curiosity took over and thrust back the emotion threatening her slim self-control. What was the nature of his illness? He had received some terrible injury, evident in the scar on his head, but was it related to the need for a crutch? Usually a head injury didn't count as "ill" like the real estate lady said.

Well, her neighbors were none of her business. She took her dishes over to the sink and ran some water. Not that sweet little boy with the poignant eyes. Certainly not his enigmatic father. And no way was she interested in knowing where Eddy's mother was. If she didn't get to know them better, it would be easier not to care. If she didn't care all that much, she wouldn't feel obligated to help them. If she didn't try to help them, she wouldn't fail. If she never had to fail, she couldn't be hurt by it. If she wasn't hurt, she'd win. If she beat the emotion game, maybe someday she could blend in here, her new home, and nothing could drive her away.

When she accidentally splashed suds on the wall next to the sink, she picked at a bubbling daisy. Underneath, the walls had once been sunny yellow.

Chapter Two

Grace was not surprised to find Eddy behind the polite ring of the doorbell at seven thirty the next morning. She offered the soulful, long-lashed child toast and jam, some of her tea, a share of the morning paper, which he declined with a swift shake of his silken head, and a freshly washed toy from the box near the door.

He drove the beat-up blue police car across the living room floor, making wonderful dinging and honking sounds. "I'm glad the rug is gone. Now we can drive straight." He didn't look up at Grace, too rapt with his play.

"It was dirty and mousy. I'm trying to clean it up." She smiled at his antics while she sorted through some laundry. "But I may have to throw it away."

"We always had mouses. Trigger helped clean 'em up."

"Trigger?" Grace looked back from the hall where she was headed with a stack of folded towels.

"My kitty. Daddy said she was fast on the draw!" At this, he did look up at her, smiling wide, big-eyed and dimpled, innocent as sunrise. He let go of the car and came toward her. She stiffened. Memories of another little boy threatened to overwhelm her.

Peace, Grace, peace. It was long ago. You don't have to go there again. You cried enough back then.

"Can I see my room?" he asked, smile gone.

She was probably scaring the poor kid to death. Forcing a smile back on her face, she said, "Sure! Which one?" and followed him down the hallway alongside the wide staircase she had yet to scrub, to the second door on the left, the one across from the kitchen. It was little-boy-sized with a closet under the staircase that tunneled through the house. Eddy went to sit on the floor in front of a dusty window which looked out on a sorry playhouse in the backyard.

"This is where my bed used to be." His voice cracked and he sniffed. "You don't know where Trigger is, do you?" Fat tears rolled faster and faster down his thin cheeks.

The clump-clump of a heavy tread on the porch steps and a shadow crossing the other window signaled another visitor, saving her from doing more than patting the child on the shoulder before answering the knock.

A different man, an older version of Eddy's father, stood outside.

"I've come to see if Eddy is here."

They both turned at snuffling sounds coming from inside.

"I'm sorry he bothered you." The man made no effort to introduce himself, and Grace was too uncomfortable in his stern presence to demand his name, although she didn't doubt he was Ted's brother, Randy Marshall, the owner of the name on the mailbox next to hers.

"He's not bothering me. He came to visit me earlier. I hope that was all right with his father?"

The man did not rise to her bait. She gave it one more try. "Yes? He is welcome to stay here for a bit, if it would be easier for you."

"No. He knows he no longer lives here. Eddy!"

Grace jerked her head as he called past her into the house. He stood with fists planted firmly on his hips, his expression stony and distant.

This was not a happy person—not at all. Should she let Eddy go with him? "He's not in any trouble, I hope? Or am I?"

A snarky eyebrow raise was his only response. The child came running, picked up his police car and skipped through the door, but not before thanking her with his expression: the faint flash of a dimple and blink of long, black, damp lashes. He did not appear fearful of the man, so she decided the situation was, again, none of her business. It was not her problem to care who watched over her neighbor's son.

* * * *

Grace continued to fold laundry into piles on the coffee table, the easy chair, and the arm of her "new" sofa. These lulling, comforting routine motions of dealing with familiar activities helped ease her into accepting this place as home. She'd tied some brown-striped sheets as slipcovers for a couple of mismatched chairs from her favorite store—the resale shop. She wondered what the local gossips had to say about her. What would they do if they really knew her and what she'd done?

Her simple touches coordinated the furniture well against freshly painted beige walls. Her walls in Tennessee had a touch of gold in the paint, but such formality wouldn't work here. At least the room no longer smelled of cigar smoke, vomit, and mouse urine. Who had smoked the cigars?

The old brown and tan braided wool carpet was sacrificed to the mouse droppings, and with it gone, she'd done her best to clean and wax the narrow planked oak floors. At one time a dog had obviously occupied the place, one which did not always make it outside to do its business. She put an end table over the biggest black stain. The drapes were gone, revealing the beautiful wood casement around the windows. The corner of one window was cracked. How much would it cost to replace the whole thing? Mundane thinking kept the other whispers at bay; the ones that reminded her of her calling, of her purpose in Michigan. She struggled to tune them out with busy work. Exhaustion would quell the dreams. At some point she'd see what kind of work she could do here. Absolutely nothing in the medical field again, though.

A ray of brilliant sun beamed though the low cloud bank at that moment, glancing off the glass on the coffee table and stinging her eyes. She closed them. *No. I told you. No.*

She ached from washing and polishing the sashes and the panes and flexed her shoulders. Think about something else, Grace, girl. Get your mind on anything else but what you'd done before.

Yeah…let's see. Maybe she could offer her services as a professional decorator. She chuckled. There were houses like this in her home town. They came from a kit and were personalized later. Marie had been exceptionally chatty at the library, filling in the gaps about

Ted's grandparents leaving the main house to their daughter and son-in-law's growing family and building this place next door. There were more touches, personal ones, made through the years in wood paneling in the living room and plastered ceilings and light fixtures. Two square rooms on the second floor looked out over the slope-roofed front porch. There was a walk-in pantry behind the kitchen and a miniature bathroom stuffed between it and Eddy's former room.

Grace could not bring herself to take one of the bedrooms upstairs for her own. Ted and the Mrs. must have occupied one of them. Just a feeling, but it was enough to keep her away. Besides, how would she carry furniture all by herself? The cupboards in the kitchen were plentiful for her needs. The former pantry was large enough for a single bed and skinny wave-front bureau.

A week after his initial visit, Eddy's father limped up the walk on her side of the hedge and found her in the yard, puttering in the late afternoon sunshine.

That hedge was not big enough. Maybe she could install a fence? An electric one with…

Neighbors borrowed things, asked questions, offering to help mow the lawn. She could assure him she was fine and send him away…

Surely he didn't need anything. He lived with his brother, didn't he? She had nothing to offer, nothing, nothing, nothing. Please, don't ask me…

"Hello, there. Nice day for a walk," she said when he came within hearing range.

"Hi." Ted settled both hands on top of the single crutch and studied the yard. He shifted feet awkwardly. "I hope you're doing well."

She assured him she was.

"Um, Shelby is in the hospital. They think it might be food poisoning. She's the only sitter Eddy's ever had. I called around but it's such short notice. There's no one else to ask. My brother, Randy, you met him the other day… Well, he's out of town on business. I'd take Eddy along to the clinic, but this is a long test. I don't—"

Then, please, don't. "That's all right. What are neighbors for?" She returned his tense smile while mentally hearing fingernails across a classroom chalk board. "He's welcome to come here for the afternoon.

I'm not—I'm not doing much, anyway. I'm not an ax-murderer or child molester, either, in case you were wondering."

The corners of his eyes did not crinkle, like happy people smile. Too much brotherly love? His skin looked papery. She forced herself to stop her automatic clinical analysis. Should she ask who Shelby was? Folks around here were so familiar with themselves they forgot others didn't know them. Not that she wanted to. Know them.

Ted leaned against a pillar on the porch. "Okay, thanks. And I wasn't wondering. I saw you go into the library. I don't think ax-murderers read much."

He could be very, very wrong, but Grace wasn't about to debate the ridiculous topic. By the time they were done, she wondered if she should have.

After he returned to his side of the hedge, Grace stalked into the house, slammed and locked the door, crawled into bed and held her stomach until she fell asleep.

When he returned the next day with Eddy in tow, he dug in his hip pocket for a slip of paper, which he held out to her with a shaky hand. "Here's my cell phone number and the number where I'll be if you need anything. I should be back by four thirty if the medi-van service is available. Eddy will eat anything you give him. He's a good kid, generally."

The subject of their discussion gave her a saucy grin and transferred his grip from Ted's hand to hers.

Yeah, right, sure.

Grace wondered about the reliability of a shared ride service. Should she offer to drive him? She had not gotten a landline yet, either, and most likely wouldn't. Her cell phone had disappeared sometime during the trip here and she hadn't taken the time to figure out something new. She did not take the slip of paper from Ted. "I don't have any way of reaching you."

His brows went up and he immediately held out his phone. "Well, why don't you take this phone, then? The number for the doctor is plugged in here."

She took it from him, holding it between her thumb and forefinger as if it might bite. He quickly showed her how to use it and then said, with a grin, Eddy could help her if she forgot. Eddy held on to her hand with a two-fisted grip. He gave her a radiant look when his father mentioned his phone-use expertise.

Despite her declaration the child was welcome, Grace felt wholly incompetent to care for a boy this age for more than a fifteen-minute checkup. She watched Ted lean down to hug his son and give last-minute admonishments. Ted wore a polo shirt and cargo shorts today. His left arm trembled even more than when they first met. She stoppered her professional curiosity once again before meeting his skeptical look. Maybe someday she could ask what had happened, but not yet.

Chanting internally "act normal, be normal, you deserve a normal life after all you've been through," she watched Eddy wave his father off to the waiting cab, apparently unconcerned he was being left in the care of a virtual stranger. Maybe the fact that he had lived here once made a difference. Maybe the child was simply a happy-go-lucky kid, used to being left in the care of others. Like the mysterious Shelby.

It had been so long…so long since she'd been alone with a little boy. What would they do all day?

Eddy took care of that fear for the first two hours as he played on the living room floor while a radio scratched out a quiet generic piano station in the background. He didn't seem to mind the lack of television and she promised they would look in the playhouse later after her laundry was put away.

Grace put the folded towels in the bathroom cupboard and followed him into her room with a pile of things held in both arms. She had scrubbed the walls and ceiling and removed most of the shelves. She was still mulling a choice of wallpaper to cover the worst of the patched places.

Eddy looked about with healthy awe from the threshold, lips pressed and hands behind his back. "This door was always closed. I peeked once when I was a little kid," he whispered.

Grace beckoned to him. "You can come in, you know."

He tiptoed up to her. "There were big boxes all over and it was cold."

The door had been closed, hmm? Every corner of the house held some secret to pique her curiosity. But it was none of her business what had happened to Ted's wife and nothing would make her ask the little boy where his mother was.

With efficient, practiced motions she remade her frameless bed. "Thank you, Lord, for my dryer," she muttered under her breath as the fresh grass and sunshine smell billowed up at her.

"What, Grace?" Eddy made faces at himself in her rusty bureau mirror. "What did you say?"

"Nothing, sweetie. Let's go look at the playhouse."

"Yippeee!" Eddy dodged outside past her.

The little house was filthy inside, strewn with leaves, and dead bugs of every type littering the floor. Chewed fragments of white plastic surrounded a play stove and refrigerator like snow, mixed with the typical brown pellets of mouse droppings and a suspicious pile of shredded newspaper and grass in a corner. It looked long abandoned.

"Did you ever play in here?"

"Uncle Randy said no, not even when we lived here. He told Daddy to keep me out. It was too dangerous."

"Uncle Randy?"

"Where we live now."

So, the stern man from yesterday was Randy, as she had thought. Curiosity got the upper hand of her vow not to care. Caring wasn't the same as knowing helpful information. Like who else might be coming around the hedge this summer. "Hmm…Where are, ah, Uncle Randy's kids, now—your cousins?"

"Just one cousins."

"Oh? Is your cousin a boy or a girl?"

"Boy," Eddy replied, swiping his fingers along a thick web in a window sill.

Twenty questions time. *How hard do I pump a neighbor's child for information and still not get too involved with the people here? Okay*—one more.

"Does your cousin live around here?"

Eddy squinted, put a hand on his chin and then crossed his arms in obvious imitation of some adult. Grace kept her smile in check.

"No, I don't think so. Jimmy only comes in the summer. I don't like him. He's lots bigger than me. He punches hard."

What kind of woman had spent enough time with him to bear his child? He was so…surly. And gruff.

She decided that was enough interrogation about the Marshalls for now and tuned belatedly back into Eddy's conversation.

"But this is your house now, right, Grace? You can let me play here if you want to, right?"

"It needs quite a lot of fixing up. Tell you what. If you help clean it up a little, we can see if your Uncle Randy is right about it being too dangerous or not. Then, only if there's nothing wrong, you can play in here when I say it's okay."

The little guy seemed satisfied with her cautious answer.

They were still outside when Ted returned from his appointment. Hazy sunshine beat down, promising a change in weather. Spring was passing on into full summer and the grass needed to be cut again.

Ted's frown as he made his way across the lawn, skirting the patch of bare earth she had begun to dig for a late flowerbed, made her wonder what was up.

Eddy threw down his little shovel and shouted, "Daddy! Grace says the playhouse is hers now, so I can play in it!"

Out of the mouths…he would get her into trouble even in his innocence. She swiftly cut in. "That's not quite it, you know, Eddy. I said we'd clean it up and see if it was safe first, then ask your dad. Remember?"

Well, not the ask your dad part. She studied Ted whose brow still furrowed. Lines etched the sides of his wide mouth. Her heart hiccupped.

"We'll talk it over, son. Uncle Randy's home. Why don't you go over there now?"

Eddy galloped across the yard to the other side of the overgrown lilac and yew tree fence row. Ted leaned on a cane that replaced the crutch today. He grimaced and cranked his neck sideways to look at her, wavy black hair falling across his eyes. He reached trembling fingers to brush it back.

Grace pushed away the desire to reach out and feel the stubble on his cheek, to soothe the line of pain along the bridge of his nose, between his brows, the clenched jaw, to massage the muscles with her tingling touch. She tightened her grip on the handle of the old splay-brushed broom she had been using to sweep out the playhouse, feeling drained.

"I have to have another MRI tomorrow," he said. "Shelby isn't able to keep Eddy yet… I hate imposing like this, but, could you…"

"Yes," she said shortly. "Eddy may stay here with me tomorrow." Pity had come and staked a claim. More than a needle stick, more than stitches, more than…say it…*cancer*…this relationship was going to hurt. Her soul already bruised deeper every time Eddy touched her, spoke to her, turned his head at her like…

She shook her head to dislodge the pain-filled memory. Sean was gone.

At least Ted didn't share any information about his condition with her. She could stand not knowing his diagnosis a little longer. The longer it took to learn, the longer it would be before that urge to touch him, that urge to care, that urge to try to help would overtake her good sense. When she failed, she'd have to run again, and she'd barely gotten settled. "What time?"

"Would seven be too early?"

"No. Is there something I should know about this Shelby you keep mentioning? Is she Eddy's mother?"

"Oh! No, no. Eddy's mother is… No, she's Eddy's regular babysitter. Childcare provider. She has a small business in town taking care of a few kids. She's known Eddy since he was born. She's really good with children. Especially since she can't have any of her own. Well, she tried… Sorry. She's just sick." He frowned. "Eddy's mother…she's not in the picture. Never really has been. We're divorced. I have full custody. I don't think what Shelby has is contagious, if that's what you're worried about."

"The thought crossed my mind."

Ted shifted his feet and took a step with his cane. "Uh, well, I can't be taking advantage of you, Mrs. Runyon. I'd like to pay—"

"I don't want to talk about it now." Grace turned on her heel and stomped back into her house as loudly as her tennis shoes would allow. Money would never be a reason to do anything. Never had been, never would be. If she ever used her gift again, it would be like an emotionless business exchange, a fair deal, and not a promise she would make it all go away. If she agreed to help someone it would be because she could, not because she had to. And she didn't have to help anyone here.

But maybe she wanted to.

She could choose to—as long as it was on her terms, doing what she *wanted* to.

* * * *

She'd resorted to an over-the-counter decongestant to ward away the nightmares when chamomile and eucalyptus failed to calm her enough at bedtime. Still, memories of Woodside sifted through her, nostalgic as the scent of the tea roses that climbed her mother's trellises. They'd brewed rose hip tea together after rounds at the hospital, when she came to pick up the baby. Her family had never lived anywhere else. Besides college, the only other house in which she'd lived was with Jonathan, after the wedding. By this time in late April the dogwood and redbuds in the yard were nearly done blooming and summer established. Everything about Michigan was foreign to her, the clothes she wore, the musty scent of the box hedge, and the grass outside. The sandy soil and the humidity. She felt out of sync, like hearing a steam whistle seconds after seeing the release. How long could she stay here, how long could this be home before she'd ruin it and have to leave?

She missed her parents, and Jonathan's parents, too, despite what she'd done and Jonathan's father's reaction. They had practiced hospitality so beautifully. Their hotel had always brimmed with return guests.

"Elizabeth," Grace whispered. "You were so kind, so helpful. Thank you for understanding," she said into the dark. "You always treated me like a daughter." Thinking of her mother-in-law left her less haunted. Maybe tonight wouldn't be so bad. She could choose, she reminded herself. She wasn't obligated to act her role in society, as she'd been in Woodside.

Back there, when someone needed her, she'd gone automatically, day or night, and loved it. Loved the praise, loved the gush of power that poured through her when she worked.

Had she loved it too much? Had she done her job too well? Maybe that's why losing Jonathan had been such a shock. Not because he'd been her husband, but because she'd never known it was possible she could fail.

Who had she failed? Jonathan? His parents? Herself? God?

But God gave her the gift. Controlled it.

Really?

She pulled back the sheets and snuggled in the smell of outside. Switch gears. Turn off the past and move on. *You're no longer that woman, the one who failed. You came here for a fresh start, and a new life. How are you going to make that work?*

The new mattress and box spring had been a splurge of her resources. Work…earning money to live. Was she ready? She stared at the ceiling, highlighted like a miniature bas relief map of the moon in the glow of the Marshalls' yard light. A crack wiggled out from the corner. What kind of patching material and color of paint should she buy? Did she want shades and curtains for the little window? If she wanted to hide here and yet buy things, she needed to earn cash.

Taking longer blinks, she relaxed.

You know what you can do to earn wages.

She had never needed the little trust fund her parents left her a few years ago. It wasn't a huge amount of money, but would help with renovations. Jonathan's estate was still there, waiting.

It would be so easy, the whispers whooshed around her. Grace turned over and pulled the sheet over her ears.

She had to be careful. Transferring the trust account to a national bank in Cadillac had been easy enough, though it meant renting a post office box.

So?

They could find her, especially after signing the deed. If she stayed here…

Of course I expect to stay. No one from Woodside is going to come here, silly girl.

A long-legged spider lazily spun a messy web in another corner of the room. Grace watched it, exaggerated in the shadow cast by the bathroom night-light she had left burning. As she closed her eyes, she wondered if it signaled she should be busy, too, finding something else to occupy her time. Since she no longer practiced medicine, there had to be something else she could do.

Chapter Three

Ted crossed to her yard late the following afternoon. The long shadow he cast crossed the patch of dirt where Grace arranged pansies and dusty miller plants she purchased the day before.

"Good news!" he called before he reached her.

Grace, expecting a medical report, tilted her head to see his head, dark with a halo of sun. Shelby Brouwer did not have food poisoning after all, he said. Eddy's babysitter was expecting a baby of her own.

"She nearly died the last time, before Thanksgiving last year, and Davy just got a vasectomy." Ted shared the news, animated excitement mingled with concern. Grace reminded herself to keep breathing. Apparently it didn't faze him to confide the most intimate details of his friends' lives to a virtual stranger.

She held up her hand. "Mr. Marshall…"

"Ted."

"Um, Ted, thank you for letting me know about Mrs. Brouwer, but I don't even know her. I'm not sure she'd thank you for sharing her life story—"

"Oh, you'll love Shelby, I know it! She's a gem. She picked us up and got us going again after…" His face clouded as he faltered. Grace was sorry the conversation turned dark. Pregnancy should be a time of joy, not fear. Ted and Eddy weren't the only ones to speak highly of Dr. and Mrs. Brouwer, as Grace had overheard snippets of conversation at the food mart and the gas station when she'd gone to pay, even at the library where a neighbor had picked up some books to deliver to the woman. A high risk pregnancy always made Grace anxious, even when it wasn't her patient.

"Well, I guess you'll want to know why I'm here." His blue eyes almost snared her, and she looked away, disquieted.

"Her doctor said if she has any chance at all of safely having this baby—"

"She has to stay off her feet and get plenty of rest with little excitement," Grace finished for him, knowing well the drill. Ted's eyebrows shot up, but he kept his mouth closed.

She continued. "No boisterous four-year-olds or armfuls of other people's babies to practice her mothering skills on."

"So, then," Ted pleaded, "I don't really know you, but for some reason, you're good with Eddy and he likes you, too. I don't know what your future plans are, but could you help us out, at least for a little while?" He twisted his head to watch his young son poke at the bushes with a long, narrow twig.

It appeared her dilemma of finding company and a little cash was resolved.

"I'll be back tomorrow—is after lunch okay? —with some details. Is there any time that won't work out for you? No? Okay, then. And, Mrs. Runyon, we can't thank you enough."

The gritty, uncomfortable discussion regarding salary took place on Grace's front porch the next day. She decided allowing him dignity was as important as refusing to work for hire; she could always put the money in an account in the child's name. She sighed and tried to pay attention. It was her choice to help or not. If she helped, it was to be on her terms. Maybe this was the job she needed, and it kept her out of the medical field. The exchange of money kept it a business deal. Business was good; it was not personal, and she could take care of the child without getting too emotionally involved.

"Eddy needs care this spring and summer. My brother helps out, but he travels a lot on business and there are days I can't manage him by myself. He is a good kid and I love him with all my heart. I want to do what's best for him. And for him to be around me when I'm not doing so well isn't the best thing for either of us." He pressed his eyes with long fingers.

"Some of the medication and testing wears me out. I still take some work, farm and orchard business consulting, from home, but it's difficult for me to concentrate with Eddy around. So, if you could keep him four days a week?"

"Sure. He can have his meals here. You, too, when you're able," she said, watching him squirm as a spasm worked down his leg. "Do you need—"

"No!" Ted closed his eyes with a grimace and then checked around for Eddy. "I'm sorry." He faced the shiny, painted floorboards of the porch. "I just need help with my son." He sighed and sank to sit on the top step. Grace followed suit.

"Eddy obviously could use some stability, which"—he pointed with the crutch at his leg—"I cannot provide at this time. It's a lot to ask, but you two seemed to hit it off and this is such a bad time for me right now. If you're on the run from the law, could you let me know now and I'll find some other way?"

He smiled at her. She wouldn't say no to Eddy no matter how desperate she got. On the run, maybe; but not from the law. Not from man's law. His little boy scent squeezed her heart whenever she breathed in. She let out the breath she forgot she had taken at Ted's initial outburst. Reaching out her hand to touch him, she remembered and stopped just short of skin to settle on the crutch instead.

"I have limited experience with children Eddy's age." Well, that wasn't a total lie. "You're right, we seem to have some rapport." She grinned as Eddy came whooping around the corner in hot pursuit of Trigger who had come begging at the back door of the house the other day, now it was occupied again. Eddy had taken the cat's reappearance in his stride, setting out her bowl of food and keeping the water filled to the brim as if it was his fault she'd run away.

"I've taken over your son's home," Grace told Ted. "Maybe I don't owe you, as it was for sale, but I feel a little responsible. For now"—she met his stare with what she hoped was a trustworthy expression—"I'd be willing to help you with your child." And if she failed them in any way, or if they hurt her, she'd fall to pieces so microscopic there'd be nothing left.

The discussion concluded with a cell phone, "It's on our plan, unlimited talk and text!" which Grace more or less tried to ignore, much to Ted's amusement. They stood as he got ready to leave.

"Didn't this Woodside of yours have electricity and outside communication? I heard the hills of Tennessee can be backwards sometimes, but honestly, Mrs. Runyon. Not even a cell phone?"

"Call me Grace," she finally invited. "Of course we had power lines and cell towers." She drew herself up to her five feet, six and one-half inch height which still only put her in view of his Adam's apple as he leaned on the crutch. She slumped again. "I simply wanted to take my time about, well, about how to make contact with the outside world. The newspaper here is very good." She dared him to laugh again.

Which he did, of course. "Yeah, the Trib's all right," he said. "But it's not like phoning home."

She tried to halt the natural instinct to wall off the sound of "home," but the defensive shutter slammed anyway. "This is home now," she said, more for herself than for his benefit. Eddy was the only one she'd let in at this point. The little piece of her heart she'd thawed was for him only.

Ted's arm began to spasm again. He gritted his teeth, successfully ending the draining conversation. Grace would not allow herself to confront his pain. She refused to listen to her soul, although this time she could not halt the gut scream that he needed her touch.

Choose! I choose, remember?

She grabbed his shirtsleeve and helped him steer along the sidewalk back through the hedge to his cache of medication in Randy's house.

* * * *

One drowsy afternoon, Eddy asked Grace to take him to visit Shelby, the only mother he had known since his own left him. Eddy did not remember much about her and never spoke of her. What did mothers do with four-year-old sons? Errands? Shopping? Cooking? Playing…putting the pieces of a shattered life together in a new mosaic. She didn't know. She'd never had a chance to know a four-year-old Sean.

She did not intend to be a hermit in East Bay, but she was cautious. She'd never had to worry about making new friends while growing up in Woodside. But how did one go about it when one was all grown up? Reinventing herself in Michigan was both a relief and a challenge.

Shelby turned out to be a practical and forthright woman who didn't hesitate to ask Grace's life history as soon as they made themselves comfortable on the wide veranda, a feature which was a prerequisite of most homes here. Her eyes sparkled with curiosity behind her glasses and as a formerly busy daycare provider she was obviously frustrated at enforced inactivity while she waited for her baby. Grace was amused at her frankness. Shelby reminded her instantly of Lena, her best friend from Tennessee, and another little piece of her heart thawed, completely without her permission.

"So, Grace Runyon." Shelby caressed Eddy's cheek absentmindedly before urging him off to play on the other side of the wraparound porch. "Eds, here, can't stop talking about you. It's nice to finally meet. C'mon and sit down. Where are you from, again?"

"I came from central Tennessee, just a small out of the way town. I lived there my whole life. But my parents had the—they were schoolteachers. We used to travel every other summer around the country." Honesty was always best. She didn't need to sweat the small stuff of remembering what misinformation she might have planted where. She'd never needed to lie, if not telling the whole truth. She'd never betray her people, even if they blamed her for what she'd let happen to Jonathan. This was her new life, and she could make new friends, if she chose to. She could decide how much to let them in.

"I've never been outside of Michigan, except to Canada once for a day trip," Shelby replied. "You don't have much of an accent. I've heard people from the hills, summer visitors you can hardly understand." She shifted a little under a lime green and purple granny-square afghan. Eddy returned, and Grace helped him pour more lemonade. She wondered how her in-laws would have reacted to Michigan ways.

She wondered, too, if Shelby was disappointed in her lack of accent or subtly rooting about for a hole in her story. "Always reading between the lines," Grace's father had teased her. How could she possibly explain her home to these people anyway? The parts she was allowed to tell.

Woodside had been founded seven generations ago. Prominent use of spiritual gifts mentioned in Scripture, like wisdom, hospitality, and kindness, were not considered extraordinary. But the mysteries of faith: miracles and speaking in the tongues of angels were easily misunderstood by outsiders who happened to stumble on the community and mistake its beauty and peace for a quaint tourist spot, like some sort of Amish village, which it was not. They did not have to dress a certain way or refrain from modern day living.

Grace smiled at Shelby and answered her personal observation in a light-hearted way. "Weel, once the tallyvision masheen cum tae town, menny younguns got ta new speak," she intoned in rhythmic deep hill county talk.

Shelby giggled. "I didn't mean to offend you." She moved her hand over her stomach. "The baby's moving. I was never pregnant long enough before to feel that."

Grace went still with the sudden rush of longing and jealousy. She inhaled deep and long and exhaled the hurt. Inhaled again, summoned joy and thankfulness. She'd had her turn. She'd refrained from making any reference to the pregnancy until the other woman brought it up, and now was the time to acknowledge it. "Congratulations. I wish you the best. Ted mentioned about your, well, past troubles."

Shelby nodded, but didn't share any more. "Yes, thanks. So go on with your story."

"I went to college in a large town, traveled some. Sort of cured me of anything remotely hilly." She took a sip of the lemonade. "Mmm, this is so good."

"I've known Ted Marshall all my life and count him as one of my dearest friends," Shelby said. "He doesn't need any more complications in his life right now. Selling his house was the latest blow. You can't blame folks for wanting to know more about you. There are others in town who would love to take care of both Ted and Eddy, so we wondered why Ted would choose a stranger to help him now. I guess familiarity breeds contempt, eh?"

Grace searched her hostess's expression for guile, envious for a moment of her pixie-cut hair.

"It's muggy," she noted, while contemplating a reply. How to respond? A little strand of silvered hair waved up from her shoulder and glittered in the afternoon light. She pulled it out with a little laugh. Honesty works best. To a point.

"I'm not sure what to say, exactly. I've never been in this situation before. I've never lived anywhere else besides when I went to school. I grew up in an old, old community, and we're not exactly progressive. Everyone there knows what to do and does it. There are few strangers. I guess I understand how you feel. I wouldn't know how to trust someone who suddenly appeared out of nowhere, either, and agreed to help me." Grace watched Shelby work out new questions in her mind while she tried to conjure up innocuous details about her former life to share, should she be asked. She didn't have long to wait.

Shelby leaned forward on the settee and set her magnified deep gaze on Grace. "So, what did you do there?"

Chapter Four

Randy's presence sent vibes of distrust and dislike emanating before his shadow turned the corner. Grace appreciated that Randy Marshall might not want to startle her but did he have to just stand there? She continued to apply quick-dry foam to seal cracks in the foundation, probably something he should have done himself before selling the place.

Shelby told her Ted's ex-wife, Jilly, demanded a cash settlement and refused to wait until they worked out a plan to come up with the money. "Tough luck you turned up—at the most inopportune time," her new friend told her last week at her third visit, "cash in hand. Well—not really, I mean."

She wasn't entirely reassured.

"I, of course,"—Shelby had indicated herself with a hand to her chest—"am awfully glad you're here. Especially now,"—the hand went down toward her stomach—"to help with Eddy. He really needs you."

Grace was amazed at the amount of trust she seemed to instill in strangers. Either that, or the people in East Bay were incredibly naïve.

Not Randy, though. He had not been happy about a stranger on his property and made no effort to disguise the fact since the first time they "met" when he came to retrieve Eddy. He gave her the shivers whenever she caught him driving around town in his dark Cougar or staring at her when he picked up his nephew in the afternoons when Ted couldn't come. So, what was he doing here this afternoon, no

Eddy, no invitation?

"Mrs. Runyon." Randy finally rounded the corner and greeted her.

She met the coolness of his tone with a rudeness she would never have guessed she possessed. This was a man she could too easily not care for. He'd never get to her, make her care. Easy. "Yes?" she replied, giving him a glance while she continued with her task. He had yet to introduce himself. A silly, pointless game, though, since she was perfectly aware of his identity, as he was of hers. She knew he traveled frequently for the fruit market co-op. She had not seen him around when Eddy had taken her on a tour of the big house where he lived and the barren fields with their neatly kept but empty outbuildings on the other side of the hedge.

She sprayed another hit of foam and smoothed it with a well-used Popsicle stick before capping the can and wiping her hand on the poor abused tee shirt she continued using as a rag before standing to face him.

"You don't hold with church, Mrs. Runyon?" It was Sunday afternoon, a day which had not escaped Grace's notice. The question was so obviously nosy, personal, and none of his business she bit her lip and took a deep breath and cleared her throat.

"Mr. Marshall," she tried, to see if her voice was still working properly through her anger. *Good.* "Mr. Marshall, I can't see how my religious beliefs are any of your concern."

Randy's thin nostrils flared. "In East Bay, everyone attends church on Sundays. We still hold to the Sabbath here, even if you—"

"Excuse me!" She held up her hand and glared right back. "I'm not interested in getting into a feud with you over this," she told him when she regained control of her temper. "That was a pretty poor invitation to church if that was your original intention. Now, if you'd like to get to know me better, then, by all means, come on inside for a cup of tea. We'll sit down and have a civilized conversation. You can tell me all about yourself and then I'll tell you about myself."

She stood her ground, chin up, refusing to look away from the dark glasses shielding his eyes. Intuition told her Randy Marshall was not going to reveal any personal information. Well, neither was she.

He backed down but not without making sure she knew he didn't consider this matter concluded. "We attend First Covenant Gospel

Church. The early service is at nine a.m., and the evening service is at six thirty." His lips thinned. "We would be pleased to have you accompany us this evening."

She turned back to her puttering at the cottage's foundation. She leaned down to pull a handful of weeds away from the next crack before she trusted herself to reply. "It just so happens, Mr. Marshall, I shall be unable to attend church with you this evening." She sat back on her knees then and smiled at him narrowly, brushing away a lock of hair that blew across her eyes. "But I look forward to attending morning worship with your family next Sunday." She turned her back, dismissing him.

Getting the last word in was petty. But it felt so good. She grinned while she pictured Randy in a tall pilgrim hat and shoes with big, shiny buckles.

He was right, though. One missing ingredient in the recipe of her new life had been church. She could try another way to worship than the comfort of Woodside's tradition. Nothing would ever be the same again. She was the one who had to adjust if she wanted to fit in here in her new home. It was her choice.

* * * *

Randy frowned on the walk back home. Instead of being furious at the way the woman had treated him, he felt as though he needed to apologize for his behavior. He had been surprised to see her crouching, taking care to make repairs on his parents' house, upkeep Dad had once been proud to perform. Mrs. Runyon had been a surprise all around, all right. A widow woman wanted to buy the house the banker told them, immediately after that vicious ex-wife of Ted's demanded he sell out and give her half the cash. A widow woman didn't seem like much trouble to have next door. Randy hadn't counted on a widow woman who looked and acted like Grace Runyon. Not elderly at all, but…trim and…fit. Maybe around his own age. Capable and independent. An answer to his brother's prayers for childcare? Though Ted had refused to do the background check Randy urged.

Randy doubted Mrs. Runyon was aware of the gossip grinding

away in East Bay. The joint owners of the resale shop where the woman had first acquired duds for herself and the house regularly visited Kaye's Café. Randy stopped in to meet up with the other members of the co-op when he was able. It wasn't long before anyone who cared to listen in on their conversation knew how the newcomer decorated her house as well as her person with offerings from the shop. He could hear their whispers even now:

"That old brown club chair, you know, we had since old Mr. Woolver was…"

"And you know the dishes from crazy old…"

"I heard she doesn't believe in church. How does that sit with the Marshalls?"

"You know that young man has her taking care of the little boy. Poor motherless thing…"

Randy didn't care if everyone in town talked about his new neighbor but he had to stop the dissection of his family. They were not going to dredge up old hurts now. Not when things were getting back to normal and the co-op was back on its feet and doing well. Forcing the widow woman to appear in public at church was a start.

* * * *

Grace knew she would further entrench herself in the Marshalls' lives when she agreed to attend church with them. But did that mean she had to act more friendly? More neighborly? How could she let them, and the others, know she was here because she wanted to be? Whatever the reason behind Randy's invitation, she was curious and hungry to hear the Word of God preached. The next Sunday she walked soberly down the aisle and sat in the Marshall family pew.

Mrs. Ten Veldt, a row ahead of them, wasted no time in turning around and loudly whispering she enjoyed seeing Grace wear her former favorite blue and white chevron striped dress. "My dear, I knew at my age I was only growing wider and shorter, so"—she shrugged—"I donated most of my wardrobe to charity." She sniffed. "It looks good on you, too."

How was Grace supposed to respond? "Thank you." She opened

her hymnbook and coughed.

Contrary to Randy's declaration, not everyone in East Bay attended church on Sundays. There were mighty gaps in the ranks of pews.

When she informed Ted on Friday afternoon she had agreed to go to church, he smirked and told her it was easier for them to go with Randy.

"I tried to argue about going to New Fellowship where some of my friends go. Better music, more kids. But Covenant was my parents' church and their parents before them. Great Uncle Harry was the pastor at one time. It's hard for Randy to think about anything else. I guess it doesn't hurt Eddy. I remember how hard it was to sit for forty-five minutes, too, until we went down for playtime. Everyone has to do it. But young families aren't staying like they used to," Ted said. "And, well, we're traditional."

Grace's first impression of First Covenant was underscored by the scent of age. Dust motes glittered through shafts of light beaming through the high, murky-colored windows. The books in the pew were cracked with age and the few well-used pages of the common liturgy dog-eared and brown. The sanctuary felt clammy and neglected. The organ loft creaked as though housing the ghosts of a long-absent choir.

Crashing organ music wheezed from a choir loft behind her, making Grace jump. She rubbed goose bumps while Eddy hung on her arm like he often did with adults until a sharp rebuke from Randy stiffened his little spine. He sat stick straight against the hard back of the pew and stared straight ahead.

The first five rows of old wooden and handsomely carved pews were empty. That must have been the expensive rent district back when pew fees were charged. She tucked back a grin, set the hymnal on her lap, and reached across Eddy to pick up a yellowed pamphlet from the holder on the back of the pew in front of her to page through.

The organ swelled to a cranky volume and then cut off dramatically as the elderly minister shuffled to the altar from a side room to begin the service.

After her first worship experience in the staid Covenant Church, Grace could never explain to the Marshalls she missed the fiery preaching of her hometown church, the thwack of the Bible on the simple wooden lectern arousing anyone who dared to doze during the second hour of the service. Joyous faith was life in Woodside. It did not appear to be so in East Bay.

She laughed drily, inwardly. She might have tried to run away from life, from God, but she'd clearly not been thinking straight at the funeral. God was here, all right. He was sleeping in the front row. Would any other church be different? Grace shifted on her feet while she looked around and listened to the latest change in medication or planting garden story or pet news.

At least they didn't seem to need to shake hands during the service and she could avoid the few who wanted to afterward by clasping her Bible with both hands and nodding a lot.

She returned in the evening to endure the second service with its accompanying curious looks, the dried hymns and monotone sermons, and the repetitive litanies, her due penance for her behavior back in Woodside…with grace.

Chapter Five

"You can*not* miss picking blueberries for *any*thing," Shelby Brouwer insisted. "We'll be lucky to find some late raspberries this year, it's been so dry. Asparagus, strawberries, cherries, raspberries, blueberries, peaches, then pears and apples." She counted on her fingers, gleeful. "We have a freezer in the basement. We missed cherries and the early raspberry season already. Please, Grace, you have to." Food was a constant topic since her appetite returned with a vengeance after the initial morning sickness and discomfort of her pregnancy.

Her expression changed to a frown, her moods jumping up and down lately. "I hated that Davy wouldn't let me out to the Cherry Festival."

"What festival?" Grace asked, intrigued. Her life in Tennessee had all been rounds, clinic, social visits, family. She'd never been interested in more than the flowers in her yard.

"After the Fourth is the National Cherry Festival. In Traverse City. The Cherry Capital of the World, you know."

Grace laughed. "As a matter of fact, I didn't. But it sounds like fun."

"Nobody told you about it, did they?"

"There are other things to think about. I'm sure it wasn't intentional. I don't expect folks around here to coddle me, you know. I have to learn my own way around."

"They're practically keeping you prisoner."

"It's not like that. You of all people should know Ted needs extra help right now. Next year, Shelby. It's an annual event, I take it? I'll take Eddy with me when we pick blueberries. It's okay for him to come, isn't it?"

"Oh, yes. We always take the daycare kids out for a trip."

Shelby offered detailed instructions about the finer points of fruit picking and which orchards and gardens gave the best deals, which ones catered to tourists and which were for "real" Michiganders.

Grace reeled with the admonitions and, knowing for certain she was a dead ringer for a tourist, she and Eddy set out the next morning on their adventure.

The child enjoyed the exercise of walking out to the rows and plucking the fruit. At first. The August weather was sticky and hot and he soon became unusually irritable.

"Gra-ace. I'm done. It's time to go home now." His little blueberry bucket was only a quarter full. She didn't want to stop picking yet and debated the wisdom of having an argument with a nearly five-year-old. Somehow she knew they both would lose.

She tried distraction instead. "Look, Eddy! A big grasshopper is on that bush. Listen to his chirping. He's singing your favorite song."

"No he's not." Eddy dropped the bucket. "It's too hot." He wiped a grubby, stained palm across his eyes leaving a streaky mask across his nose. "There's hoppers at home." He kicked at his bucket and pulled at Grace's arm when she reached into the bushes for another handful of berries. "Let's go home and jump in the pool!"

"Eddy—hold on there, big guy." She picked up his bucket. "We're almost done. Why don't you go sit over there by Mrs. Overstreet for a little bit while I fill up your bucket, okay? It won't take long. There's her dog. You can pet him."

She waved a hand to shoo away the little gnats away from her damp face. She was uncomfortable too, but intrigued by the great gifts of western Michigan. Mrs. Overstreet was a member of the co-op and clearly respectful of Eddy as the nephew of their marketing chief. She recognized him right away when they drove up, inquiring about picking for the day. Confessed ignorance of the fruit season gave the woman a chance to look her up and down, frowning, and Grace did not want to further annoy her by not getting a decent picking. Besides, they drove a half-hour south to find the recommended farm and she was sharing the picking with her friend.

Eddy trudged over to the tent occupied by Mrs. Overstreet. Grace waved hesitantly when the woman looked over at her. Was she breaking some child labor or neglect laws? Her neighbors picking on either side of her smirked and nodded at each other. She picked faster.

* * * *

Randy came to the house that evening to take Eddy home.

"We were at blueberries today, Unca Randy! By Mrs. Overstreet. I played." Eddy was in a much better frame of mind now he had been given lunch and was splashing in his wading pool. He'd slept all the way home, much to Grace's relief. He rarely took a nap and had obviously been tired that morning. Now he went giddyupping in his tiny brown swim trunks around the pool, water flying everywhere. Randy backed up, a smile barely making his mouth change shape underneath his dark sunglasses. He was dressed soberly as always, the perfect front man for the local marketers. He obviously took the responsibility seriously. Too seriously.

She invited him to join her on the front porch while Eddy dried off. "How's Ted today?"

Randy did not look at her. She watched him swallow before answering. Not that she cared overly, but since the rest of the townspeople held him in such high regard, she supposed she should stay on his good side. Maybe they could reach a mutual understanding, some sort of respect, even if they didn't actually get to the liking each other stage.

"They'll be keeping him another day at the hospital," he replied in measured tones. "More prodding and poking. He complains."

Randy sighed. Then, for the first time, he showed his vulnerable human side to her. "We just wish someone would figure it out, but so far..." He shrugged.

She wasn't sure how to take the change in attitude and kept her tone neutral. Just going for respect at this point, she reminded herself. No need for gory details. But no need to wound him, either. "I'm sorry. It must be hard on you as much as Eddy."

Randy turned his head in her direction but Grace could not read his expression through the reflective lenses. He nodded while staring at his twined hands. They sat on the top step, leaning on opposite pillars to watch the sun inch lower on the horizon.

She lifted a hand to shift the hair on her sweaty neck. A truce? Is that what he offered? How far would he take it?

"Um, Randy, can I ask about the place? About the orchards? After being at Overstreets' today, I was wondering what happened here, if I'm not being too personal."

Randy pulled off the sunglasses and leaned back on an elbow to study her. His eyes were a faded imitation of Ted's. The family resemblance in nose and cheekbone was obvious. Pain etched both their faces, each in his own way. Randy kept his steely hair military-butch short. He brushed his hand over the bristles.

"I don't know what folks have been telling you," he said while looking down at his hands.

She sat back and wrapped her hands around her knees. "I haven't heard anything around town." She smiled. "I don't get out much, besides church."

Randy looked her way again, his lips pursed and a stern line between his brows. "I guess we've taken advantage of you."

"Not at all." Grace straightened. Eddy zipped up the steps between them, shivering. "Time to change your clothes buddy," she said.

He stamped his brown feet and nodded his head up and down, then slammed the door behind him. She called after him, "Remember to leave your suit in the tub, Eddy. Not on the floor, okay?"

She looked at Randy, wondering whether to share a piece of her own history. "In fact it was an answer to a prayer to have some company," she said instead. Maybe later. She wanted to know about the farm first. "But we were talking about the orchards."

Randy faced the barren field that stretched past the big house along the rural road. Where rows of fruit trees once marched, only mounds of stumps and overgrown grass remained.

"This far north in Michigan is more cherry country," he said. "Our father had a kind of apple he wanted to try, one from New England. It actually did very well and we had good yields. He passed away quite suddenly four years ago. Heart attack."

"I'm sorry."

"He was a good man," Randy said quietly. "Neither Ted nor I really had any interest in working on the farm. He knew that and, yes, was disappointed but didn't try and make us feel guilty about it. I went for a degree in business management and am happy to work with the fruit grower's cooperative. Ted started his own consulting company. Ergonomics, efficiency in farm practices—you know." Randy looked at her. "This place influenced us deeply even if we didn't want to do the same kind of work Dad did."

He tapped his glasses against his knee. "It's natural to think your parents will last forever. We didn't plan ahead too well. Anyway, Ted's wife, Jilly—ah, ex-wife, that is—did management studies, too, at MSU. When Ted brought her here after they got married, she and Dad put their heads together. He liked her. It never even bothered him when she smoked cigars. She spoke well and was enthusiastic. At first, she did have some good ideas. We all discussed it, and he let her gradually assume management. Mom had been gone a long time by then." Randy checked the screen door and spoke quickly, quietly. "I don't know. Maybe he was just happy having a woman around again. Not that anything improper was going on." He stared hard, challenging her to deny him.

She didn't respond. He could tell her more if he wished. She wouldn't encourage him, but she didn't feel the need to stop him, either. Knowing something didn't mean she had to make it part of her own life. But it might help her with Eddy if he ever asked about his mother.

"When the apple maggot got out of control, Jilly refused to see how serious the situation was. Despite the agent's concerns, she would not order the treatment he prescribed. She tried to save money and go natural, but in the end we lost the trees here. Then it started spreading to the neighbors." Randy grinned at her, humorlessly. "She wasn't the most popular person in town. In fact, the car accident that nearly killed Ted happened on the way home from a town meeting. Growers wanted her to take responsibility, make her pay damages. I always assumed she and Ted musta had an almighty row." Randy shook his head, rubbing a callused hand over his scalp again. "Ted refused to say exactly what happened in the car. Jilly left town four months later."

He stared out once again at the hot wind leaving rippling wakes in the tall grass. "We did pay the co-op to help out the others who were affected."

He didn't mention his father, Grace noted, or how he felt about the circumstances or the underlying reason why his sister-in-law took off.

"We would have started planting cherry trees, but then… Dad became sick. Other things got in the way."

Eddy came slamming back out through the door. Randy stopped the story. She didn't press, as she was pretty sure what "things" he meant.

"Come on, feller," Randy said. "Let's you and me ride 'em broncos back to the stable." He took Eddy, whooping, on his shoulders.

She followed them down the sidewalk to the driveway. "Thank you, Randy." He nodded. She gave Eddy a big smile and gave his fingers a shake. "And thank you, Eddy, for your help today. We'll take Shelby her berries soon, okay?" The little boy yipped and kicked his heels into Randy's chest. Randy winced and then winked at her before swooping his nephew to the other side of the hedge.

Grace picked up the inflated colorful plastic ball Eddy played with and brought it to the porch before going inside. Randy wasn't such a bad guy, after all.

* * * *

Ted returned from the hospital and took Eddy on a promised overnight fishing trip, leaving Grace truly alone for a few days in a row; the first since she'd moved in. The hours stretched. She went to visit Shelby.

"Please, Grace—just go out to breakfast or something, at Kaye's—anything—and come back and tell me the latest of what you hear. This bed rest is driving me nuts. I never hear any good gossip anymore." A dog-eared magazine slipped from her lap to the floor of her living room.

Grace was naturally curious about the local lunch counter. But no way would she walk in there alone. "I'm gossip fodder enough. I want to go, but I'll wait for you, until you're better."

"Somehow I knew you'd say that." Shelby couldn't hold a pout, though she tried. "I guess I'd feel the same way, you know, if someone dumped me in the middle of Tennessee where I didn't know a soul." She closed her eyes and leaned back.

Grace hurt for her. She and the baby weren't out of danger yet. Her friend's exhaustion permeated the little house. "How about I read to you?"

Shelby nodded, a ghost of a smile on her pale petal lips. "I'd like that. No one else would think of it, you know. I'm so glad you're here." She turned on her side and reached for Grace's hand. "When I'm better, I'll make it up to you."

"Hey." Grace squeezed her hand and prayed silently. "That's what friends are for."

Shelby pressed back. "Yeah." She took off her glasses and sighed. "How about where you left off in the book about the sin eater? It doesn't make sense without you reading it."

"Sure." Grace rose and fetched the book from the basket by the rocking chair, settled in, and began to read.

* * * *

A couple of days later Grace stood at her screen door, answering Eddy's summons. Ted, Randy, and Eddy had obviously been primed by Shelby. The trio showed up with a lunch invitation to Kaye's. Eddy squirmed with delight and swung like a monkey from his uncle's big hands.

"Come on! Let's go!" His enthusiasm brooked no argument.

"I can't imagine why we haven't come before," Ted said into her ear as he leaned over to close the car door after she got in.

She met his apology with aplomb. "I'm glad we're going now."

Kaye's Café and Natural Foods was a street front shop in the quaint downtown of East Bay. Grace was enchanted with the rolled-out striped awning and round blue lettering showing outward on the large windows. The message announced the day's special of turkey subs and Tanya's Tuna Salad.

Eddy, barely containing his excitement, helped his father out of the car and handed him the crutch Randy pulled out of the trunk. Eddy matched him pace for pace up to the entrance of the café, then let go of his father's hand suddenly and rushed forward. Ted stumbled before he could catch hold of the swinging door and stop it from slamming into his good leg. The boy continued to bound into the café where he scampered to the counter and clambered onto a round red-leather and chrome bar stool.

Grace reached for the door to hold it open for Ted, curious neither Ted nor Randy reprimanded Eddy. She would have held on to Sean. Of course he'd been too little to run like this. Ted raised his eyebrows as he passed. "Eds hasn't been here in a while," he whispered.

Once inside, she followed Eddy's innocent antics. He folded his hands on the breakfast bar and checked his neighbor's dishes. Mr. Jeffries from church sat two stools down. Eddy waved and made a show of licking his lips and rubbing his tummy in exaggerated appreciation of Mr. Jeffries's huge gooey cinnamon bun and big cup of hot chocolate with whipped cream.

Grace blinked and caught herself short. She'd almost run right into Randy, who'd halted in the entry. She checked his profile, curious about the pulse under his clenched jaw. She swiveled in the direction that held his attention. A uniformed woman leaned over the counter to greet Eddy. Her blond hair was caught up in a net that made her appear exotic in an old-fashioned way. She had to be Kaye. Hmm, not only was Randy not an ogre, he had a heart firmly attached to a beautiful woman.

As if the moment never occurred, time started again when Randy moved ahead, steadying his little brother on one side. He nodded to various customers and picked up the state newspaper as they walked past a haphazard pile stacked on the end of a vacant booth.

Ted shuffled across the gray-patterned tiled floor, his head bent and his shoulders hunched. Grace couldn't bring herself to offer the embarrassment of a second helping hand and continued to glance around as they made their way toward a free table. Were they going to call Eddy over? Kaye continued to engage Ted's son in animated conversation. The blonde looked up once and smiled broadly right at Ted who was studying his laminated menu as if he'd never been here before.

Grace gnawed at her lip and hoped Randy hadn't seen the bold appreciation the café owner threw at Ted. Of course, she could be mistaken about the identity of the woman behind the counter. Her intuition whispered she wasn't. She took a deep breath and looked around the place, antsy and nervous to meet people who might have talked about her. She recognized three of the customers from church and smiled at them. One of the women who worked at the resale shop was seated at a sunny table under the big window. They exchanged nods. No one approached them, though. Well, whatever. They were probably just as flummoxed about a stranger trying to move in on their homeboys as she was attempting to pretend she could be one of them.

She was glad she knew about Jilly. Randy might be a regular here, but Ted obviously was not, and his flushed face hinted at his embarrassment. He had once been popular, Shelby told her. Now Ted undoubtedly thought of himself as broken and crippled, pitiful. And probably ashamed of his former wife's actions.

When Grace caught both Randy and Ted looking at her, she nodded over to Eddy at the counter. Three older ladies pinched his cheek or patted his head. "It's a shame no one pays any attention to him at home," she commented dryly. The grooves on either side of Randy's mouth deepened for a moment and his eyes twinkled. Ted relaxed, sagging against the seat.

Clattering plates and silver provided a cheerful backdrop to the smell of sweet onions over chocolate and pancake syrup perfume. A coffee bean grinder whirred. To their right another room opened up with a variety of shadowy boxes and bags on shelves. Must be the natural foods side of the business. Since she'd assumed the café only served natural foods on the menu, she hadn't gone inside before.

Now she wished she had come earlier. She and Jonathan had belonged to the little natural foods co-op back in Woodside and she missed it. Maybe the store could order some of the special whole grains and herb teas she was used to drinking back home if it didn't already stock them. She reached for a menu as she watched a tall teen glide up to the table, tablet ready. Pretty girl. Somewhat aloof, but not snobby. More…professional, like she was trying to play a part.

"Grace, meet Kaye's niece, Tanya," Randy said. Tanya Smits, a waif-thin teen with mature brown eyes, flipped her pad to a clean page.

Ted had explained on the way downtown Kaye took the girl in when her brother needed a long stay at a rehabilitation hospital a few years ago. The situation suited all of them and Tanya stayed on after her father's successful treatment. No mention was made of her mother. Another motherless child.

Grace smiled. Tanya hesitatingly returned the smile with a hurried glance at Ted Marshall, then an even quicker check of her aunt who was filling a coffeepot with practiced ease, her attention still lasered on Ted. The smile drifted blankly over Randy, then cooled considerably as it passed on to her.

Grace hadn't connected all the dots yet around the hometown relationships, but she was beginning to pick out the outlines of this particular picture.

Chapter Six

Jimmy Marshall's annual two-week visit was scheduled for the end of summer. One afternoon when Ted came for his son, he filled Grace in on the sordid details of his brother's son with little encouragement on her part.

The cousin who "punches hard" according to Eddy was the only child of Randy and his former wife who now made her home in Sault Ste. Marie. High school angst, prom night, and longing for the girl who wouldn't give him the time of day apparently led to some bad decisions on teenaged Randy's part.

Grace wasn't surprised. Hope deferred makes for a sick heart.

"I guess we could say my eighteen-year-old brother, Righteous Randy, the president of the church youth group, dealt himself and Jenny Walden a bad hand," Ted said. "They got married then divorced after Jimmy was born. I think Jenny loved him, but…Kaye Smits was her best friend."

Ted's tendency to gleefully share personal news about people in East Bay sometimes made Grace squirm, but she was glad to know some of the facts about Jimmy. "The Kaye from the café?"

"Yeah, her. Randy sure had a bad rep at church," Ted said. "Dad was upset and told him he was glad Mom was gone. That hurt Randy most about the whole thing, I think. Jimmy's an okay kid. I liked Jenny fine, too, but…well, it's water under the bridge, now. Jenny helps manage the kitchen at the big restaurant in Soo. Have you ever been to the U.P.?"

"Yoopee?" Grace asked.

"Upper Peninsula—of Michigan," Ted explained.

"No, Ted, I haven't been up there. Is it far? What's 'soo'?"

"A half-day drive. Soo is short for Sault St. Marie." He spelled it. "Old French. It's a really pretty town. The big lock and dam to get through to Lake Superior from Lake Huron is there. It's fun to watch the big ships go through. A lot of sailors and merchant ships stop. Eddy loves it. And you can go across the bridge into Canada. Have a passport?"

His enthusiasm was infectious and she smiled back. It was sweet to see him happy about something instead of morose and feeling sorry for himself as he sometimes was before a hospital visit. She had not yet asked a direct question about his symptoms and their possible underlying causes.

"Maybe I'll visit up there sometime," she said.

Ted looked at her as if she'd just announced she wished to visit the moon and needed directions. "We'll all go," he said. "I'll take you."

* * * *

Jimmy arrived the next day. Grace had been invited to meet him at the family campfire pit after dinner. The young man stood shoulder to shoulder with his father. When he finished filling out, he would take after the paternal line with a straight nose and deep blue eyes like his uncle. He wore his hair fashionable curly and streaked, and proclaimed his joy at being away from the hot restaurant kitchen where he washed dishes. The job was okay, he told her in a growly voice. "My mom's the manager and makes the soup du jour. She knows my schedule."

Grace nodded, seeing right through his sullen-on-the-outside act. Jimmy fidgeted. Although Randy spoke with pride of the good grades and musical honors Jimmy earned, they probably didn't get together enough to be comfortable with each other.

"So, you're a junior?" she asked him. He nodded. "What are your plans after high school?"

"I dunno." He shrugged his young giant shoulders. "I haven't decided about college yet."

"Hmm." Grace poked the fire with a stick. Orange and yellow flames licked at aromatic apple wood, while a gentle breeze wafted the aroma. Eddy chased fireflies near the lilac bushes. Jimmy shifted with restless motions, ill-at-ease, probably, with hanging around the company of older folks and one energetic little boy all day. Several kids from the church youth group were going to Sleeping Bear Dunes on the lakeshore the next week and Randy signed Jimmy up over his protests. But Grace understood about being in the company of strangers and felt sorry for him.

He crouched on the grass in front of the crackling bonfire pit, rocking back and forth. As if suddenly remembering his manners, he turned to ask, "Um, so, Uncle Ted, how are you feeling these days?"

Ted craned his head back at his nephew, a smile reflected in the firelight. "Thanks for asking. I'm actually feeling okay, Jimmy. Mostly tired—and tired of being tired." He impaled another marshmallow and handed his roasting stick to Eddy, who promptly stuck it in the ashes.

Jimmy bent his head. "I can't imagine, man, feeling that way and nothin' anyone can do. Don't the doctors have it figured out yet?"

"Not exactly. They can tell me what they think it isn't—which isn't saying much, is it?"

Ted was rarely this candid about his condition, and Grace was surprised at the conversation. She looked over at Randy, curiously, to find his eyes on her. He shook his head slightly, agreeing. They had spent longer moments together lately talking comfortably and companionably about many things. Ted's brother certainly stored emotion deeply, something she had only recently come to understand and appreciate. Who would have thought they would turn out to be kindred spirits after the contentious first couple of weeks?

The quiet talk continued between Ted and Jimmy. Grace caught hushed snippets of high school antics, the trumpet, cars, and girls.

She smiled and tuned it out, eventually getting up to hunt for Eddy. It was bedtime. After setting the little guy in the tub and leaving the door open to listen to him sing and splash, she sat down to read the guidebook she found in the Marshalls' living room. A visit to the famous Lake Michigan dunes climbed to the top of her wish list.

"Hey, Eddy!" she called and then went to stand near the bathroom. "Has anyone ever told you the legend of the Sleeping Bear?" she asked.

Eddy slapped bubbles with a frayed brown terry washcloth. "I don't think so," he sang, in time to the splashing. Grace smiled.

"Listen. It's from Ojibway Indian stories. Long ago, in the land of Wisconsin, Mother Bear and her two cubs swam into Lake Michigan to save them from a raging forest fire. The cubs swam strongly but the other side of the shore was too far away. They fell farther and farther behind and sank in the waters. When Mother Bear reached the Michigan side, she climbed to the top of a bluff, pacing and looking back across the water, searching in vain for her cubs. The Great Spirit saw her and took pity on her vigil. He piled up the two Manitou Islands to mark the place where her cubs vanished and put Mother Bear to sleep."

She set the book down and went into the bathroom. She reached into the cooling water of the tub to pull the plug and wrap a big fluffy towel around Eddy as she hauled him out.

"Why did the mommy bear have to sleep?" he asked, rubbing his eyes.

"So she could have good dreams about her children, I suppose." She cradled him, rocking gently, reveling in her good fortune to be part of this little guy's life. "Let's get you in bed and see what kind of good dreams you have."

* * * *

The spasm of misgiving that taunted Randy since he signed his son up for the youth group trip grew into a heart attack of doubt when he dropped Jimmy off at the church parking lot. About twenty kids and five chaperons milled about with parents or siblings. Beach bags and coolers were being loaded into the back of the bus and someone already had a guitar strumming. Jimmy gravitated slowly toward the music. Randy's heart shimmied when Kaye arrived with her niece. They didn't attend First Covenant Church, so what were they doing here? Tanya's friends must have invited her along on the trip to Sleeping Bear Dunes.

Randy stared at Kaye, the hunger and longing a slow ache that had never healed over twenty years. And now… He cocked his head. What was with the kid? After complaining about rising so early to meet the bus, Jimmy changed directions mid-pace to meet up with Tanya.

Randy paced by his car, thinking maybe he should tell Jimmy not to go after all. This was not a good development. The whole business had started three days ago at the diner when the kids met at lunch. Sparks between his son and the waitress could have lit a fire. Not good—not good at all. Nothing good comes from high school romances. He should know. He couldn't help it; he had been short with the girl. He'd complained about the coffee first, knowing that ordering hot coffee in the heat of August was a mistake. The pot had obviously been left over since breakfast and tasted stale. Still, a good waitress would have made fresh.

He had ignored her when she brought a full pot several minutes later. Tanya, with uncustomary shakiness, spilled a few drops on his silverware. He gave her the look then, and watched her retreat, breathing hard, her face scrunched and red. A good waitress shouldn't sweat the small stuff. Of course his attitude fed the animosity Jimmy carried as a chip. Jimmy got on his case then.

"Dad, why'd you have to be so hard on her?"

Randy ignored him while he drowned his French fries in ketchup.

He had been unprepared for Kaye's steely eyed assault when she brought their check.

"What gives, Randy?" she had asked point blank.

Randy was already ashamed of his behavior, embarrassing his son like that. He didn't make excuses. "Sorry. Bad morning." He left a twenty on the table and muttered, "Have to get back to work. See you at home about five," to Jimmy, who stuck to the booth.

Now he wished he knew how long Jimmy had stayed. Randy kicked some gravel with the toe of his shoe before he got into his car and drove to work.

In the evening, when Randy went to pick up Jimmy, he watched a familiar car pull into the lot. Kaye emerged, held a hand up to block the glare of the setting sun, and then brushed back her heavy swath of hair set free from the confining net she wore at work. He lounged against the warmth of his own car door, hoping not to be noticed so he could keep on watching her. She saw him anyway, waved, and sauntered over.

"It was a nice day. I hope the kids had a good time," she said, skipping over a greeting.

"Hmm."

"Jimmy goes back Sunday?"

Not a moment too soon. "Yes, I'll drive him up home. School starts soon."

"Look, Randy, I think you should know something." She held her hand up to her eyes again, turning toward the road as if to spy the bus. Randy slumped against the side of his car and crossed his arms, head bent, sure of the news to come.

"You know I'm not really much into the parenting scene. I love Tanya, but she's easy, not like when we were kids, you know?"

Randy shifted against the warm side of the car, irritable. Of course he knew. He sighed. "Yes."

"We had a good talk, your boy and me. He's nice, Randy. You and Jenny did well with him."

"Jenny did, you mean."

"You, too, Randy. I mean it. But Tanya's not ready for anything serious. I don't want that for her. She's never asked me for time off before, like yesterday—and today. I already said yes to this trip before Jimmy came, so that was okay. But, yesterday? You know they spent the whole time together, don't you?"

He hadn't. Jimmy hadn't said anything besides "hung out with some peeps" when he'd asked yesterday evening what Jimmy had done all day. "Thanks for telling me. They just met, and Jimmy's leaving. They'll forget about this by the time school starts. Don't worry."

"I hope you're right."

The bus pulled in. Parents herded over to pick up their various progeny and friends. Kaye held up her hand again, shielding her eyes from the last blast of sunset. She caught her breath and Randy turned to look, too. All the kids had exited the bus except for one last couple tangled together in the back. Randy beetled his brows under his aviator sunglasses and he started forward. Kaye put her hand on his arm.

"Wait. Randy, it's only a kid thing. Don't fuel it or make it worse. Please."

Randy looked down at her neat hand and let out the breath he didn't realize he was holding.

"If we make a big deal out of it that will only encourage them," she said.

"You're right. Okay." Randy sighed. "Yeah. Jimmy goes back on Sunday."

One of the chaperons hustled the kids off the bus. Randy thrust aside the old, old feeling of regret he had every time he thought about Jenny. When he saw his ex-wife again, he had to be collected or she would wonder if something was wrong. He didn't see enough of his boy as it was, and he did not want to alienate Jimmy or his mother. Not this late in the game. Jimmy was almost a man. He forced a smile. "You sure you're not into the motherhood thing? You seem to have good instincts around Tanya."

His compensation was the pleased look on her face, the softening expression in her eyes. It would have to be enough to hold him. She'd rejected him once but she'd never gotten over his rebound to her best friend either. He watched her lead Tanya to her car, whispering heatedly in the girl's ear. Tanya turned for one last look at Jimmy. Neither waved or acknowledged the other.

Jimmy got silently into their car. Randy hesitated at the wheel, wondering what to say.

"Save it, Dad," Jimmy stated. Randy immediately bristled until he realized his son was simply on guard against what he assumed would be a natural reaction.

He let go a deep breath and turned on the ignition. "It looks like you had a pretty good time," he said mildly, and was rewarded by Jimmy's gape. Randy smiled. "Close your mouth, son. You're lettin' in sand lions." They both laughed.

On Sunday they had the best trip back into the Upper Peninsula he could remember. This must be the start of something good. Kaye had sought him out to talk and he and Jimmy found a reasonable place to meet each other half-way. The long wait for God to answer his prayers had been worth it. Please, God, for Ted. Now for Ted. Heal him.

Chapter Seven

Ted Marshall had become accustomed to tingling pain sparking up and down his limbs and spine, and having various parts of his anatomy betray him with trembling and total collapse. He frowned and flexed his left foot. Something was different. He was reluctant to even hope his range of motion seemed easier these last couple of weeks. His last headache had been—well, he couldn't remember when the last one laid him out. The physical therapy must be starting to kick in. His left leg had all but stopped its twitching, he realized, though the arm had not.

He and Eddy had a good time on their "men's" fishing trip earlier in the summer. He felt strong enough to guide their boat out. Swimming did wonders to ease the trembling. It had been the most pleasant summer since Dad passed. Since Jilly. Since the year of the apple disaster. He finished a complicated schedule for pruning and spraying at the Woolver's orchards, profiting Eddy's trust fund. He also worked out a rotation of needed housing between the migrant workers and the several housing facilities maintained between the co-op and the larger marketers. The clients were pleased.

Ted eased himself onto the lower step of Grace's house while he watched his son stalk the cat, Trigger. Grace's house. He realized it didn't bother him, being able to move on. The house had been his—his and Jilly's—for a few years first, and Dad's. Life here with his wife had not been all that pleasant. Except for Eddy.

He twisted his lips as his hand slid down the length of the cane which replaced the crutch. He set it aside, wishing he could be out there playing with Eddy and Grace. He was still too unsteady to move quickly on uneven ground. *Maybe soon, if I keep improving.*

Grace waved at him, brushing her wind-blown hair away from her lashes, and clamped her silly floppy green hat back onto her head when the breeze threatened to take it. They had been to church that morning and she had not complained about complying with the unwritten rule of headgear for women. She had not yet changed her clothes from the full skirt and light top she had worn to the service. She had, however, removed her sandals and ran barefoot in the lawn. If he felt more like a healthy man with a future, something to offer a woman like Grace, he might think about getting into the dating game again. What had happened to her husband? Had he been elderly, sick, or had his death been a sudden shock? He rather thought the latter, although he had not felt right about asking. She should have been a mother. He loved watching her with Eddy.

Ted grinned at the sight of his son who screamed with delight and kicked his heels when he finally touched the marmalade cat's tail. It streaked by the boy when he almost had her cornered.

"Daddy! We almost got her!"

Ted gave him a thumbs-up. Eddy had gotten a haircut, he could see—probably yesterday when he had been working. Eddy turned five a week ago. Grace made a cake which she served with ice cream to four of his favorite Sunday School friends.

Kindergarten would start soon. Did that make him feel old? The thought of giving up the last bit of control over his only child, another reminder of losing things, hurt. The world was so big, so scary. He wanted to keep the little guy close, not let any of the terrible things touch his innocence and break his trust.

Ted leaned back on his elbows and lifted his face to the late afternoon warmth. Grace's flowerbed rioted around the circle she had dug, dark purple alyssum bordering the taller mix of annuals. The couple of things he recognized, cosmos and statis, swayed in the breeze.

Grace dropped by his side after a moment, gasping for breath and leaving Eddy to frolic after the cat who had left a roly-poly jumble of kittens in the playhouse. No worries there—it was now spick and span with floorboards safely repaired. Eddy's zeal to reclaim his pet kept them wholly occupied during most of his days spent with her and filled his supper and bedtime chatter.

"Weather's changing again," Ted said and nodded to her. "We get a lot of snow in the winter—lake effect, we call it. It's strange to think about snow so early but, in case you're worried, Randy usually has the place plowed. We'll work something out to keep your driveway cleared."

Grace studied her fingers, knit together on her lap. She ducked her head and looked at him out of the corner of her eye in a way that made his toes curl. "I didn't know. It's, um, well, nice, to think that far ahead."

As he gazed around the yard it occurred to him the holiday season approached, too, along with the snow. He was able to be detached at this point, as if Christmas was something he could choose to have happen or not as he saw fit. Past Christmases had been dull for Eddy with only him and Randy for company, although the poor kid didn't really know the difference. This year, though, kids in school were bound to compare.

"What's 'lake effect'?" Grace asked, bringing him back to the present.

Ted stretched his legs out straight and crossed his ankles. "Lake effect snow storms happen because we live so close to Lake Michigan. The air picks up extra moisture from the lake and dumps it on us. Happens with fog and rain some, too."

"I can hardly start thinking about next month, let alone winter. Isn't there a fall in there, somewhere? The weather's not quite as changeable as home."

Ted noticed her use of *home*, but he didn't think she was aware of it. Unless she wanted to relay some subtle message, like she wasn't planning on experiencing a Michigan winter. Maybe he'd never learn to listen right to a woman.

"It's not as hot, either," she was saying now. "The breeze is nice here. Does it trouble you, to feel the change in the weather—physically, I mean?" She tucked the skirt underneath her and clasped her knees with her arms. He envied her comfortable suppleness.

"Not so much anymore." He flexed his leg, bending the knee and swiveling it from his hip. "It seems to be better these days. It's good to be able to walk around easier. Swimming has helped quite a lot." He watched his son cavorting in the yard.

"Do you," Grace asked, emphasis on the *you*, "need to take Eddy shopping, or anything, for school? Kindergarten starts in two weeks."

Ted slid his glaze back over to her, groaning inwardly. Shopping. With a five-year-old. He had no idea what to do. "Um, I haven't done this before…so I thought we'd look through his clothes later this weekend." Her legs had taken on a great bronzy tan over the summer. What he wouldn't give to slide his hands down her smooth calves to her ankles.

Bad Dad!

Lame!

"He's five years old and has a wardrobe. How did that happen if you didn't take him?"

"Huh? Uh, well," Ted's face felt warm and she shifted. "Shelby," he said and ducked his head. When Grace didn't respond, he changed the subject. Sort of. "I brought the supplies list from Miss Jones, his teacher," he said hoping to regain some respect. Crayons and folders he could do. He frowned at her stillness. She'd turned into a statue. Why? "You brought it up."

She took a breath. "Well, I never did this before, either. What makes people think any woman just knows what to do with kids? It's one thing to let Eddy ramble all over my house and to feed him and tell him not to stick his hand inside the wasp nest and read stories to him—" She thrust herself to her feet and paced two tight circles beside him.

"I'm sorry. I'm sure there's plenty of help for you at the stores," she finally said and abruptly went inside the house.

Ted watched her go, surprised and hurt. "What did I say?" he asked out loud. Grumpy, he struggled to his feet. "Eddy! Time to go home."

* * * *

Grace worked out a flexible routine with the Marshalls for Eddy's care when school began. It left her more hours to herself, something she was not looking forward to. Volunteer positions were limited, and with a natural cut in salary, working the gas station cash register was looking like her next job unless she wanted to start making regular trips to the bank in Cadillac, a half hour away. She shivered at the thought.

Ted gave her an appointment calendar with his therapy and client appointments. But his next question left her unsettled.

"All right if he shows up in the mornings sometimes to wait for the bus here?" he asked.

"Do you want me to come and walk him over here?" *Shows up* and *five-year-old waiting for a bus* didn't seem like a great sentence combo to her. What did he mean?

He alternately flushed and paled. "It's just… I'm pretty uncoordinated in the morning. When Randy's not there it takes me a while to start moving." Ted frowned and looked away. He folded his arms defensively over his chest. "I don't want Eddy to see," he mumbled.

"Ted…" She'd never told him about her work in Tennessee. Then again, he'd never asked, not like Shelby, who'd earned a very cautious and innocuous reply about her former job. Which no longer hurt to think about. "It won't be every day."

Men and their pride. "He'll need a good breakfast." He wouldn't meet her eye. "Maybe he should stay here once in a while when Randy is gone, too." Short of moving in, what else could she offer without demoralizing the man?

"Maybe." He shuffled away. "Thanks," he called over his shoulder.

At some point she should find out more about Ted's illness, but the days passed and she let it go. Eddy dressed himself in the mornings before the bus came. Occasionally he would come and have breakfast with Grace, but more often he told her he wanted to stay close to his dad. The little guy eventually stayed with her after school to "help" when she needed it. They had dinner together, giving her an excuse to experiment with cooking. Really, she was so glad not to be alone every night. When Ted felt up to it he joined them. Not quite a family but more than simple babysitting. The numbness she'd wrapped around her heart had more than half melted. She no longer stomped on the little bits of love that occasionally escaped in the form of forehead kisses and hugs. Eddy would never replace what she'd lost, but maybe she could make up for what had happened by paying forward a little of her gift. As long as they didn't know what she could do, and neither of had expectations she was certain she would fail, maybe caring about all of them some would be all right.

The last Saturday in October was chilly. She leaned on her rake in the yard to watch the child whirl among the rain of tie-dyed sunset and old hay-bale-colored leaves fluttering to the lawn. Loving Eddy didn't make up for what she'd done, of course, but perhaps if she was good and kind and obedient God would forgive her, though she'd never forgive herself. Of that, she was unworthy. She could love them a little, help them to understand she wasn't a bad person, that she hadn't meant to hurt anyone. Perhaps he wouldn't make her—

"Let's make a scarecrow!" Eddy, smelling of little boy and fusty crackling grass, jumped into her arms.

"Let's!"

Eddy helped raid her laundry, looking for an old pair of pants and shirt they could stuff. She dragged out a tattered lawn chair from the garage for their creation.

They studied the figure slumped in the chair.

The child unconsciously copied her usual thinking pose: right leg forward, elbows bent, and hand covering chin and mouth. "He needs a head. My ball!" Eddy raced into the playhouse where they stored the summer toys and came out with an old rubber ball starting to lose its bounce. Grace found a ragged knit cap, which they stretched over it.

"Perfect! Let's make supper. Race you inside!" She pretended to grab at Eddy who giggled as they ran through the brittle leaves in the yard. They raced up the porch steps.

"Stamp your feet, son!" They left their damp shoes at the door and went inside to the light and warmth of her cozy kitchen.

Ted stumbled in at dark. She heard the hesitant footfalls on her front porch, turned on the light, and met him at the door. His expression needed only one look before she turned to distract Eddy with her computer. She quickly found some children's games and set him down before it, ignoring his wide-eyed wonder. The computer had been off limits before.

"Let's see if you can beat my score," Grace gushed out. He complied for once without question.

Ted had made it through the living room and grabbed at the entrance to the kitchen with a shaky hand. "Hey…there, Eddy." He lurched with the next step he took. "I think I need…"

She grabbed him before Eddy saw his near tumble and led him to her room, struggling mightily with his tall frame to direct him down the hallway and angle him across the bed. She deftly pulled the cover back before he landed, making the bedstead creak. His shoulders settled in slow motion and she waited while he adjusted to being prone. When she knew he wouldn't be sick all over her bed, she gently untied his boots and lifted his emaciated legs, accidentally coming into contact with his skin above the socks. A familiar tingle began along the webbing between her thumb and forefinger and she pulled quickly away, breathing hard and fast. How could she have forgotten? So far away from Woodside... She'd never tested the gift, of course, but assumed it wouldn't work here. Definitely didn't want it to. No…she'd never try it, for she would surely fail. There were other ways to take care of him. She had the knowledge—she could always use her training without the gift.

Ted moved restlessly, hissing in a breath. "I don't know if your hands are warm or cold," he rasped.

There was no alcohol smell on his breath; nothing else strange to indicate this behavior. Perhaps a reaction to medication? Some sort of stroke? What had happened? "What's going on? Did you take something?"

"Nothing I shouldn't." He flashed a half-grin. "So tired. I forgot to eat lunch."

"Rest, then. I'll be back in a little while with some food for you."

He grabbed for her hand when she turned to leave. "Wait!" His voice barely rose above a whisper. "Wait. I want, I—thank you—I want you to know…" His voice trailed off and his shoulders began to shake.

Grace sighed and grabbed a straight chair and pulled it close. What had caused him to lose control? She hadn't been able to cry about anything in two years, despite all she'd gone through. She might have wanted to, but she'd dammed tears behind her lids, where they belonged. Weren't men bastions of stoicism? Jonathan had never shed a tear that she recalled. Certainly her father never had.

She gently dislodged her hand from Ted's convulsive grasp. Her legs itched to run again; right now she'd like nothing better than to run from this little family with their strange problems. Everything had happened so fast. She wanted to be left alone to build relationships for herself at her own pace. Excuses drizzled through her mind—all the reasons she should leave Michigan and go somewhere—anywhere else. Somewhere safe.

This house had been too good a deal. She moved too quickly to purchase it. She hadn't explored the neighborhood enough. The real estate agent misled her when she said the brothers next door wouldn't bother her. How wrong she had been. They both bothered her in different ways. She wasn't a mother any more, not a wife, not a professional anything. Why did they have to ask her and ask her and keep asking her to do things for them? Couldn't Ted see she was as tired as he was?

He gasped and brought his knee up, clutching his calf.

"What do you need? What can I get for you?"

"No-nothing. Just a—spasm. It'll—pass. Wait."

He gulped in air and sweat ran down his temple. She felt as helpless as she did watching a patient in labor. Not much she could do until it was time to push. Michigan? Why had God brought her to Michigan?

Grace had not counted on there being an Eddy and a Ted. The Ted who now wriggled like a taser victim on her own bed and whose tears wet her pillow.

She breathed in and out, setting a calming tempo and urging him to follow. He slowly relaxed then sighed and turned over to look at her with eyes gleaming in the dim lighting. "Jilly left me after the accident when the sickness started."

He swallowed, the noise exaggerated in the dimly lit room. "The first seizure, she freaked. By the third one, she was gone. Didn't even take Eddy. He was only a year old. What was I supposed to do?"

He was really laying it on thick, feeling sorry for himself again.

"Eddy's been through too much for a little kid. All he'll remember when he grows up is he never had a mom and his dad got sick and died."

Grace blinked at her internal burst of sarcasm and squashed her emotions into the pit of professionalism. Whatever his diagnosis, he had regained strength since she first met him. Until today.

Normal life…no professional or otherwise mix of life and business. That's what she'd craved with every cell of her person. She'd been so raw upon arrival, the wound barely scabbed over from her own losses, she could not reach out to anyone else. That God would need her, demand she use her gifts so soon had been repulsive, a hurt beyond deep. Another betrayal sent her reeling.

The caring piece of herself was buried with Sean and Jonathan in Woodside. She had nothing left to give; no desire to, for that matter.

But the gift, had she left it there, too? Was it time?

No…not tonight. If ever.

"What are you talking about? You're so much better. What happened to bring this on? You and Eddy—you're both doing fine. Who says you're going to die?"

Silence. Sniff.

"Other than we're all going sometime." Trying to coax him out of his mood, she said, "Come on. You must have had a bad day. Rest, and I'll bring you something to eat."

Ted closed his eyes. "It's not right I tell you my problems," he allowed. "I hardly know anything about you. And you're right—no one's actually told me yet."

He lay back and rubbed the prominent scar at his temple. "The seizures stopped six months after the accident, but then I started losing control of my muscles. It's a good thing Jilly wasn't here then. We were in pretty rough shape for a while." He scrubbed at his cheeks, grasping again at her hand. "Half the time I don't know if I'm getting better or worse. Stay a little longer, please? Eddy will be okay. I never asked you before. Do you have any family?"

Grace snatched her hand away and jumped up. "I'll let you rest now. You'll feel better soon, I'm sure."

Ted grabbed at her hip as she turned in the tight space and reached for her wrist to pull her close with a surprising surge of strength.

Grace resisted the urge to fight him. She held her breath, not wanting Eddy to hear anything. She had to strain to listen to Ted's soft croon.

"You've been so good to me and to Eddy. Why?"

She let him stroke the hair at her temple. She let her lids drift and caught the moan before it escaped. So long…so long it had been since anyone had touched her like this. She felt his fingers move across her cheek to trace the corner of her mouth, letting the tingle turn into a shiver of desire. She reached for his hair, letting her fingers weave through it.

"Can I make love to you?"

For the first time since she put him to bed, she felt a reluctant smile cross her stiff lips, the desire dashed with cold water, reason returned. Eddy was right behind that door, probably wondering what was taking so long. Good heavens. She pulled away, put her hands on her hips, and looked down at him. "You wish."

Chapter Eight

The smell of buttered toast and something steaming, sweet and delicious-smelling, roused Ted from his drowse. She must have left it only moments ago on the chair by the bed. The thought of her seeing him vulnerable in sleep sent prickles up his arms. The tea he recognized as her special blend. A few sips revived him and after a while he was able to stand straight without tipping. He used the bathroom and splashed water on his face, scrubbing at the tear tracks on his cheeks, embarrassed, remembering his near break down in front of her. He would have sneaked quietly out the door without seeing or speaking to her, but there was Eddy to think of.

Fact was, he had no idea how to act like a single man in front of a single woman to whom he was attracted. Three years since Jilly left. Five years of marriage before that, and one tumultuous year of living together before deciding for sure they wanted to marry and live happily ever after.

Not so happily ever after, after all. Four long years of being sick and struggling to raise his son as best he could all on his own left little time to think of anything other than figuring out what was wrong with him. Randy helped, or he wouldn't have been able to do it. But Eddy deserved a mother who could adore him. Someone like Grace.

Ted moved as quietly as possible down the hall past Eddy's former bedroom. He glanced through the door into the empty space, forlorn in the baleful glow of the yard light shining through the window. No boxes, no stuff people usually had. Who was Grace? Was it true she'd come here with nothing but the clothes on her back and enough cash to plunk down for the house? He wouldn't have sold, but for Jilly's demands.

He lumbered up to the entrance of the living room and stopped short. A hand over his heart checked to be sure it still beat.

Grace had Eddy cuddled close as they snuggled on the sofa. She stroked his head while they looked at a book. Her hair reflected the lamplight and silver filigree earrings lay across the hollow of her cheek in the place he longed to rub his thumbs. His fingers twitched in memory of the feel of her skin. Funny he didn't recall touching her before, although they must have. That strange tingle, like they said was supposed to happen when there was some sort of electric attraction… Had she felt it, too? But it was the expression on Grace's face, though, made him take in a breath and hold it until he got dizzy.

He recalled the incredible pain after the crash while he lay on the side of the road on the ice and nuggets of windshield with his head gashed open, of not being able to call out to know if Jilly was alive. He added that to his wife's betrayal of the family orchards, of her running out on them when he first got sick.

Together, it did not match the suffering emanating from the entire being of Grace Runyon.

His selfishness made him turn his head in disgust. He knew almost nothing about her—just instinctively she was good for his son and made this house into the home Jilly never had. The pain—what would cause her that amount of grief? He could simply ask her. Were they ready for that level of intimacy?

He turned back. She was watching him now, detachment in her expression. Her expression of a moment earlier might have been a figment of his imagination. Relief. Yes, what he had seen, a nano-second was all, really, had simply been leftover dream. There wasn't much they could bring up in front of Eddy.

"Hi," she said, her voice softer than the one she had used on him earlier.

Eddy slapped the book shut. "We had dinner, Dad. I helped. Do you want some?"

Ted stepped forward. "Sure, kiddo, that would be fantastic." He watched his boy trundle out to the kitchen, pull a chair up to the counter, and laboriously ladle up some casserole into a bowl.

Heat prickled along his scalp as he recalled his question after she had helped him lie down and watched him cry over—what? Getting that stupid letter from Jilly had been the last straw to a really lousy day. He'd turned into a little boy looking for his mommy instead of an adult propositioning a woman he desired.

What had he wanted from her, anyway? Despite his jerk-wad question, he hadn't been drooling with lust. He'd been desperate for the touch of her hand. Touch—just touch, was all. He could not remember anyone besides Eddy who touched him out of need, or desire. That tingle on his skin, right before the spasm…when she'd lifted his legs onto the bed, she'd touched him and the warmth made him feel like pulling her into his arms right then and there.

Eddy carried a bowl into the room, holding it with both hands and walking with exaggerated care. Ted sat down next to Grace first and then took the bowl from his son. "Something smells powerfully delicious. I'll have to start calling you Chef Eddy."

Eddy's grin erased his discomfort.

Out of the corner of his eye, he caught Grace's stare. She reminded him of the physical therapist, not letting him get away with anything less than acute discomfort as she worked him like a demon.

"You look a little better," Grace now said, unnecessarily, in his opinion.

He hid his grimace by leaning his face over the dish and inhaling. He patted the stool in front of him and Eddy sat down anxiously to watch his reaction to the creation of lean burger, green beans, carrots and potatoes. Ted gestured generously in big circles with his spoon, making a sloppy grin, which threw Eds into fits of giggles.

"I peeled the carrots. Grace showed me how," he announced. "It was easy once I figgered it." With a sideways glance at their hostess, he added, "Grace says she peels her thumb. I didn't do that."

A flash of a smile tilted her lips. When the entertainment of watching his daddy eat wore off, Eddy wandered away.

Grace did not move, even when he leaned into her personal space.

Over the casserole, delicate scents he associated with her mingled and seeped into his brain. Mint from her tea, the scent of aloe from her pores, and lemon in her hair. She held herself very still, watching him. He gobbled the food, hunger not a lie, before he spoke to her.

"This is really delicious. Could you share the recipe with us? Anything Eddy likes, I say, is a go."

Grace's pewter eyes flashed in the light. "Grandmother Eames would thank ya," she said in a molten twang that seemed to fit both her personality and the evening, "but would nevva consent to sharing a fam'ly re'cip."

She smiled. "'Sides, I have a hard time following a recipe for food." She dropped the hill speak. "To me, food begs for experimenting. Hence, you will never be served the same thing twice at this establishment."

Ted set the bowl aside and leaned his elbows on his knees. "Grace, can we talk?"

She curled up and faced him. "Sure. Will it change anything?"

"We've been pretty good about avoiding the things that really matter, haven't we?"

"Oh, I don't know. What really matters to you, Ted?"

He hadn't expected this turn of the conversation and felt like he'd lost control. Maybe he'd never had any. Which way next? Left or right? Up or down? "What else is there to care about, besides my son?"

Her lips pursed. "That's a start," she said after a couple of seconds.

Eddy came in with a plastic bug jar in his hands. "Can I go out and catch fireflies?"

Ted wasn't sure to whom the request was made. He looked at Grace first before nodding to him. "Sure, Eddy. Stay away from the road like always, though, okay?"

Pounding feet. He was out the door. *Slam!* Ted watched Grace wince at the second bounce of the screen door. "Sorry. I keep reminding him not to let go of the door."

"So do I."

He reached out to touch her arm. She flinched at his sudden contact and moved away to pick up his bowl.

Okay...don't surprise the woman. But he wasn't finished with the conversation. "Grace—wait. Leave the dish. I'll wash them for you later. It's the least I can do to say thank you for—for all you've done for us."

He studied her hesitation, needing to convince her, to apologize for his earlier behavior. "I'm harmless. Really."

He settled back, indicating the nearly useless leg, trying his most charming smile, feeling a betraying tremble start along the side of his arm. "As long as you can run faster than I can, you don't have anything to worry about, right?"

She did not help him out with a response, but curled herself on the sofa, restless and ready to run at a scent of distress.

"About—before, what I said, you know." He looked down at the floor. "Um, I'm sorry." He glanced at her face again. "I don't usually go around propositioning women."

Silence.

"I had a long day. Then there was a letter from my ex-wife, complaining about everything past and present. She didn't even ask about her own child. I guess I stressed and let myself get worked up about things."

She inclined her head, untangled her legs, and stood.

How to make her stay? "You're not exactly what I expected, you know," he told her, changing tack.

She eased back down. "Oh? You were expecting something in particular?"

"Well." He arched a brow. "The agent said a widow was interested in the place." He touched his chest. "I naturally pictured a little old, blue-haired lady with pearls."

Grace laughed then, sending relief washing over him. "Sorry to disappoint you."

"Not at all. You're forgiven." Ted enjoyed the tiny triumphant shiver. "Am I?"

Their mutual stare intensified and she skittered away, nervous as a kitten. "Y-yes. Of course. Just don't—don't let it happen again."

He reached to soothe her forearm, but sprang back when a spark leapt through the air. "Wow! It must be dry in here. That usually doesn't happen until winter. Grace? I saw, before, when I came in here before..." He wanted to curse his clumsiness. He didn't know how long her husband had been dead or how much she mourned him. *Stupid! Slow down!*

"I mean, the look on your face. It was so-so—well, sad, maybe, hurt about something? I, Eddy and I, that is, we don't want you to feel sad. If this isn't working out—"

"No! Don't! Wait, Ted. You don't understand." When she pulled away he let her go. "I want—excuse me. I'll be right back, okay? Just give me a second."

She snatched up the dish and hurried to the kitchen, splashing it into the sink full of sudsy water. She clung to the edge of the counter, swaying.

Ted watched her through the wide passage. Should he go after her?

She brought two cups of coffee five minutes later. He reminded himself he should no longer feel comfortable here, that his house belonged to a stranger now. Somehow Grace had changed everything. He felt more peace than he had ever known. It was a restless peace full of promise. Ted couldn't put a definitive answer on what the promise might hold but he knew he'd be content with whatever happened.

He followed her change of conversation, never once hinting at anything more personal than grocery shopping and open house at school. He took that memory home with him, the despair and longing on her face as she turned the pages for his son.

Chapter Nine

With Eddy comfortable in Kindergarten at Wind Point School four long days a week, Grace crossed off the aimless march of her days on the calendar. Eddy was thoroughly in love with Miss Jones, the pretty teacher in her second year in East Bay. When Ted had not stopped smiling all the way home from the first Open House, she'd felt mildly jealous. It was something she was not proud of. She needed to stick to her resolve not to become too involved with the neighbors. Even if they spent every afternoon at her house.

The time had come to think seriously about a job. Not the gas station, not the school. The library was as staffed as they could afford. Not the café. Not the resale shop. Maybe some volunteer work. Not PTA, though. That would really fuel the fires of gossip. Her fingers tingled.

She sighed. She was fully and properly trained. Everyone wore gloves these days. Maybe it would work. But…how? Who did she talk to, without raising too many eyebrows?

The next afternoon she went to spend some time with Shelby who was more bored than she was.

"Your husband is a doctor, right?" Grace asked. "But not here in town."

"Davy's at Bay Bridge. He's an endocrinologist. It's not far from here, so Greg sends patients there who need more than he and Matty can offer."

"Matty? Greg?"

"Oh, you probably haven't had any need to go to the clinic," Shelby said. "Greg Evans is our local GP. If you can believe it, we only have one doctor in town, but at least he's full time. East Bay's one and only clinic." She pulled her afghan around herself again. "Hey, come to think of it, Davy was talking about Greg's search for help again. Everyone hates waiting in line so long, but we've never been able to bring in another GP." Her voice lowered. "Everyone specializes these days. More money, you know."

Grace *hmm'd*.

"Greg would probably be grateful for even part-time help." Shelby hugged a pillow to her middle. "They take in a lot of Medicare patients. He can be a bit gruff, but the kids love him. He'll do house calls once in a while, and he's even accepted a casserole in payment. Some of those folks up the valley don't have much."

Grace found the casseroles hard to believe and just raised her brows.

Shelby plowed on, excited now. "His nurse, Matty, is a saint, a wonderful person. She's getting up there in age, though. I bet if you went over there he'd hire you on the spot."

Grace exhaled. She twitched her lips. Was this an answer? Maybe…maybe not. Was she really ready? "It's not that easy. I promised Ted I'd take care of Eddy."

Shelby thumped the pillow. "Yeah, it's a tough one. But you can't pass up a good opportunity. Your experience in that clinic where you came from…I'm sure it's enough. Even another practical nurse would work out. What are your qualifications again? Anyway, Greg would probably work out a deal so you could be home most afternoons."

"I left that life behind. I don't have a current license for Michigan, and I really can't…" Grace's protests might have sounded mild, but inside she was quaking. Could she do it? Go back to work? What if she did something wrong? Failed someone…again?

"You're more than a babysitter, girlfriend. I know it."

Grace took in a cleansing breath. "How about I read some more? Where were we?"

Shelby pouted but accepted the change of subject.

But the idea of working in the clinic grabbed Grace and wouldn't let go. Just plain working…nothing different. Nothing…unusual. She actually drove slowly past the little health services building on her way home that afternoon. There were four cars in the parking lot. The low building had a row of dark windows all along one side. The exterior was a rusty orange and someone had planted asters which bloomed with purple ferocity.

She pitched her idea to Ted later at night. It wasn't that she needed his approval or anything to get another job. She had agreed to be Eddy's caretaker first but owed it to Ted to discuss the possibility, if by some miracle she was hired at the clinic and did her best to work part-time, there was a chance an emergency might interfere.

They were sitting together after supper, reading the paper in Grace's living room when she broached the subject. Ted's glower and pout rivaled Shelby's.

"I didn't know you were looking for another job," he said, bending a corner of the business section to look at her. "I'm sorry. Look if you don't want to babysit anymore or if you need more money, I—"

"Ted!" They were sitting on opposite ends of her sofa. She faced him, pulling up a knee and curling her ankle underneath. She wrapped her hands around her leg and looked at him. "It's not the money. It's something Shelby said about the clinic. It sounds like they need help." *How can I explain my calling? Even when I ran away from it?* She was no longer terrified of admitting who she was. At least not the practical side. That much she could handle. As long as she was careful.

"Um, you may not know this but I am a PA, a Physician's Assistant. I'd have to look into getting certified in Michigan but that's my training, what I did back home." She tried some levity. "I'm not ready to retire, no matter if I'm a little old widow lady." When he frowned, she rushed on. "Not that taking care of Eddy isn't important. And I love it."

She started to reach out to touch him, pulling back only at the last second. "The funny thing," she said, trying again to lighten up the atmosphere, "is I really didn't want to have anything to do with heal— um, medicine, again. I left Woodside not thinking I would ever return to work in the field. But here I am in Michigan, thinking about the same old thing."

"Of course I didn't know that about you!" Ted's mouth was tight, his lips pale. His blue topaz eyes sparked. He turned away from her. "You tell me so little about yourself, even when I ask you. I know hardly anything at all about you! Whether you have any children, how old you are, whether you had any pets when you were growing up."

Grace leaned her face against her knee, wondering where that outburst sprang from. It was a little late to get personal after all these months. Why had he held back? She knew why she had, though her once-proud claim to choose whether or not she cared about her new home and its people was a long-lost idiosyncrasy. Their unspoken agreement to act as though they had no history, as if life started last spring, had worked so well for her. She sighed. "I don't have any children, Ted. I'm ancient, and as a kid I had a white rabbit like *Alice in Wonderland*, named 'Rose,' of course, and two hamsters for a couple of months until I forgot about them and only smelled them later. Mother was not happy but she refused to interfere when I promised I would take care of them. I'm an only child and my parents are dead," she added for good measure. "There. How's that?"

"Better. I'm sorry about your parents. And Rose. So you worked at a medical center in Woodside? A PA, huh?"

"Something like that." She jumped up and started dancing a strange jig in surprise. She'd sat long enough for her feet to fall asleep and the prickles were literally shocking. Ted laughed. She tossed her head and marched relatively straight into the kitchen to check on Eddy. He didn't even look up from coloring pumpkins and turkeys for her front windows with oddly scented markers. The markers had all been uncapped and left to mingle on the table like so many abandoned fish. She wrinkled her nose and started to turn aside, not realizing Ted had slowly drifted in her wake.

She continued the conversation, ignoring what his proximity did to her heart rate. The last time he'd gotten to her, she'd almost lost it and touched him. No way could she let that happen. He might be looking a little better these days, but he was not well, either.

"So, I thought I would just check into it, Ted. I don't even know if they really want help, could use mine, or how much time it would be. I will ask the clinic hours not interfere with Eddy's school schedule before I decide anything, okay?"

"You don't need my permission to get a job." His easy laugh of a moment ago was gone. Eddy looked up from his turkey project, eyes wide under his heavy swath of bangs. Ted put his hand on his son's shoulder.

Grace smiled to reassure the boy nothing was wrong.

It didn't work. "You're getting a job, Grace? Who's gonna take care of me?" His anguished face nearly undid her plans right then. "My mom wouldn't have gone and done something so stupid."

Grace ignored the paper cut to her heart Eddy's words caused as she gave a smoldering flame-cheeked Ted "the look" out of the corner of her eye. She swiftly went to put her arms around Eddy while he sat at the table. Kids at school must have been talking.

"I'm only thinking about helping Doctor Evans out at the clinic while you're at school, Eddy. I'm not sure if he needs help. You're my most important job right now. I'll still be here almost all the time when you need me. It's just sometimes someone has an accident or gets sick when I want to come home, but I have to help them, too."

"Oh. I like Doctor Evans," he said. "And Matty puts me on Ranger Robot bandages," he continued, clueless about mixing up his words, clueless of the effect of his earlier words about his mother. He went back to coloring, relaxed. "I can come and see you there, too, can't I? I didn't know you were a doctor. But I did know you're smart as Miss Jones. I love you!"

"Yeah, well..." She ruffled his head as she stalked past the little man's father out of the kitchen.

* * * *

"Time to start moving, Eds," Ted told his boy, Eddy's work apparently done here. Grace's unspoken admonishment worked its way up and out of his spine. So the cruelness at school had already begun. Should he talk to Eddy about his mother? He'd ask Randy first how to do it. Shelby, too. Eddy hadn't acted traumatized. Maybe he should just brush it off. Grace...again, she surprised him, made him uncomfortable in so many warring ways.

All the way home he heard her voice in his head. Ancient, hmmm… and he caught the present tense in her answer about children. What did she mean when she said she didn't think she'd ever want anything to do with medicine again? What had happened back in Tennessee? He'd never pried, never felt the need to. He'd trusted her from the moment he'd first seen her, one of his old ragged tee shirts wrapped around her hair as she cleaned cobwebs Jilly had never bothered to notice the growing filth. Then, he hadn't done much about it except childishly use it as poison on the marriage.

He should have asked for references at least, before he hired Grace Runyon to take care of Eddy. He had meant to. Somehow, he'd never gotten around to it. Shelby's opinion seemed more than adequate. Maybe he shouldn't have been so hasty.

"Bedtime, kiddo," he said as they crossed the threshold.

"Dad!"

"What clothes are you wearing tomorrow? And where's your school bag? Let's pack it up. What papers did you bring home for me to see?"

During their evening routine, thoughts continued to swirl. There must be a better way to learn more about her. Shelby and Davy could help figure out where this Woodside clinic was. Somewhere in Tennessee…

* * * *

Grace returned to Doctor Evans's clinic and this time went inside. When she explained her reason for stopping in to Nancy, the receptionist, there was no mistaking the young woman's wide-eyed look of relief. "Wait right here!" Nancy disappeared down a hallway and returned three minutes later. "When can you come back and talk to the doctor?"

On a mid-November Friday afternoon, when Eddy and his father were home together doing whatever fathers and sons find to do, she paused in the driveway in front of the clinic. The parking lot was an ominous three-quarters full, car windows glinting in the fading light, and wind rattled the remaining brown leaves still clinging to skeletal trees.

She clutched the pristine envelope with her diploma, CE credits from Harvard and certificates from Greenville declaring her duly bestowed with all the privileges of a Physician's Assistant, along with references she never imagined she would ever need. It had been a sort of joke in Woodside, keeping the papers in her emergency bag in her car. Now she was glad to have them even if she could not believe she actually wanted—ached—for the feel of steel instruments in her hands, the look of children and mothers who begged her to help them feel better, the brisk scent of rubbing alcohol. Gloves. She'd have to remember gloves at all times. She pushed open the glass doors, thinking up reasons for the amount of cars in the parking lot.

The office window was dark and deserted, a sign-in chart left haphazardly on the counter, a pen tied to a string swung below the clipboard in a lazy arc. The waiting room overflowed with a dozen people in varying degrees of discomfort, an unsmiling mother holding her youngster over the garbage can in the corner where he unreservedly vomited. Two other children and a dad looked ready to join him. Grace walked down the hall, as apparently no one was available to invite her to her appointment. At the door marked "Doctor's Office," she knocked.

She took the resulting groan as an invitation to enter. A sandy-haired man in a white doctor's coat slumped in a maroon leather desk chair. His eyes were closed. "I just need a second, Matty," he said faintly.

"I'm Grace Runyon, Doctor, ah, Evans, about the job. I see you're busy, though, so I'll…"

The man's eyes snapped open at this, and as quickly, closed again.

"Oh, yes. I'm sorry but we're in the midst of an early season flu outbreak and I really don't want you catching it. If you could come back later, that would be great."

"I never get sick."

Doctor Evans opened one lid to reveal a foggy hazel eye. "Never? Really? In that case, you're hired." He carefully got to his feet. He'd probably unfold to at least six-two standing fully straight.

"No, wait." He rested his knuckles on the clean desk top, hunched over, and watched her. "What do you do for the flu?"

She wondered at the trick question. "Um, not much, unless there's obvious dehydration determined by patient information, skin touch, and a look at the eyes. Then we re-hydrate, IV if necessary, watch for spiked temp and bring it down if pushing one hundred three for more than a few hours."

"Okay, how about a busted collarbone?" he asked, without apparent need to impress her with technical jargon.

"Well, again, not much. Visual exam, X-ray. MRI if suspected soft tissue damage or internal fixation is needed. Otherwise, stabilization with a sling, painkillers, and follow up, possible PT," she said, curious about the nature of these two obvious tests.

"Okay, now you're hired. I'll check your references and see about transferring your license later." He offered a tiny smile. "Actually, Davy Brouwer told me you might come. Right now, we have patients who need to be told there's 'not much' we can do for them, and Tony Vandergroot, age eleven, who needs a sling. I have about half an hour,"—he looked up to the ceiling, rising to his tiptoes, stretching and taking a deep breath—"I think, before I collapse. Matty is done in, and Nancy went home about ten this morning." He turned his computer screen with an obvious X ray toward her, watched while she studied it for two minutes, then ushered her back into the hallway. "Come. You get to tell Tony no skateboarding for six weeks."

He grinned weakly. "Baptism by fire, as they say. Welcome to East Bay Community Clinic."

* * * *

The schedule Greg set up for her was perfect. Grace worked six-hour shifts for the most part, Mondays and Tuesdays and Thursdays, trading some on-call days when Greg and Matty needed extra help. The job offer had happened so fast, she'd been stunned, giddy. Piece of cake. She'd called Shelby to crow.

"I owe you big time! What do you want?"

"For you to be happy," Shelby replied. "And a healthy baby, of course."

"Your desire shall be granted." Grace giggled and hung up,

squashing down a flare of doubt, maybe jealousy if were really honest, replacing it with relief. Then wonderment at what she'd gotten herself into. She quickly booted up her computer and started to read through last year's medical journals.

* * * *

The doctor was not nearly as young as he first appeared to Grace, so exhausted as he sat at his desk. On closer inspection she noted fine lines around the outside of his pale hazel eyes and silver woven through his thick, blond hair. He had been surprised to know she was the new neighbor at the Marshall place, and her primary reason for working the short hours was to care for Eddy.

"I'm not much into the local gossip," Greg said. "I developed this habit of listening with just one ear. Then I never have to remember if I'm told something in confidence or not, though everything is supposed to be confidential," he said, in much better health and humor, now the mini flu epidemic was over. "I'm always amazed at what I hear at Kaye's a half hour after an accident, though."

Grace wondered how much he knew about Ted's condition, and if he would talk about it. She didn't even finish the thought before he answered.

"Ah, yes. Ted Marshall. Had to turn him over to Beardslee in Lansing," he said in his shorthand speak when referring to medical cases, regret in his voice. "Terrible accident. No reason to think it's the cause of the deterioration, though. Can't put my finger on it. Should be…ah, well. But it isn't. No known viral or organic. I checked out some interesting stuff on the net. Shouldn't be happening." He looked up at her. "All hypothetical, of course."

"Of course."

At a staff meeting at Bay Bridge Hospital before her next shift she met more of the medical community. The group arranged itself in a loose circle on folding metal chairs. Despite the navy padded seats the backs of the chairs were cold. Closed navy drapes and abstract prints hung on the walls, removing any sense of coziness. Deeply padded carpeting muffled the conversation and the "new" smell competed with antiseptic from the hallway oozing in whenever the door opened to admit another arrival. Before the meeting, Greg officially introduced her to his inherited nurse. Matty of the famous bandages had been ensconced when he first joined the local medical clinic fourteen years earlier, an invaluable help, the doctor said. Grace had only seen the backside of Mathilde Van Ooyen disappearing into the restroom at the clinic when she'd first interviewed.

"Grace, here's our Mathilde—the best nurse at East Bay Community Clinic."

"The only nurse, you sly one. Call me Matty," she told Grace. East Bay's nurse was in her late fifties at least, judging by her iron-gray hair. Her rich labials and slurring sibilants identified her as a non-native speaker. Pleasantly well-fed, Matty appeared to enjoy life. Grace did not dare compare Greg and Matty to the medical people back home. It was past time to move on with her life. Woodside was over.

The three of them stood together before the huge silver coffeepot, embellishing the thin brown, harsh-smelling contents of their foam cups with various powdered offerings. Grace ignored the large sugar cookies and stale-looking donuts arranged on a paper doily near the pot. Matty revealed her origins during their easy conversation. As suspected, she was born Dutch. The nurse smiled quizzically at Grace, head cocked, eyebrows rising to some inner rhythm of thought as the doctor droned on with the introductions.

"I was just planning to fulfill an obligation to the university, to practice in a smaller, less prosperous community before I went on to bigger and better things," Greg said. "I went to med school on a community grant and scholarship and the university helped pay part of the costs. Once I got here, got to know some of the people, I didn't want to leave. Where else would be better to live?"

"Grace, dear, anything you can do to help out this poor, tired, exhausted soul. He can't keep up with me, you know," Matty stage-whispered conspiratorially and gave a wicked wink.

The doctor grinned. "These Dutch women are so demanding," he responded and turned away to shake hands with another of the hospital staff.

The nurse gave Grace a soul-searching look which she took in good humor. Establishing a good rapport from the first was mutually beneficial. When Matty reached out her hands, Grace automatically met them.

"Ja, good, strong, warm, useful hands," she happily observed, squeezing. There was no spark, no tingle; nothing but firm pressure. Her hands were warm, tough, and square with deep calluses. The older woman leaned close then and held Grace in a narrowed focus.

"You have it, don't you?" she asked.

A chill ran up her spine. "Ha-have what?"

"The touch. Yes, I can feel it."

Grace tried to pull away. "I'm not sure what you mean." She broke eye contact.

"Yes, you do. The touch of someone who feels what's wrong and wants to fix it. The special gift that makes a healer."

Grace gasped and let go, panicked at the woman's potential reaction. Could she tell?

"Not ever'one has it," Matty said, turning to bob her chin at the pepper-headed man at Greg's side.

Grace relaxed.

"Him, for instance, Mathews. Has the technique, but not the call." Matty looked at her again. "Not the gift." She sniffed. "So, come, I'll introduce you."

Chapter Ten

Grace noticed the change in the atmosphere when she went out in East Bay now to do her errands. People who recognized her from the clinic or church greeted her with cautious friendliness. She enjoyed these small signs of acceptance. She had come a long way since spring when she was the usurper of the Marshall property, the stranger who bought her clothes and furniture as cast-offs from the community. Home at last. This could work. Everything could work out very well, and no one would ever have reason to accuse her of anything.

Tanya greeted her when she stopped in at the bustling café for an aromatic morning coffee and roll, and to buy her mint and pekoe tea blends and some other things the grocery stores in town didn't usually carry. Carob was a favorite, although she didn't ever let on to Eddy that he was not eating real chocolate chips in his cookies.

Kaye, though, was another story. The woman sniped ever so subtly about her clothes (ah, I see you're wearing van Ooyen again), her hair (Livvie at Stylish does wonders, let me call for you), whether she sat in a booth (bad light, dear, it will make more wrinkles when you squint) or table (oh, not there, dear, you're alone, sit at the counter) whenever Grace went in to order tea or buy some other goods. Grace stopped trying to stay for a cup of coffee and to read the paper, the anger vibes creating disharmony the rest of the day. Too bad, because Grace wanted to like Kaye. The underlying problem obviously revolved around those bothersome brothers. Snide little comments about having the attention of not one or two, but three Marshalls got on her nerves. The woman's obvious hots for Ted, and Randy's long-suffering looks at her, drove Grace crazy. As if she was some kind of competition. Which, of course, she was not. Even if, upon occasion, Ted made her remember just exactly what she missed about being married. Anyone who thought widows were out to catch another husband did not understand the concept of the soul-rendering loss. It's not like husbands were easily replaceable, mix and match. But why didn't Randy tell Kaye how he felt about her? Had the woman once rejected him? Ted never mentioned her, except as a community business leader and aunt to Tanya. Grace doubted Ted even noticed the unrequited lust going on in front of his nose.

None of your business, woman. Just live—breathe, eat, sleep, work, worship. Not necessarily in that order. East Bay was no different than any place on earth with its little intrigues, busy-bodies, love and life messes. There was room for her and she was gradually adjusting.

* * * *

Greg caught her up as she left the clinic after an unusual early evening shift she'd agreed to. Today was a birthday she had no intention of sharing with anything other than a pint of cherry macadamia nut chocolate ice cream and the latest cheesy Nicholas Sparks film.

"Hey! Wait a minute!" He came running into the parking lot before she opened her car door. "Could you possibly do me a favor and take this over to the hospital? Our Internet server just went down and the admitting doc there wants to check out this file. Would it be too much trouble?"

Grace bit her lip, but let go immediately. "Of course not. I'll drive up there now."

Greg waved as she drove off. She saw him in the rear view mirror as she turned the corner. He cast as long a shadow as Ted Marshall. A shivery echo of the feel of Ted's touch along her cheek made her jerk the gear when she shifted into fourth.

Eat, sleep, work. You don't need anything else, Grace. Eat, sleep, work.

She wandered the halls of Bay Bridge Hospital not thoroughly lost, but candidly enjoying the "long way around," as she told the couple of nurses who asked if she needed help. A faint tang of antiseptic made her feel at home and she could not stop smiling. In Tennessee, Lena had told her she was nuts, but Grace's sense of smell was acute and she learned the brands of disinfectants almost like the vintages of fine wines.

Someone fell into step with her as she walked along. She looked up and then stopped in her tracks.

Her companion stopped, too, inquiring grin on his face. "Ah, yes! Grace Runyon, new PA over with Greg?" He held out his hand, knocking away the stethoscope nestled around his neck.

"Yes. I'm afraid you have me at a disadvantage." She sneaked a look at his ID badge as she shook his hand, but it was inconveniently covered by the stethoscope cords.

"Sorry."

She could tell he wasn't sorry at all and delighted in taking her off guard. He was probably the latest McDreamy at the hospital, fresh, good-looking enough to know it and confident, well-dressed, and purposeful. Brown hair, clear eyes, she noticed as he introduced himself. "Tom Rawlins, DO, if you can believe it. We met a few weeks ago at one of the long, dull staff meetings."

"I apologize for not recognizing you, Doctor. I'm still getting used to things and people." She continued walking. "Don't let me hold you up."

"I think you might have exactly what I need."

At her raised brow, Rawlins smirked, indicating the file in her arms.

Grace felt the flame on her cheek. "Oh! Right. I'm so sorry." She looked at the name she had written on the little drug company notepaper, clipped to the file. "Doctor Rawlins. You, I presume?"

"Yup," he replied, cheerfully. "Call me Tom. Why don't you follow me to my office? It's just down the hall, here."

He held open the door for her, clicking the lights on and taking the file. He flipped it open, indicating absent-mindedly she should sit in the chair opposite his at his desk. Grace did so slowly, while looking around. A couple of nicely framed prints of birds on the wall besides his various diplomas, two very much alive and healthy philodendrons in brass pots flowing along his book shelves, a mess of papers on a small work table under the now dark window made a comfortable tableau.

The doctor continued to read through the short file, then looked up at her. The corners of his eyes crinkled as he leaned back in his chair. "So, how do you like Michigan?"

This time of evening was not a great time to have a getting-to-know-you conversation, especially when she was tired. "Ah, just fine, Doctor." She tried to erase the worry lines between her brows and took a calming breath. "Was there anything else?" She gathered her little clutch purse and rose, hoping to escape before she forgot to stay aloof and polite.

That brought Rawlins to his feet in a hurry. "I'm so sorry to keep you. But I wondered if you didn't have any other plans, if you'd care to have dinner with me tonight." He came around his desk and made a show of settling her coat over her shoulders.

What on earth? He couldn't be…could he? "Well, um, I'm flattered." She stared at his chin for a minute and raised her eyes to his. The hopeful expression said, yes, he certainly was making a pass. Too bad he wasn't remotely attractive to her. He didn't raise a single goose bump or tingle. Certainly nothing like—"I buried my husband a few months ago, Doctor, you see, and I'm simply not ready for…" She let the words fade, hoping it was enough of a hint. No need to crush a guy for trying.

He paled only a shade. "I understand. Can I call you sometime?"

No. "Perhaps in a couple of years." Grace walked out to the parking lot, head high, and chuckled as she got into her car, wondering if Greg had set her up. It had been a long time—twenty years, in fact, since she had been asked out on a date by anyone other than Jonathan. She doubted Rawlins was really interested, but still…

"Okay, not bad for thirty-six! Happy birthday to me." She giggled as she drove away.

* * * *

Grace's first Thanksgiving in Michigan was over, celebrated low-key with dinner and church service. Snow had fallen several times, covering her driveway and showing her the real reason for a garage. Snow. So much already. Eight inches over three falls. How did people manage? Dark, dreary all the time. Why did anyone want to live here?

Eddy's first school program had been held the evening before the Thursday of Thanksgiving in the school gym. She was tickled to coach Eddy on his two sweet little lines, and sat with Ted at the program, returning the nods and little smiles from those she recognized. She stared down their smirks, knowing their tiny evil minds drew livid pictures of her relationship with Ted and Eddy and probably Randy Marshall.

Sometimes she worried if the speculations would hurt them, but remembered, choice, it was her choice. She chose to let life happen. And it was a good life, working, breathing, giving something back, something that helped, not hurt, others. Earning her way back to forgiveness, so to speak.

Though she hadn't sent any holiday cards, she'd received one from home earlier in the week. She put it on her kitchen windowsill after reading the message and turning it over and over. It took a couple of days before she could look at it without feeling nauseous. The last time she had driven to the bank down in Cadillac, Mr. Harris, her account manager, had a folder waiting for her. It contained a letter from her attorney in Woodside and the card.

Elizabeth Runyon's handwriting flowed as beautifully as always. She had signed on behalf of Roger. Had her former father-in-law known?

Nice of you, Elizabeth. Yes. Very nice. And Elizabeth had been nice. When Grace's parents died, Elizabeth stepped in. Not to take their place, but to do the things a mother had to do, to be what they needed, especially with Sean and then when Jonathan was diagnosed with cancer.

Would she ever be able to face them again? Had it been enough time since his death, his funeral? Was there some other way she tell them she was sorry, and she was trying to make it up to them by helping others? Grace considered writing back, a little frightened maybe they'd ignore her. Or worse, that someone would come and find her, take revenge, as she deserved. She might send a Christmas card. Maybe even a card and letter to Lena, her closest friend. Time might be the universal healer, but not near enough of it had passed for her to feel completely at ease with her past. Maybe it never would. On the bright side she could probably open an account at the bank here in East Bay if she didn't have to hide anymore.

A welcome knock on the door put an end to her dilemma as Randy and Eddy came stomping in to claim their hot chocolate after shoveling snow from her sidewalk.

"Ted wasn't kidding back in August when he told me about the snow in Michigan." She pinched Eddy's tasseled hat and pulled it off, smiling at his rosy cheeks and runny nose.

Randy unbuttoned his coat, but left it on. "Who's afraid of a little snow?"

"Didn't you have snow in—achoo!—in…" Eddy managed to rub his nose on his sleeve before she could reach him, "in Ten—" The rest was muffled under Grace's tissue and command to "blow."

Randy's assessing eyes made her tense. They might have reached a point of common familiarity, certainly respect, but not the level that called for this type of inspection. There were plenty of things he didn't need to know about her and her past, for instance, that would certainly unlevel the playing field.

If he could check her out, she could return the favor. He had let his hair grow a little longer for the winter.Instead of looking like a bristle brush over his scalp it covered his head in a smooth wave, softening his expression. In fact, everything about him was softer than their first meeting on her front porch last spring. Whatever the reason, he no longer terrorized her, even if she wasn't as comfortable with him as with his brother. She answered Eddy.

"Not like here, Eds. It snows a little, but doesn't usually stay around much. Sometimes we get great ice storms." She tried to measure up to their pride in showing her their world, offering up their experiences.

The little boy helped himself to the cocoa mix on her kitchen table, leaving a dusting of the brown powder. "Hey, Grace, where'd you get the turkey card?"

She snatched Elizabeth's card and stuffed it in a drawer. "Just someone I knew in Tennessee," she said quietly. "Don't I need a snowman for my yard? Let's make one after hot chocolate!"

* * * *

"Hey, Grace, grab your coat and come on. You're gonna love this—it's right up your alley! Oh, and bring some of your goo—the hot stuff with the Capcaisin." Greg Evans was on the run, pulling her along with him. "Hold down the fort, Nancy, and reschedule until three o'clock, okay?" He didn't stop for her affirmation before hauling his carry bag out the door and to his car.

"We don't do a lot of house calling, but once in a while," Greg started to say, before concentrating on getting out of the parking lot past the unsmiling elderly couple driving in, and down to the old country road leading out of town, driving over the hard-packed snow as if it wasn't there. Grace still couldn't force herself to do more than thirty-five.

"Anyway, once in a while I'll go up and see a few people who can't come in to the clinic."

"What do you mean, 'right up my alley'?"

"A lot of your Tennessee folk came up here in the nineteen forties and fifties to work in the auto industry, which is, for all practical intents and purposes, no longer the promise and hope for the future it once was. Of course these people, second and third generations of them now, stayed and continue to live like they always did—no offense."

"None taken, I'm sure," she replied a little huffily. What—did everyone really think all hill folk were backwoods country idiots?

She caught Greg's glance and twisted her lips in a terse smile.

"It's not a crime to be poor," Greg commented.

"It's not a crime to be a hillbilly, either. Not everyone from my home is backwards or indigent."

Greg touched her hands. "No one said they were. I thought you might like to meet some of these folk. You know, you told me you did this kind of thing back around Woodside."

She relaxed. "You're right. I miss that, going up to see some of my patients. I used to keep an emergency pack in my car and everything. People knew my number, and I'd go when I had to. Sometimes Jonathan would become annoyed when I went alone out at night." She turned to look out of the car window, watching carefully which turns Greg made. "So, what's the case today?"

"It's Elvira Brown. Everyone calls her Granny B. Severe arthritis. I'm trying to get her to do some simple exercises, but, well, you know what they say…"

Grace snorted. She followed him out of the car and treaded carefully through wood soot-dusted piles of snow to a faded house with a stream of smoke climbing from a chimney.

"She always has a plate of rock-hard cookies or shortbread or some of her preserves set out." His voice whispered conspiratorially as they knocked on her dilapidated door, "Stay away from the lemonade-looking stuff. It's made from sumac. And a little something extra."

She raised her brows. "Lemonade in winter?"

Greg laughed.

Chapter Eleven

The trouble with Thanksgiving was that Christmas caromed right afterward.

Grace searched through the gaudy boxes of Christmas cards in East Bay's variety store. The flash of a familiar bulge caught her eye.

"Caught ya!" she hissed, from just out of sight in the next aisle. She giggled as her pregnant friend jumped like a kid caught lifting the tape on a wrapped gift under her mom's bed. She peeked around the corner.

"Honestly!" Shelby pulled her coat tighter around her middle and looked back and forth. "I thought Davy had the bed rest cops out again. Here I was, hoping not to run into anyone I knew. After the last time, I can hardly go to the bathroom by myself when he's home. I'm going crazy all cooped up."

"Did you sneak out? At least the weather's nice. I hope you only toddled these three blocks from your house."

"Of course! How about you come have a tea with me?"

"You betcha!" Grace giggled. Midwestern slang showed up in her vocabulary when she least expected.

Back at the Brouwers', she helped Shelby with her boots and coat and bundled her up in the afghan on the sofa.

"I don't know if I'll ever be able to wait on anyone else again. I'm getting used to this royalty treatment," her friend said.

"I don't think you need to worry about that when the baby is here."

"You bought some Christmas cards."

Grace nodded, wary.

"Eddy told me someone sent you a Thanksgiving card from Tennessee."

"Hmm." Little pitchers…no secrets with the boy around. She might as well have taken out an ad in the paper. She bent over her steaming mug, praying her friend would drop it, yet hoping she could talk to someone about the overwhelming nostalgia. Last year she's spent the holiday with Jonathan and his parents in the hospital. They hadn't been able to stay long. She could do without that particular memory, but there'd been others. Her first married Christmas. Sean's first tree and gifts. He's stared at the lights in bald, drooling fascination, cooing and gurgling.

Shelby drank from her own cup of Mystic Orange. "This is your first holiday on your own, I think, isn't it?" She held out a tissue.

Grace grabbed it like a lifeline. "Y-y-yes, it is. I didn't imagine it would b-be so h-hard."

A soothing touch felt like a blessing on her bent head. "It's okay, Grace. Someday you'll feel like things are working out, life is more than simply sleeping, working, and breathing. You'll see. It's about time you let go of some of that anxiety for the holidays you've been carting around."

"You've been a great friend. You've made me feel welcome, helped me so much. I'm not sure I would have stayed if you hadn't been so nice." Grace sniffed and wiped her eyes.

"Yeah." Shelby rubbed her bulging tummy. "Well, I doubt I'm the reason you stayed. But thanks. Sometimes, when you've known people all your life, you don't really have anyone to tell things to 'cause they already know it!"

It didn't hurt as much as she expected when Grace cracked a tentative smile.

"So, you've been exactly the friend I've needed, too," Shelby said. "Ooh!"

"What is it? Are you okay?"

"Yeah," she wheezed. "Just an extra tug. I think."

Grace put her hand on Shelby's belly to gauge the bubbling spasm.

It soon eased. Another pillow under her knees would help, along with a foot and ankle rub. Shelby wasn't too swollen, but enough to merit a reminder bed rest was an order.

An enervating conduit of peace passed back and forth between them with her touch, a comfortable reminder of the gift slowly recharging inside of her. She wasn't fully prepared to admit how much she'd missed it, even as Sean's laughter echoed around her skull. Why now? Why were these memories surging out of their neatly labeled boxes she'd thought safely locked in the attic of her soul? A baby…so precious. She'd practiced as a midwife last year before having Sean, visiting expectant mothers and fathers, acting as doula or delivering at home. The joy of that first breath, that first cradling hold, so right in her hands. The pulsing of the warm umbilical cord reminding her of attachment, but also of the need to let go. Trust. So hard.

"There. Stopped," Shelby declared. "The doctor said not to get too excited unless my water broke or the spasms didn't stop. Early contractions or something, he said. You should have seen Davy sweat the first one last month!"

Grace passed off her automatic professional smile, but she worried about her friend. The story Ted had told her about the last time they'd tried to have a baby and almost died lingered on the surface of her consciousness. She'd never let anything happen to Shelby and the baby. She must remember…do nothing unusual. Only what she'd trained for. If she did everything right, Shelby and the baby would be fine.

Grace walked to the other side of the room and took her coat from the closet.

Shelby pulled the colored afghan around her shoulders. "Hey. Thanks for your concern. You make me feel safe, you know. Everyone says how great you're doing at the clinic." Her smile grew conspiratorial. "Mr. Jeffries won't even see Doc anymore. He only makes his appointments with you." She winked, and Grace laughed.

"The people are very kind. I'm so glad to be here. I'll take off now and let you two rest."

For once her friend didn't protest.

* * * *

A week later another of Grace's dilemmas was conveniently solved. She laughed at the sight of her neighbors' special delivery upon answering the door.

"We brought you a Christmas tree, Grace!" Eddy pranced into her living room. Randy carried in a fresh cut fir and Ted followed, hunched into his coat against the cold.

"Why is it, just when I'm really wondering what to do, my prayer gets answered?"

"What prayer?" Eddy galloped around the tree.

She grabbed him and hugged him tightly. "Why, how to find the perfect Christmas tree, of course! And here you are, my favorite guys, bringing one right to me."

Whoops! The words popped right out before she considered them. Ted leaned forward, both hands folded over his cane, bemused smile on his face, while Randy spared a fleeting glance as he turned the tree for the best angle in front of her window.

"Eddy—fetch the stand, boy. I think we left it outside," he told his nephew. A blast of cold air filled the living room when he raced out and back in again with a red metal stand clutched in his arms.

Grace tried to cover her awkwardness with exaggerated cheer as she imagined herself wiping that smirk off Ted's face. "We'll string some popcorn and gingerbread guys on it, Eds."

"I'll make you some!"

"You're my best decorator," she told the little boy as she helped Randy settle the pretty little tree into its stand. Randy and Ted then examined the multitude of paper snowflakes taped to the front windows, some on large lined paper, some misshapen, but all made with love.

"I think we can send over some stuff, Grace," Ted said. He plopped into her little bentwood rocker. "Mom had a lot of decorations and most of it's in the attic yet. We never did a lot of decorating after she passed away."

"Oh, I couldn't use your mother's things," she replied, appalled he would say such a thing. She gave the tree a critical eye. "I'm sure now that Eddy is older you'll enjoy decorating with him and use them yourselves. But thank you for thinking of me. I have some things of my own I could bring out."

A large box had been shipped up from Tennessee last month, in fact. Still wavering over how long to stay here, where else she could run that wasn't inundated with snow or sick people, she had directed her lawyer to close up the house for now. As she wrote a detailed list of what to send she wondered how much he'd get right and laughed at herself when she reread some of her directions. "A box in the downstairs closet, underneath the steps, marked Holiday 2, not General Ornaments…" "A set of eight dishes, the bird ones in the cupboard to the left of the refrigerator, the ceramic ones, not the white china set…" Poor guy earned his pay.

But what she'd finally understood was no more secrets back there. If they'd wanted her back, they would have asked. Lena's letters started coming two weeks ago—three newsy missives—catching Grace up on news of Woodside. Lena conveniently passed over anything too personal, memories that might have proved too sad.

Grace had replied with a postcard. Just an appetizer, she told Lena. It would take awhile before she felt comfortable writing at all, let alone talking about her new life. She wasn't ready to start e-mailing or even texting her friends, either. In time. Let the memories fade a little more, allow the blame to burn away. They might forgive her eventually, if there was more distance and she had more proof she was doing good things.

She roused from her muse to catch Ted watching her, telltale sympathy in the gentleness of the lines on his face. Randy stared past the tree out of the big window.

Yeah, so? Widows deserve a little sympathy.

Ted pressed to his feet, gesturing for Eddy to come and put on his coat. "Well, Grace, us favorite guys gotta mosey on. I hope you don't mind we took it upon ourselves to bring you this one. We didn't give you a chance to pick it out or even knew if you liked living Christmas trees."

She flushed, feeling him pick at her thoughts. "I love the tree." She buttoned Eddy's coat and wound the scarf around his neck. "I can't thank you all enough. I'll see you tomorrow, then, for church? Would you three like to have dinner here? It's the least I can do."

She waved them gone from her porch and turned back inside, daunted by the thought of actually having to open some of the boxes from Woodside.

* * * *

On the floor of Eddy's former bedroom, the contents of the largest carton of her belongings from Tennessee spread in a loose arc around her. Her tea the other day with Shelby seemed to breach a dam of pent-up emotion. Tears rolled non-stop down her face and dripped on her sweater. She took out the bubble-wrapped framed photographs of her parents, Jonathan's parents, of herself and Jonathan, and finally, of Sean. She put those of Sean away to look at later and held up the one of Jonathan and herself sitting on a big rock at Acadia Park in Maine where they had vacationed once. The ocean sprayed across their smiling faces. They had been wet and so happy. There had been so many good times before he got sick.

She smiled as she unwrapped some of the pinecone ornaments her mother had decorated with paint and tiny glued-on birds, beads, and glitter, and one she attempted as a child. Four glass birds from her collection. It was a big chance sending them through the mail, but they had been carefully wrapped and cushioned. Eight doilies her great-grandmother crocheted, taken from her living room chairs. They were yellowed with age, quaint dainty little things. Grace held one up to the light, marveling still at the microscopic stitches, then set it aside on the bare floor, smoothing it with her forefinger.

She brushed hair behind her ear as she bent forward again, pulling out the dozen books she requested. She smiled, thinking of whoever was kind enough to search through the numerous titles to pull these favorites for her: Sir Walter Scott, Tennyson, and Kipling. Eddy might like some of Felix Salten's *Bambi: A Life in the Woods*, the early parts, if he didn't already know the non-Disney version.

On the bottom was a heavy packaged set of kitchen dishes. She was tired of the unmatched and stained plastic odds and ends she picked up at garage sales and found leftover in the cupboards. Ted said Jilly took away most of what they had when she left. Grace had always liked the chunky country-art set of eight she and Jonathan had found on one of their weekend rambles. The plates and cups were moss green with folk birds and birdhouses around the edges, in old blues and deep reds and mustard yellows. He'd done well, her attorney, or probably Gina, his paralegal. She heaved herself off the floor and hauled the dishes out to the kitchen to wash, her river of tears mingling with the dishwater.

A few hours later she answered the door to Ted who stood alone on her front porch, fist raised mid-knock.

"I just came with a few of Mom's old decorations, even though… I just thought it would be a kick, getting them out and I wanted to share…to tell you about some of them. I guess, really just to talk. If this is a bad time, though…" Ted stammered. "Can I, um, do anything?"

Grace focused on him, wondering why he was really there. He drew his eyebrows together, as if concerned about something. Someone. Her? She rubbed tear tracks from her cheeks.

He shifted a box under his arm and held it out. "Here. Just look at them. If you can't use them, I'll take them back."

"Okay."

Ted stared past her into the living room. "You're unpacking."

"Yes. I had the house in Woodside closed up and a-a few things shipped," she replied, pressing her lips together. She squirmed under his scrutiny. She had put the picture, the one of her and Jonathan on vacation, younger and untried, on her end table.

Ted swayed against the doorjamb. "Ah, well, maybe I'll come back another time, then."

Had he come for a reason? She was so tired. She shook her head and blinked. "Excuse me?" She wasn't supposed to have Eddy, was she? He wasn't here? No, it was the weekend. She was alone with the ghosts of her past. "Thank you. I'm sorry, Ted. What did you want?"

Ted took a deep breath and straightened. "A cup of sugar?" he said with the hint of a smile. "I was mostly showing off. Look—no cane, no crutch, but—I'll go. I'm sorry I keep turning up. Just because I live next door doesn't give me the right to drop in any time, unannounced. Although you don't have the phone turned on, so I couldn't call ahead and ask."

Grace tried to smile, a real and honest one, but she felt confused about how she should accept his news, his visit, his gifts. "Yes. I don't. How wonderful for you. And, thank you," she said, without any sense or order.

Ted cocked his head. Silence ensued. "Okay, then. I'll be off."

And to her dismay and confusion, she let him go. All these ghosts reminded her of what she'd been incapable of in the past. She couldn't risk hurting anyone now…certainly not someone as vulnerable as Ted. It was better, so much better, if he left her alone. She couldn't help him, anyway.

Chapter Twelve

Grace gazed out on her snowy front porch and considered sweeping the wide boards. The wet probably wasn't too good for the wood. She had not had to worry about things like that in Tennessee. She let the lace panel fall back into place at the window as she turned and wandered back into her living room.

Mmm. Aromatic cedar branches she had brought in three days ago and placed around the room whirled their Christmas scent every time she breezed by. She decided to put in a rug after all and bought a short-napped rust-colored area one. Eddy could still run his trucks smoothly across it and not scratch up the polished oak floor.

The prints she'd found at a local craft store and hung on the wall across the door were perfect. Apple orchards at dusk, the green and rusty reds in early Americana, had a primitive feel. The lamplight was low and intimate, casting long shadows on the drop ceiling panels. This was more than a nice house; it was becoming home. Running anywhere else could wait until spring.

What do people do about gift-giving here in Michigan? She brushed moisture from her eyelashes and struggled to keep back tears at the memories of past holidays. The first Christmas with Sean had been so much fun. Everyone had been right. Christmas with a baby was special. Bittersweet memories.

A card had come from Lena. A few colorful notes and cards from patients and some of her new friends here made a little respectable pile in her Amish apple wood bowl on the coffee table.

Grace sat down on the sofa and picked up her list. Scarf and leather gloves for the men in her life, new pads of colored papers, smelly markers, and squiggly cut scissors for Eddy, new hot pads for Matty who complained her husband Harold burned up her last nice one when he dropped it in the oven.

She twirled the pen in her fingers as she contemplated her options for Christmas Day. Matty had invited her home.

"Harold, my man, will make you his famous Christmas punch. That's a drink, you know." There was something definitely mischievous about this punch, judging by the twinkle accompanying the declaration. "The children all come home with their own—thirteen so far. *Und* a neighbor or two who may be alone." She waggled her plump fingers. "You never know. Then the cats and turtle… Harold has this snapper—big as a plate! Feeds it burger. The little ones love it! The cat always tries to play, but Georgie, that's what Harold calls it—he don't play too much. Ja—no one should be alone on the holy day."

Matty pronounced it as two separate words, letting Grace know she held Christmas sacred.

* * * *

Grace wrapped up her mincemeat pie in a couple of dishtowels to keep it warm while she drove to the other side of East Bay where the Van Ooyens kept a small hobby farm. Matty had come to the United States from her native Netherlands when she married Harold, whom she met while he was studying abroad at the Hague for a semester. She was already a nurse who had no trouble getting a license in Michigan and worked while Harold finished school. A few years ago, Harold retired from the engineering firm he worked for. The two of them enjoyed their growing family, the animals, and a small orchard.

"Mincemeat!" Harold exclaimed upon opening the door. "Reminds me of home with grandma. I'll take care of that for you. Oh, and Merry Christmas."

Grace laughed and surrendered her coat to Matty who grinned hugely and kissed her cheek. "We're happy you could join us!"

Grace strolled around the living room, alternately looking at her friend's lifetime of odds and ends and dodging grandchildren of various ages and scrambling pets. She sipped cautiously at the punch which Harold had given her accompanied by a wink, a sort of tart apple mulled with cinnamon sticks and cloves. Aromas familiar and tantalizing wafted from the huge farm kitchen. The boisterous, joyous, and homey atmosphere enveloped her.

"No one should be alone," she repeated softly to herself. She jumped at the unexpected sight of her boss, hands in pockets, admiring the other side of the tree.

"I didn't know you were coming," Greg said, as surprised-looking as she felt.

Grace took a nervous sip of the punch. "Merry Christmas to you, too."

"Yes, yes. I suppose so." He sighed. "Matty and Harold collect strays, as you can see," he told her, eyes full of chagrin and discomfort. He reached for her hand but didn't meet it as he was nudged out of the way by a rambunctious waist-high little boy, closely followed by a petite curly headed girl chasing one of the cats.

"Well, anyway, I'm so relieved to see a familiar face, no matter whether Christmas is merry or we're all a bunch of strays getting together for a good time," Grace said. "Are you really not a fan of Christmas? Does your family feel the same way?"

"I get back home every couple of years. In between, I'm invited here." He indicated the pager at his hip. "A couple of us take turns watching the shop over the holidays."

Happy chaos continued to unfold around them. "I suppose for years I've associated Christmas with accidents and work," Greg said in a low voice. "My family is pretty staid. The folks are gone now. I have two sisters, one older and never married and one younger with grown-up kids. Christmas is supposed to be more like this, don't you think?" He waved his hand at the ruckus of children and pets and the heavily decorated tree in constant threat of toppling over. A fairy of a girl lay on her tummy, chin in hand and ringlets running riot over her head, eyeing the pretty packages spilling from underneath it.

Warmed by the punch and the commotion, Grace agreed. She

drew a ragged breath at the memory of a little boy who once looked at a brightly lit tree with rapt amazement.

Right then, Harold, dressed in an old white butcher's apron proclaiming "Kiss the Cook," banged a ladle against the lid of a pot and announced, "Feeding time!" It was a mad scramble for the table. Greg ushered her to a corner seat, her mouth watering in anticipation of the flavors emanating from the various covered dishes.

Greg's tranquil baritone was another surprise when Harold started singing. She joined in. "We gather together, to ask the Lord's blessing…"

Everyone at the table knew the words. She smiled inwardly at the Norman Rockwell moment around the table, the faces glowing in candlelight and every mouth open in praise.

An hour later the scraping was done, the dishwasher humming, and the refrigerator boasted leftovers for a few easy meals. Grace joined the intimate group to watch the exchange of gifts; all of them arranged about the living room and spilling back into the dining area. Parents begged the children to go slow, be properly thankful and figure who gave what to whom. Greg somehow worked an arm across Grace's shoulders and whispered in her ear, "And what would Grace like for her Christmas gift?"

She sat still, flushing like a victim of early menopause, unsure how to read the situation. She liked him and did not think he would turn on her if she rebuffed him—or wasn't that what he was doing? Making a pass? He hadn't acted like more than a friendly uncle during work hours and she had only bumped into him a couple of times in town while shopping, once at the diner. Maybe it was the punch. She hesitated, trying not to twitch her shoulders but failing. The arm was immediately removed.

"I'm sorry. I didn't mean to—"

"Oh, no, please," she hissed, checking around to see if anyone was looking at them, feeling her cheeks unnaturally warm. "It's not…" She risked a peek at him. She leaned back again and closed her eyes briefly. "What Grace would like this Christmas is just being here" —she gestured at the room—"with my new friends." She included him in her smile. "In my new home."

He nodded, pursing his mouth as if he understood. Matty brought over a small package. "Thank you, dear, for the new hot pads, then," she told Grace. "I'm keeping Harold away from them."

They laughed.

"Here's a small token of my esteem for you."

"Why, thank you." A beautiful blue and silver box revealed a small bottle of perfume. She applied a touch of scent to her wrists and wafted it toward everyone within reach.

"Thank you," Grace said again to Matty, who had taken Greg's place beside her when he got up to admire something with Harold. The two men stood looking out a side window.

"We bought a new snow blower," Matty explained. "Beddar dan jewels when you get old as us, and more romantic!"

An hour later, after a quiet cup of tea, Grace declined dessert and said she had to be going. Greg helped her with her coat. She stood mesmerized by the sight of one of the daughters rocking her sleeping toddler. She shivered and turned to find Greg looking at her, asking with his expression for answers she could not give.

At least, not here. Should she ask him over to her place for coffee? What would he think?

You're a grown woman, Grace. The situation couldn't get any more awkward. "Greg, would you like to stop in for some coffee?"

He quickly agreed. "Sure. See you in a little bit. It's still slippery out there. Be careful, okay?"

Hugs, thanks, and waves were all that remained between home and a coffee date for which she had no answer why she'd made the offer.

* * * *

Greg started talking from the moment she opened the door to him forty-five minutes later. She served aromatic chicory coffee and some of the shortbread cookies a patient had given to her a few days earlier. Lights from the Christmas tree glowed softly.

"Did you know Ernest Hemingway spent his summers near here?" Greg asked. "In nineteen-nineteen he came to recuperate from wounds he received in the war and then, in nineteen twenty-one to get married. The museum in Petoskey is interesting but…"

He paused and looked at her, next to him on the couch. Grace flicked a strand of hair behind her ear and offered what she hoped was an interested smile. Now that she was in her home, so close to the hedge, she couldn't help but wonder what might be going on at the house on the other side. What were the Marshalls doing for Christmas? What was it like with Eddy there? Did he get up early…

"It's only open in the summers. Although this time of year there's skiing and other winter sports. Actually, it's cold and snowy usually right through Easter. I don't know if you like that kind of thing, but would you like to go sometime? We can stop for a nice dinner…" His voice trailed off. "You haven't blinked in the last two minutes," he said, giving her arm a little shake.

Oops. "I'm sorry. It's been a long day. I'm not used to so much activity, I guess. You were talking about Ernest Hemingway."

"Hmm. Yes, well." He picked up the framed photograph on the lamp table. "This was your husband, I assume?"

"Yes. Jonathan Runyon. MD."

"You look very happy."

"We were. It was good, until the end when he was so sick. Cancer." Please, no medical talk today. "It was—well, everything possible was done. Now it's over."

"Oh?"

She took the picture from him and stood up. She put it back on the little table and glanced out the window.

"And now you live next door to another sick man."

"Yeah. I thought, when I first met him, what a great cruel joke on me, God. Thanks a lot."

"People talk. You spend a lot of time together."

"I take care of Ted's son."

"Is that all?"

"I beg your pardon?" Grace snorted. "Not you, too. Enough with the insinuations." He sat there on her sofa, wearing a fuzzy moss green sweater and nice khakis: healthy, clean-shaven, sincere. She cocked her head, wondering why he should care.

He shrugged. "Sorry. Idle gossip."

"Not that it's any of your business," she kept her tone light, "but when Shelby couldn't watch him anymore… I like the Marshalls. I didn't know them when I bought this house, and I thought you didn't pay much attention to what other people said. Perhaps the next time you listen to idle gossip you can set the story straight. I told you the circumstances and what kind of hours I would be available to work and why when you hired me."

Greg set his coffee cup back down with a sharp clink. He got to his feet and walked over to the tree, reaching out to touch one of her small gingerbread men.

"You're right. That was rude and I apologize." He turned back to look at her. "I never thought I'd need a policy about not becoming involved with my staff. There's always just been Matty. Or Nancy. Of course, it goes without saying there would never be anything romantic with active patients. When I found out you'd only been widowed a short time, I waited. I watch you with patients, listening to Nancy with her family problems, at home with Matty today. You have so much life, so much to give. So lovely in every way." He fingered a dried cranberry strung with popcorn. "Oh, Lord. Look, Grace, I wondered, um, I mean, I naturally assumed… No, that's not right, either." He sighed as he faced the door. "I only mean that I hoped, ah, maybe, you…and then…"

He went still. Grace heard it, too—firm steps across the porch, followed by staccato rap.

"But, I suppose not."

She moved toward the front door. "Wait a minute, Ted," she called out, already guessing who her visitor was. "I, well, I just don't think I'm ready yet—for anything romantic with …um, well, anyone." No matter how her thoughts wandered next door, or how she longed sometimes for Ted to come over when she and Eddy were just hanging out, reading a book, pretending to be a family.

She opened the door. "Ted! Merry Christmas. Come on in out of the cold."

"Are you all right? I saw a strange…oh, Doctor. Hello, and Merry Christmas." Ted glanced from her to the doctor, one eyebrow arched and a frown belying the friendly greeting.

Greg folded his arms and stared back at Ted. "Mr. Marshall. And

Merry Christmas to you, too."

Grace did her best not to giggle, but rolled her eyes as she took their empty cups out to the kitchen. "Would you like some coffee, Ted?" she called back. "Or tea? I'm getting us a refill."

"Oh, well, no. I thought I'd stop by and see what, ah, how you were. How was it at Matty and Harold's?"

She answered from the kitchen, wincing at the echo. "Just crazy! Wild. And so much fun. Great food." She brought their cups back, filled. "How was your day?"

Neither man sat. She plopped the tray on the coffee table and made herself comfortable once again on the sofa. She helped herself to a cookie, trying to make this situation out to be perfectly natural. Ted acted like a lion defending its den and Greg was sizing up Ted as if determining the most efficient way to remove a major organ without ruining her floor.

"Ted?"

"Um, pretty quiet, really. Kaye and Tanya stopped over. We had a good phone conversation with Jimmy, Randy's boy. Thank you for the gifts, by the way. We all liked them."

"Good. I'm glad. Thank you for your gifts, as well."

"Well, I guess I'll be heading back, then," Ted said after another awkward silence. "I'm sorry if I interrupted anything."

"That's all right," Greg assured him and helpfully opened the door for him to go out into the cold, dark night. "And Happy New Year."

She looked at Greg over the rim of her cup and decided to say nothing.

"Why do I feel like my grandmother just scolded me?" Greg complained when he sat across from her again.

Grace laughed. "All right, boss. Maybe we could try this again, hmm? What do you want?"

"Boss, huh? Honestly? What do I want?" He sighed. "I'm not sure. I like being a bachelor—most of the time." He grinned. "Half the town wonders why I'm not married for one reason or the other. I like women. I go on dates. I never wanted, well, just to settle. No one ever made me want to stay home for Christmas before. For years I always assumed I would be moving on and didn't want to take a chance someone wouldn't want to move with me. Then it was sort of too late to meet anyone new. Until you came along. And I saw how you looked at Marshall." His gaze slid to the photograph on the lamp table. "I always thought I'd have that someday."

Hot stabbing pain started in the corner of her eyes and made her mouth tremble. "Don't, Greg. Don't want that. Because when it's over, you wonder why God could be so cruel. You wonder why you should bother breathing anymore. You try to run so far…and you end up—"

"Marshall's prognosis isn't very encouraging."

Grace took a deep breath and lifted her face to the ceiling. When she felt in control again, she leveled a look at her guest. "You're the one who keeps bringing him up, Greg."

He frowned and plucked at the fringe of an afghan slung over the arm of the chair, a gift from Shelby who couldn't do much more than work her crochet hook.

"I've never hidden my beliefs, my faith. You know that. I'm not ready to give up on Ted. God has been known to perform miracles when we let him."

Greg nodded. "You and old Mrs. Brown can really go at the religious stuff, I've noticed. She's perked up a good deal since she has someone from her part of the world to talk to."

"What I can do, what I've always believed was true as far as these hands,"—she held them up between them—"is God wants me to touch people, both inside and out. I admit, I can be a little, um…" She dropped her hands and looked away. "Well, it got to the point where I thought I could do pretty much anything. Then the good Lord saw fit to teach me a lesson."

"I won't believe in a God who takes away your husband simply to teach you an unwarranted lesson in humility."

She shook her head. "I don't believe that's what I said. No one can be too sure of anything, even medical prognoses. Back home there was always hope."

"What about me? Can I hope?"

Grace lifted her chin and looked down her nose. "Please don't let me stop you. But I don't think you've decided for sure what you really want. Things will be changing next year, I can feel it." She looked at the photograph of her husband. "We all have time to consider our steps carefully. We've only just begun to get to know each other, all of us. No one can predict the future."

She picked up her teacup with shaky hands. When had she become such a sage. She sounded like some turn of the twentieth century social worker. "I'm not sure how it happened, but I woke up and found myself in the motel one morning. Literally," she said to Greg's raised brows. "I barely remember the drive from Tennessee. I was in shock. I'm here for a reason, obviously. That much I accept from God. But I don't know yet for sure what that reason is. Ted needed immediate help with Eddy. There may be more in the future, I'm not sure. I'm helping people at the clinic like I did back home. With hope…and patience. I'm learning not to be so…arrogant? And I'm so newly widowed I don't know how to act around…men. I never had a boyfriend other than Jonathan. I'm learning how to be alone and that's okay with me for now. The Lord says, 'My grace is sufficient for you,' and I'm figuring out how to accept that."

Greg stood and took restless steps back and forth in front of the little tree. He put his hands in his pockets and hunched. "All those self-satisfied little remarks come to mind. You know—'I bet God can't keep you warm at night, or shovel your driveway,' or…"

He shook his head. "My grandmother again. She's here, looking over your shoulder at me. She believed—like you seem to. I never considered God any more real than in a church on Sundays." He pulled his coat off the rack near the door and put it on. Grace trailed him to the door, feeling like she just lost the opportunity to take part in something big and good. He deserved better and wished she could give it to him.

Before he left, he put his hands on her shoulders and sighed. "I guess no one can define 'fair,' can he?"

She smiled. "Fair doesn't have much to do with reality, Greg. You see it every day."

"True. Thanks for the coffee…and conversation…and"—he gave her shoulders a little awkward pat—"food for thought. I'll never look at your hands in the same way again." His faded blue eyes were very close. His lashes were very thick for a blonde. Grace's breathing slowed and a spark leaped when he tugged her hand to his mouth to gently kiss her fingers. But not like the spark Ted made. "Goodnight."

"Goodnight, Greg."

Chapter Thirteen

Ted didn't wait for an answer to his knock the next morning. Sheer frustration propelled him across the threshold into Shelby and Dave's little house. "All right. What's wrong with me? I just don't get it. I'm trying, I really am. What does it take? I admit I've been out of touch for a couple of years, but I'm outta my league, here. What can I do?"

"Yo, slow down, man. What are you talking about? And Merry Christmas!"

"Doc Evans is ruining it. Her. You know him. I mean, Dave knows him. We all thought he was…I don't know, gay, or something. All of a sudden…I mean, does she even know what she's doing?"

"Nice to see you, there. How's Christmas vacation going?"

Ted blinked. "What? Oh, yeah. Fine. You and Grace have gotten to know each other pretty well, haven't you? How long does it take to get over losing a husband? When do you know you're ready to get involved again? I mean, well…" He stopped, unsure how to go on.

Shelby looked puzzled with her head cocked at a funny angle and her brows all scrunched up. Then she snorted a great raspberry. "Ted Marshall, I declare, you thinking 'bout fallin' in love again?" She giggled and clapped.

Ted sat back and heaved a great sigh. "It's not a joke. You have to help me out here. I'm drowning. You're a woman. What do women want?"

Shelby plucked at the afghan she was wrapped in and heaved her great bloated belly around. "Yeah, I'm a woman, hard as it may be to believe. But I don't know, Ted. I couldn't ever imagine getting over Davy if I lost him. I hate to have to point this out, but being widowed is different from being divorced."

Ted pursed his lips and drew his eyebrows tight.

"Come on, you said it yourself," she continued. "If you're angry or not in love anymore, or betrayed, you divorce and move on. If someone dies on you, it's not like you had any kind of choice in the matter."

Ted pushed himself up and started a hesitant pacing. "But what if there's someone else, someone better—"

"You're not using your cane or anything!"

Ted stopped in front of her and put his hands on his hips. "Yesterday, I was thrilled. Today—hey, don't change the subject!"

Shelby grinned. Ted shook his head and went back to pacing.

"I guess I've been so wrapped up in thinking I was going to die that I didn't try to live after Jilly left us. I was worried about my little boy and what was going to happen to him. I didn't ever want to feel like there was a chance for anything else, for a future with anyone." He stopped to look through her window out into the snow-covered yard.

"Now I think maybe, I can get better. Maybe there's something more. An opportunity to start over. Do something right." He knelt and took her hands. "Do you think it could happen? Grace is so special. She came into our lives for a reason. I just know it. I feel it. How can I help but love her?"

Shelby stared at his hands. "I know what you mean, Ted. I never could carry a baby before, but since she came I knew it would be all right this time. It's like we connected immediately. I've never known anyone like her. But it's not like everyone instantly falls in love with her. She has a purpose here, I agree." She held Ted's gaze with her own. "But I don't think she's here only for us. I haven't been able to get out to church lately you know. When she comes over, she reads Bible stories sometimes with me, besides other books."

Ted jumped up. "Yeah. That's nice. So?"

"There's a lot to our girl we can't understand. Anyway, we were reading from the book of Romans, about Paul wanting things, following his goal. She got this far-away look—you know—almost like she went to another place. We talked a lot about why people do the things they do, why some things happen, girl stuff mostly. You wouldn't be interested." Shelby stopped and twitched her lips. "Funny. I went to church all my life and never really considered the Bible as anything much more than something people read at church. She told me she tries to read almost every day. And pray, too. How about that?" She shook her head. "It's positively mysterious. Anyway, did you think, Ted, maybe she's the first woman you've been attracted to in years and it's only a phase, or something? I don't mean to offend you, man, but it's been a long time."

"Well, yeah. That's what I'm trying to say. It *has* been a long time. I need…advice. You have to tell me how to handle situations like…last night."

An alarmed look flashed across her face. "What did you do?"

"Me? Nuthing. At least… Well, it's Christmas. So, yesterday, last night, I went to her house. I saw a light on and knew she was home. There was a car in the driveway. I was concerned." He twisted his lips. "I was. Don't look at me like that. Maybe I should have turned around, but I had to see—"

"Had to?"

"Yes. Had to. It was Doctor Evans, from the clinic. They were pretty cozy. He acted like, well, like…I don't know, not exactly boss-like."

"Boss-like?"

"Isn't he gay?"

Shelby laughed.

Ted lowered himself to a chair and stared at the floor. "I just assumed Grace and Eddy and I…you know. We were so perfect together."

"Like a family?" Shelby pushed the granny squares away.

"A guy can dream. Look at you! I remember when we…Jilly…I mean—"

"Eddy's a doll. You got the best part. Never forget that."

"Yeah. Cripes. Here I am, complaining. How's it going with you, anyway? Things okay with the baby?"

"Oh, sure. Third time's the charm."

"Are you scared?"

"Well, I was for a while, you know. But since Grace checks on me," her voice dropped, "and prays, I know this time things will be all right."

"I need her, too."

"Calm down, Ted. Give her time, okay? If it's meant to be, it will work out. Don't push it. I think Grace and the doc were both at Matty and Harold's yesterday, weren't they? He probably only stopped in for a few minutes. Everyone knows you have to tread lightly around your boss. If I'm not mistaken, you and Randy had company yourself, didn't you?"

"So?"

"So, I didn't hear her getting all bent out of shape because Kaye and Tanya spent the day with you. Why didn't you ask Grace to come over?"

Ted felt the heat cross his scalp and ears, burn his cheeks. "I forgot. I thought I had, or at least I thought she'd know she was supposed to come. What a dope! When she didn't come, Randy went over to check and she was gone. I can't believe it."

"Sometimes a girl needs to be invited."

"I'll keep that in mind."

"And for the record, Ted, I don't think there's much wrong with you."

He raised his left brow and squinted. "Much?"

"I don't think a swelled head would help you anymore."

"Gee, thanks."

Shelby patted her tummy. "You asked. So, no cane?"

He stood and turned in a circle. "No cane."

* * * *

Alyssa Ann Brouwer arrived on January 27. On St. Valentine's Day Grace held the tiny, squirming girl on her lap. Shelby sat on her sofa, worn out from walking her bundle of joy.

"If she's not gagging at nursing, she has a rash. She's got Davy's sensitive skin, poor girl. Two and a half weeks old and diaper rash you wouldn't believe. I've tried four different brands of diapers, no diaper at all, powders, salves…"

Shelby's tears came close to matching her daughter's.

Grace cuddled Alyssa close, then held her out to peer into her navy blue eyes. "Yeah, girl? What's with that, huh?" She spoke to Alyssa's mom without taking her gaze from the baby. "You want me to take a look?"

"Oh, would you? I simply can't run to the doctor with one more complaint."

"Sure. Come on, little love." Grace took the baby down the hall to the bathroom and set her on the padded, railed countertop. Alyssa kicked her little legs when they were unsnapped from the terry suit.

Grace hissed when she saw the bright red skin and chafed patches. "Ooh, yeah, baby. You have one sore bottom. How could you do this to yourself? Hmm, and what can we do about it?" She loosely re-wrapped the infant and took her back out to her mother where she immediately began to cry again.

"I have something in the car that might help. I'll be back in a second, I promise." Grace patted Alyssa's head and hurried out.

She brought in a jar of her homemade salve, mostly of aloe and vitamin D. It wasn't a cure, but a great prop. Props were necessary when she needed a good explanation for what she was about to do.

Back in the bathroom with the baby once more, she warmed up a scoop of the stuff in her bare hand and began to smooth the ointment on the little girl's red bottom, making sure her fingers and palms soothed over the skin first. Alyssa burbled with satisfaction as the healing began.

When the little tingle prickled quickly across her own bottom, she jumped. Just as quickly, the sensation was gone.

"Very funny," she said, rolling her eyes heavenward. Alyssa's skin became less irritated with her touch and the homemade ointment. A new diaper fastened, and they were ready to return to the living room.

"Here we are," Grace announced, but did not surrender the baby to her mother yet. It just felt too good to hold a tiny one so close. She and Alyssa exchanged wide expressions.

"You've done this before," Shelby stated.

"Yup, lots of times."

"I mean, for yourself."

Grace went still, keeping eye contact with Alyssa. "Mother's instinct, then?"

"Why don't you tell me about it?"

Why not? The healing touch had returned; maybe it was time to share more of her story. But how much? Cuddling Alyssa against her heart, Grace leaned back in the rocker to center her soul. Where to start?

"Jonathan and I…wanted to wait a while, you know, to get settled and such before we, well, had a family." Alyssa took longer and longer blinks. She made little sucking noises against the side of Grace's neck, and rubbed her nose at the collar of her sweater, drawing up her little terry-covered rump.

"We were married for five years before we felt ready. Med school, and all that. Jonathan did his pediatric internship while I worked since my degree didn't take as long." Grace rubbed the baby's back and pulled a blanket around her. "It took another two years before we realized things weren't working out. Then a few more months before we figured what those things were. We were advised on, um, adjusting our, ah, strategy, and it worked—eventually. We had Sean."

Inhaling Alyssa's sweet baby scent, she whispered, "He was beautiful—perfect."

"What happened?"

Her long, shaky breath sighed out slowly. The quaking started in her toes. "He died. With my parents. They took him for a long weekend on our anniversary to give us some time alone. He was sixteen months old." Her smile wobbled. "Amazing the damage a semi can do to a Continental on a twisting mountain road."

Silent tears streamed down Shelby's cheeks.

"It was an accident. We accepted that. It's not easy, it never will be. But it's done. We forgave. It was quick and they didn't have time to suffer. Reverend Edwards said they went to a better place. We had to believe. We do believe." Grace closed her eyes. "We'll be together again."

"Ted doesn't know, does he?"

"We haven't discussed it."

"Oh, Grace. I knew there was something else besides Jonathan to make you so sad about Christmas. It must be hard on you, taking care of Eddy. Practically your whole family gone in one fell swoop. How can you stand it?" Shelby poked at her eyes with the edge of cloth diaper hanging over her left shoulder.

"I have to. Maybe Sean would have been something like him. I've come to love Eddy. He's such a sweetheart. He's been put through a lot. If there is any kind of normality to look for in a weird situation, the least I can do is attempt to provide it. I moved into his house. I'm not trying to take the place of his mother, but he's welcome in his old house. Someone should be there to meet him after school, make sure he eats well and has time to play like a little boy."

"What about the little boy's father?"

Grace hunched and shrugged. "I don't know." She leaned back and sighed. "I ran so fast. You know, I left—no I ran away,"—she changed her first thought—"right during Jonathan's funeral."

"I didn't know. You said he got cancer. That was…after Sean? How awful. No one should have her whole family gone like that. What made you come here to East Bay?"

"It seemed like the right thing at the time. I woke up one morning in a little motel on the beach and here I was." Grace glanced at her friend again. "I think you know what I mean when I say it was one of God's little whispers." She rocked back, staring at the silent television. An African violet plant bloomed pale pink on top of it. "I can't possibly think about anyone else. I never want to go through anything like that. Ever again. It's too much to risk." She cleared her throat.

"I think you should know people saw Doctor Evans's car at your place on Christmas. There may be talk," Shelby told her.

"People will always find something to talk about. Anyway, who told you?"

"Oh, it's not important."

Through pinched eyes she watched Shelby pick at a thread from the baby blanket hanging on the arm of her chair before answering.

"Yeah, people will always find something to talk about. Alyssa seems pretty settled. Thanks to you and your magic."

"Never that, girlfriend. Only miracle."

Chapter Fourteen

Tony Vander Groot's blood-curdling scream made Grace's fingers twitch.

"What in the world? Tony—what's the matter?" She withdrew the needle from his arm and pressed cotton against the entrance wound. She then pulled the arm straight up with her other gloved hand.

"It hurts!"

At his shout, Matty came through the curtain.

"Tch!" The nurse reached past her to the cotton pad which had bled through. Grace withdrew her hand, perplexed and worried.

"Get me another one!" Matty commanded.

Greg, mouth pursed and arms folded, joined them.

It took nearly five minutes of pressing firmly against Tony's inner arm and positioning him on an examining bed when his eyes rolled back before they brought the matter under control. Tony had rained down vociferous protests until his near-faint quieted him.

"It was a routine draw!" Grace hissed when they had Tony lying down, an ice pack on his inner elbow and Mrs. Vander Groot soothing his forehead, glaring at them. Greg had vanished into an examining room with his next case.

"We talk later." Matty's forehead resembled a roadmap as she padded out of the exam room.

* * * *

"I've done this a thousand times, Greg. I can't tell you what went wrong."

Grace, Greg, and Matty sat around the desk in his office after lunch.

"There was nothing unusual about Grace's procedure, Doctor," said Matty.

Grace smiled her thanks.

"This kind of incident has never happened to her since she's been here. Even a through and through wouldn't cause such distress. She is so gentle and careful. And you know the young ones ask for her. Perhaps young Master Vander Groot wriggled. That would explain much."

Greg picked at the remains of his lunch. He swiveled to look out of the window at the trees leafing out and the lawn greening up nicely.

The women waited patiently while he twiddled his fingers, and then brushed back his hair. He turned back and smiled at Matty. "Thank you. Why don't you go check on the afternoon schedule, okay?"

Matty, obviously not used to being dismissed, frowned and left the room.

"Grace, did you make up a new batch of salve for arthritis lately?"

"No."

"Granny B was admitted to the hospital this morning with a blistering rash."

"And you think I'm to blame."

"We have to consider the possibility. It was pretty ugly, sore. The fact Elvira consented to go to the hospital is an indication of how serious it is. I saw her on rounds this morning."

Grace looked down at her lap, clutching the arms of her chair, thinking back. Had she done anything differently the last time she made up the salve? The recipe was always the same. She was extra careful, despite what she had told Ted once about not following recipes for food. She pushed herself upright and began pacing. "After the Tony thing this morning, I don't know what to say any more. I suppose she could be reacting to the salve after all this time. It happens."

"Let's get a jar of the same thing you're using on her to the lab, okay? And we'll call this blood draw incident a routine complication for now."

She stopped behind her chair and pulled her white jacket onto her shoulders.

"And, Grace? Let me watch you for a while, okay? Until we're sure these are isolated—ah, matters."

Stunned, she nodded. Unsure whether she was to see patients alone that afternoon, she left Greg to finish his late lunch while she went to check the schedule.

Matters, hmm? No one had ever questioned her practice in the past. No one. What was going on?

* * * *

Grace held the letter up to the sunlight in her kitchen. She let it fall back on the table.

A year had passed—an entire year since that shocking day in Woodside at Jonathan's gravesite. A letter from Reverend Mayor Jeremiah Edwards invited Grace to a memorial service and plaque dedication at the cemetery in Woodside in honor of Jonathan, their son, Sean, and her parents. "Jonathan Runyon was a respected pediatrician, town leader, and naturally is dearly missed," the Reverend wrote on official letterhead.

She smiled at the phrasing—so pompous. "Yes, I did know that about my husband."

"Your parents also, Mrs. Runyon, were a great loss as fine educators in our community. We would be honored with your presence on…"

Grace got up and took the letter with her into the living room along with her cup of tea. She had splurged on a couple of nice bookcases, a pretty little lamp, and a new easy chair in olive suede. Memories of Tennessee were the last echo of a dream these days. Woodside was another lifetime in another realm. Their home there had felt empty after the loss of Sean, emptier still as she and Jonathan spent the last month of his life in hospice. The house threatened to suck her into nothing when there was no one left but her. She couldn't face returning there after the funeral—one of the reasons she had simply taken off.

Late spring snow was melting, making the snowman she and Eddy had made look as though it was curtsying. Michigan was more home.

What was missing? Ah, yes. There he was. The subject of her thoughts came limping up the walk.

The good health Ted had gained over fall and winter regressed faster than the snow melt. She clenched her fists as he resorted to the crutch again when his muscles let him stumble. He could no longer grasp things well with his left hand.

Letter forgotten, Grace went to greet Ted at the door and invited him to sit.

"Eddy's at the Robertson boy's birthday party."

"He was excited. I'll fix us some tea."

She returned to the living room to Ted's white face, his shaking hand holding her letter from Tennessee. Her first impulse was to grab the thing out of his hand and scream at him. She locked on to his raised eyes. Betrayed. That was Grace's next crazy thought, she'd somehow betrayed him.

She took in a deep breath as she set the tea tray down on her coffee table. She seated herself and then sighed the used air back out.

Ted held the page out to her with a quivering hand. "I'm so sorry, Grace. I shouldn't have, ah, even… But it was just lying here, and…I'm sorry."

Grace pressed her lips together and blinked away scalding moisture.

"Why didn't you ever say anything?"

The question sounded so anguished she couldn't help feeling sorry for him, despite her dismay.

"My past was never anyone else's business," she said quietly. She retrieved her letter, folded it, and put it in the drawer. "You knew I was widowed when I bought the house."

"But you had a child. A son. Grace! All this time and I only now find out. How did he die?"

"Ted, please. I don't want to talk about it. If you're worried I can't take care of Eddy, that I'll hurt him or something, don't be. My son died in a car accident and I wasn't there. Just…let's pretend you never dug into my personal affairs, okay?"

He closed his mouth. "Now I'm not sorry," he said mutinously. "And that was a totally rotten, unfair, mean thing to say. How could you have kept this from me? From us? Don't you trust me?"

"It's not a matter of trust! It's a matter of privacy. I didn't ask you all about your divorce, or why you sold your house and had to move in with your brother. That's none of my business, like I'm none of…*your* business."

Ted passed a hand over his face. "You had a child. You told me you…wait a minute! I wondered what you meant, 'I *have* no children.' Shelby knows," he accused her. "You told her, but not me."

"I think you'd better leave now." Grace was surprised at how calm the directive came out. She rose, ready to usher him out.

Ted didn't move. "Eddy. You seemed so comfortable around him. How could you be around him—or was that it?" His eyes narrowed and he leaned forward. "You found out I needed help and you came here so you could be around my son as a substitute for yours."

"That's ridiculous!" Grace lost her emotional equilibrium and dove at him, jerking his arm to pull him off her sofa and push him out the door. "You go home, Ted! You're being childish, now. Insane! I didn't know anything about you. I don't want… How could I want—"

All the emotion she had stuffed away so carefully came flooding out. Dealing with Sean's death as if she was supposed to be thankful in all things had left her numb and angry at God. The double blow of Jonathan's illness and her helplessness without her parents to lean on made her feel as though she had stepped out of her life and watched a copy of herself meander through it instead. Grace no longer had the strength to fight the emotions and Ted.

"It hurt so much at first. Sean… Eddy could have… Sean was only a baby. I didn't know…"

She crumpled against Ted on the sofa, leaning against his side, where he clasped her tight with his good arm and rocked her to her internal mantra.

No tears. Stop crying. Dry eyes. Deep breaths.

He spoke, muffled against her hair. "I'm so sorry, Grace, so sorry. I shouldn't have pried. If I had known about Sean, I never would have asked you to keep Eddy."

His bristly cheek rested on her forehead. His warm breath flowed over cheek, infusing her with a sort of reverse energy.

"I don't know anyone braver than you." He hesitated. "Or more selfish than I am." His hand made heated circles on her shoulder blade. "You must hate me."

Grace let him think his distracting ploy worked. No, hate was not what she felt for Ted. Not pity, either. It couldn't be love. Not yet. It wouldn't be fair to Jonathan. She pulled away to look up at Ted, smiling slightly, recognizing his appeal to get them moving on and change subjects. But she couldn't answer him yet.

She blinked and rested her cheek against his chest. Fear. Fear of losing him, and not being able to help him, as she had not been able to help Jonathan, locked her heart up tight. She moved away, took her tea, and drank. She set the mug down and smoothed her hair. *Deep breaths, deep breaths. Dry eyes. Go home. Go home.* No one will hurt you ever again, remember? He—they—are not your concern.

Ted struggled to his feet. "Grace…please. I—we—need you."

When she stayed silent, he limped to the door. She watched, detached from the scene as if watching a stage play. Ted stopped at the door. "You know how I feel, Grace. About us. Nothing's different. I can't hope for a future. Now—this moment—is all I have. And I want to share it with you."

He left.

Things had changed between them. But for better or worse? She wasn't sure.

* * * *

Grace flew out to Knoxville for a long weekend, driving over to Woodside and staying with Lena and her family. She did not go to her former house or even consider spending the night there. Only a year had passed—a year and a lifetime. The ceremony at the cemetery had been undemanding, respectful, well thought out, and low-key. The bronze plaque was elegant. Permanent. No one asked her to speak. She endured the photographs and said a calm thank you for the newspaper and radio and couldn't wait to leave. Reverend Edwards spoke to her formally, stiff as his letter had been, asking kindly about her new life. She answered him as plainly and soberly about her work at the clinic, the little boy next door, and his sick father. They knew each other well enough to understand without words the emotional and spiritual cost for her to attend another sick man.

"I never cease to marvel at the wondrous wit of the Lord God," Reverend Edwards said, barely a hint of a humor twisting his mouth. Grace watched him mull over the thought in his mind and predicted the title of next Sunday's sermon.

Few others spoke to her. She was the one who'd left them and they didn't like it, no matter the cause.

"Who said, 'you can't go home again'?" she asked Lena a little while later. The Woodside clinic had been deprived of two medical specialists and it would be another year before another doctor was ready to join them. Woodside preferred homegrown professionals.

They sat in Lena's quiet, darkened office with only the dim fading afternoon light from the window illuminating the room. They shared a cup of green tea, companionable but strangers, too, after all this time.

"So, you live in an old apple orchard?" Lena asked, smiling.

"It's the mother-in-law place on the homestead. The main family house is across the driveway. The orchards have been abandoned."

Grace hesitated over how much more to add. Lena always seemed to know her heart and this time didn't press for details. "Michigan is very nice. Cold, snowy, but great food," Grace went on. "Church is pretty dried up, though."

They shared a grin, thinking of Reverend Edwards's rapturous, loud, arm-waving sermons.

"That was nice of the town, what they did today," Grace said after a while. "Thank you for your part, too." Lena had spoken about Jonathan and Sean, and brought the crowd to tears.

"A small thing. I'm just glad you've landed on your feet. I miss you."

Guilt broke the sense of companionship. Landed on her feet? She felt more like she had been shoved to the ground. The view from the floor was not all that great. She needed a strong arm to raise her up— something Ted Marshall did not possess, nor could she give it to him. How could she tell Lena she was about to fail, big time, again?

"I miss you, too. Thanks for finding me and writing. I'll be better at staying in touch. Promise."

* * * *

Elizabeth Runyon welcomed her for a quiet reunion at dinnertime, speaking soothingly of the hotel and a few incidents that occurred over winter. Grace told her about her new church, the Michigan tourist trade, Shelby and the baby, how different and alike her new patients were, and the hill folk who resettled around Grand Traverse Bay after the auto industry tanked.

"And, you, Grace. Are you happy? Did you discover your purpose?"

Elizabeth would be the one to bring that up. Grace could never claim to have simply wound up in Michigan through fate, or running out of gas. Everything under the sun had a specific purpose. "I thought I did. When I first came up there, this man and his little boy came right to me. Ted was limping. I was sure I was there to heal him."

"And now? It's been a year."

"I know." She stumbled over her thoughts admiring her mother-in-law's serenity. "I…" She looked down at the lace doily place mat under her tea cup and swallowed. "Well, I didn't want to, at first. Heal him, I mean, not after, after…Jonathan." His name came out whispered, fraught with guilt. "Now I don't know if I can anymore. There were a couple of accidents at the clinic recently. I'm not sure what happened." She described the trouble with Tony's blood draw and the rash of the arthritic woman.

"The gift is not yours to wield at your disposal. You've always known it to be so. It is for God to say the right time and place."

"I hate that!" Grace jumped to her feet, agitated, itching to run away again. "When I thought I was supposed to, then I didn't want to use it. Now, when I want to, I can't."

"What changed your mind about helping that man?"

How could she admit to her former mother-in-law if she could thaw enough to have feelings, she might find love with someone else?

"My dear, you're a young woman. It's natural to want to love again."

Grace blinked. How could she know? "What if he dies? Li-like

Jonathan? How can God ask me? To love him and think he can be healed, when he can't?"

"You don't need me to remind you the Lord only gives as much as He knows we can take."

"I'm not that strong, Elizabeth."

Elizabeth smiled. "It's a good thing you don't have to be. You are not alone, no matter how hard to try."

* * * *

Grace returned to East Bay, mixed up; wanting to leave one day, stay the next. She might be better off somewhere else. Someplace where no one needed her and there was no chance of hurt.

Spring in western Michigan was a promise and a tease. Verdant grass, daffodil and tulip buds conflicted with the ice still piled up on Grand Traverse Bay. Steelhead migrated from the big lake upstream to spawn. Rafts of snow slunk among the off-road stands of pine, oak, and birch. The fruit orchards took their time responding to the warmth and longer amounts of sunshine with leaves and eventual buds.

Patient care remained routine and incident-free at the clinic. But that was a concern to Grace in a way she couldn't share: routine was routine. No sparks, no energy, no sped-up healing of infections or wounds. Greg stopped watching her every move. She wished her state of mind were as asymptomatic. Shelby proved to be a good sounding board, and Grace was grateful for her friendship.

On a beautiful, quiet Saturday in Grace's back yard, Alyssa slept in her carrier on a blanket in the shade of a big maple tree while she and Shelby chatted. Eddy explored a new ant colony taking shape at the corner of his playhouse, counting out loud for them the number of soldiers snaking out in a long line.

"What a great day. So warm." Shelby lifted her face skyward. "We can still get snow this time of year."

"Wow." Grace bent over the baby and watched her purse her little mouth. "I feel so restless these days. Ted and I need to discuss what to do about Eddy over the summer when I'm working at the clinic, too, if I stay here in East Bay."

"Well, I can help, Grace. I'll be happy to keep Eddy two of the days. That should ease your mind a bit."

Then she widened her eyes, searching Grace's face. "Wait! What do you mean, 'if I stay'? You're not thinking of leaving, are you? You only got here! Where would you go? What would we do without you?"

Grace snorted. "It's so hard. It seems the reasons I felt I had to run away from Woodside were all in my head, now I've been back, and talked to some of the people there." She looked at Alyssa, making little sucking noises in her sleep. "But yet, it didn't feel entirely comfortable, either," she admitted. The quiet thing inside her head, the real fear that the healing gift was gone for good after its brief appearance, she couldn't share.

"You're worried about Ted, aren't you?"

Grace swallowed before she answered. "More like afraid. He's slowing down quite a lot again. We're all frustrated. It's almost like watching my husband die all over again." She swallowed, tasting the acid and lowered her voice. "It's hard to explain to Eddy. He's a little trooper about the whole thing even though he doesn't really understand what's happening to his father. I don't know where exactly I fit into all of this, how much I want to fit in, or for that matter, if it's any of my business."

"I hope I never, ever, have to go through what you did, but Ted has come to rely on you," Shelby finally said. She skewered Grace with a piercing gaze from her brown irises. "I've never considered myself a busy-body or matchmaker, or whatever." Tears overflowed. "Ted went from having no will to live, to fight this, whatever, attacking him, and hardly knowing what to do about his child, to finding a reason to beat this thing. It's not fair, I know." She sniffed and used the edge of the cloth diaper on her shoulder to wipe at her eyes and nose. "It's just that I care about you both so much. You've been there for me when I needed you, and for Eddy and for Ted. And we give you nothing in return."

Grace disagreed, but waited for a moment to put her thoughts in order. "Of course it's not like that, girlfriend."

Eddy wandered over to them, plunking himself in her lap with a cookie he picked up from the bag they'd brought out with them earlier. She hugged him and jiggled him until he giggled.

"I was so wrapped up in myself, back in my former life. It finally doesn't hurt to think about what went on those last few years," she said, surprised at the confession.

Shelby sniffled loudly. "Go on."

"It's true. I admit it. I became complacent, and I think, so did Jonathan. Everything always went right for us. Having a baby worked out, eventually. We didn't question giving any more or less to anyone around us than they asked. We stopped doing anything we didn't feel comfortable with and took whatever was handed out, proud of ourselves and our blessings and our talents, our lifestyle. Then, of course, my world fell apart."

"That's putting it mildly."

Grace nodded and folded a sleepy Eddy against her heart. "My way of handling things was to run away."

"I can't imagine what I would have done."

"Like you said, I hope you never have to. I reacted the same way I lived, by hiding and doing whatever I could to make me comfortable. Always for me. So I think it's time I give back. I need to do things for others. In a way, it helps me, too, keeping my mind off of myself, healing my heart."

She thought for a moment and added, "Of course it's not all one-sided. Your support"—she rocked Eddy—"and companionship,"—she looked around the yard—and this home, have been the solace I needed. Loving involves giving. I think I'm finally beginning to understand that."

"Oh, Grace. I still don't think it's fair."

She reached out to touch Shelby's arm. "Thank you."

"I want you to stay."

Eddy squirmed. "I'm going with you."

"What would your daddy do without you, little man?" Shelby asked.

"Daddy will come, too."

Grace pulled him into a giggling swinging hug. "Maybe we'd all better stay here, then."

At least for now.

Chapter Fifteen

Randy shut off his headlights as he pulled into his driveway. Kaye's car blocked his spot in front of the garage. He knew Tanya had gone back to Detroit to be with her father over Easter vacation. So what was her aunt doing over here?

Randy turned off the engine and rolled down his window to the cool damp night air. He watched Kaye head toward Grace's front porch. The way the house faced, he saw what she did through the window: the silhouette of a man. She paused. Before she lost her nerve she knocked.

Little boy giggles spilled out and echoed around the front porch when the door opened. The warmth and inclusiveness hit Randy in the hollow pit of his stomach. He couldn't imagine what it did to her. In the yellow porch light, he saw her stiff back and her clenched fists held behind.

"Kaye! How nice to see you." Grace's voice floated on the evening air. "Come in. Did you need help with something?"

"Happy Easter. I was just next door, and, ah, no one answered. I happened to notice you were home."

Eddy popped into the doorway. "Kaye! Yeah! Look, Dad, it's Kaye! What are you doing here?" the little boy demanded. "Who's making lunch at the diner if you're here?" He whooped again and dove back into the house, out of sight.

Randy had reached the edge of the yard before he realized what he was doing. He paused, listening, knowing he shouldn't.

Ted appeared next, apparently as comfortable and homebound as if he still lived there. "Hi. What can we do for you?"

"Hello," Kaye said, bringing her hands away from her back. "I was out for a drive, and wondered what you were up to. I thought maybe Grace might know where you were."

Ted looked back before shuffling out to the porch and tugging the door closed behind him. "I'm here."

"I see. It's nothing, really. I thought maybe you'd like to have Easter dinner with me."

Randy sucked in a breath, misery, fury, embarrassment all vying for dominance. Why had she said it like that? Why not invite all of them? He turned away. Kaye shouldn't throw herself at Ted.

"This isn't really polite," Kaye said next. "I don't know why I came over here when it was obvious you weren't home. I apologize." She turned and began to hike down the steps.

Too right. Randy twisted sideways to duck behind a branch.

"Wait! Kaye!" Ted shuffled after her. "Thank you. That's really nice of you. I'll check with Grace and Randy and see—"

"It's okay, Ted. I don't want to intrude."

Randy watched his little brother grab hold of the rail by the steps, looking as if he'd have followed if he could have. Why did everything have to be so backward? Ted shouldn't be crippled and Kaye should know how—

He stepped from behind the branch. "Hello."

She put hands over her mouth in obvious surprise. Without a word she stomped around him, ripped open the driver's side of her car, and started the engine with a terrific grinding of gears.

Randy pounded on her window. She bent her head before fumbling for the switch to roll down the pane of glass separating them.

He pretended ignorance. "Were you looking for m—us? What do you want?"

She killed the engine. He had to lean close to hear her breathy speech.

"Randy, what do we know about this Grace person? Really? She came here with only the clothes on her back. Is she running from the law? Is she a criminal? How can we trust anything about her? And didn't she pay cash for the place? Who has that kind of money, anyway?" Kaye searched his face, eyes dark and bright in the moonlight.

Randy squatted at her side, hands on the open frame, his face close to hers, inhaling the slightly yeasty sweet smell of her. She must have been setting a batch of rolls to rise for tomorrow's baking. If only she knew. How could he ever convince her he was every bit as good as Ted? He could love her and care for her better? He had never been involved with another woman after Jenny. Only a miracle would reverse Ted's condition. They all knew it. She did not need to be jealous. Maybe…maybe if he did something to prove his worth, Kaye could see him for who he was. "I did a background check. Ted trusts—"

"Ted!" Anger spewed with the word. "What kind of shape is he in to make judgments? It's Ted we're all concerned about, isn't it? And *her*. Who knows what she's really after? How can you let her live here for a year and still know virtually nothing about her? I hear things, Randy." She unbuckled her seatbelt and swiveled toward him. He rose and stepped back, opening the door and grasping her elbow. She shrugged him off.

"I don't know what you mean." What else could he say?

"You travel all the time. You must know where she came from. You probably pass through Tennessee all the time on the way to Charleston and Atlanta. You could just, um, take a little detour sometime, check it out. You know, find out something…" She let her voice trail, silence speaking for her.

"Everyone likes her." Which wasn't exactly true. The prime example stood right here.

"She works at the clinic. People have to be able to trust her," Kaye insisted.

"Don't you think that's Doctor Evans's problem? You order things for her from your store."

"So? That's business. Her money is as good as anyone's. Besides, what harm could it do? If she has nothing to hide." She put her hands on her hips and tapped one foot on the gravel. "Randy?"

"Yeah, what harm could it do?" he replied. "I have an appointment in Birmingham next week. I could take a day then."

Her smile glinted in the cold moonlight. She had already slid back into her car by the time he opened his mouth again. "Maybe, when I get back—"

Her car window glided up, shutting him out as she drove away.

* * * *

Randy emerged from the rental car he picked up at the airport and looked up and down the short main street of Woodside. He had been glad of the air conditioning on the drive from Knoxville. The trees were already leafed out and flowers bloomed in their pots along the main street. White and pink dogwood blossoms wafted their spicy sweet fragrance. Several people window-shopped in various multicolored and textured storefronts.

He asked around about the Runyons at the Woodside version of Kaye's Café, at the hotel, at the gas station, but received very little response. It made him wonder what folks in East Bay would say about him, should any stranger ever come into town looking for information about the Marshalls.

He met a former patient in the parking lot after asking at the clinic to speak to anyone who knew her. The young woman told him Grace had left a year ago, after the deaths of practically her whole family. People wondered what happened. She'd had a large patient list. They hoped they hadn't upset her. Nobody seemed to get better as fast as when she treated them. The woman had a little boy with a bad case of poison ivy—again—and Grace had always helped him. She was missed. Did he know her? When was she coming back?

Another passerby had mentioned a ceremony in the cemetery a few weeks ago. "If I hadn't been out of town, I'd have confronted her myself," the prissy elderly woman said. "I'd have told her how sorry we all were. I'd have begged her to come back. Her house is so empty. Just sits there. Sad."

Grace's house? "Where did she live?"

"Why, it was just, over"—the woman turned and pointed—"down Bradley Street, there, the pretty Cape Cod. Douglas Kirby mows the lawn, you know. Misses the edge every time between hers and Kitty's."

"Thank you." Randy had already looked in the courthouse for personal records, death certificates of Grace's husband, and found her parents, even a child Ted never mentioned. He hated to think Kaye had some right to be concerned. What mother wouldn't admit to having a child or talking about him? Grace had plenty of pictures of that husband of hers. What about the kid?

After strolling down the street past her blank-eyed house, Randy walked through the rows at the cemetery.

A striking, young woman with spiked orange hair strode up to him. "Can I help you find someone, a missing relative, or family history, perhaps? I must also remind you, if you are a tourist, this place is private and dear to us. We ask you to respect it."

He studied her square-rimmed, gold wire glasses and narrow lips, incongruous with the hair. Had she ever cracked a smile?

"Someone told me a whole family was buried here, and there was some interesting story behind it. I was looking for a plaque or something, telling about it."

"Oh? Did you catch the name?"

"Runyon, I believe."

The woman glowered behind the glasses. Her hands clutched her elbows. A long white coat billowed out about her in a puff of wind.

Between the coat and a stethoscope thrust into her pocket, Randy took a guess. "You wouldn't, by any chance, be from the medical center, would you? Did you work with Grace Runyon?"

"How do you know her?" The woman's mouth bunched into a small, tight bud.

Now he was on to something, Randy was unsure how to proceed. He turned and gazed down a row of headstones nested in neatly clipped brilliant grass and bumblebees explored azalea bushes. "She bought my house, lives next door to me in Michigan."

The orange-haired woman stuck out her chin. "You must be Ted."

Randy took off his sunglasses. "No. Ted is my brother. I'm Randy Marshall. What made you think I was Ted? And who might you be?"

A puzzling angry glint appeared in the woman's eyes. His first estimate of her age changed when a cloud passed over the sun. Crepe skin showed under her jaw where the short reddish twists of hair ended. She would be a little older than Grace, then.

She kicked a divot in the smooth lawn. "I'm Lena Roberts, a friend of Grace's. She's written to me and stayed with me when she came here for the dedication." Lena indicated a monument a few rows over. "That's the memorial we put up to honor her family. Was there something you needed to know?"

Randy opened his mouth when he caught site of an intimidating bearded man in a knee-length black cloth coat leading a uniformed police officer toward them. He heaved a gusty sigh and grimaced.

"Look. I like Grace. She's a private person. We—I—just wanted to know a little more about her. She's been taking care of my nephew and I had some…missing pieces to fill. Nothing serious, but he's going to be my responsibility, eventually. And I heard a strange story about her whole family dying. I wanted to check it out for myself."

"You are obviously here out of some…concern…about Grace. She would tell you anything you needed to know."

The men had joined Lena, facing off against Randy.

Lena made the introductions. "Reverend Edwards, Officer Grenich, this is Randy Marshall, come from Michigan to pay his respects to Grace's family. He's her neighbor in Michigan where she lives now."

Randy offered his hand. "Sorry to intrude. I was simply passing through on business and thought I'd stop in."

"And what business are you in, sir," the officer asked, not really making it sound like a conversational question.

"Fruit grower's cooperative, Officer. I'm the head sales rep for the company." He named the organization which brought smiling, nodding recognition to all of their faces.

"It's nice to meet you. We're all friends of the Runyons, here. Was there something in particular you wanted?" the Reverend asked.

"No, sir. Like the lady said, I'm only here to pay my respects."

He hoped Kaye would get over whatever bugged her, as it seemed there was nothing remotely dangerous about Grace.

* * * *

The biggest monkey wrench in Randy's summer plan to prove himself to Kaye turned out to be Jimmy.

Randy went up to Sault St. Marie earlier in May to watch his son graduate from high school. The boy had been accepted at his alma mater, Michigan State University, in East Lansing. Randy still expected Jimmy for his usual two weeks before heading out for campus life and was surprised to arrive home late one evening to find him, dressed in ragged shorts and tank top, high-topped sneakers and no socks, draped all over the front steps to his house. Jimmy's hair was shaggier than ever with a bleach job grown out to about the level of his earlobes. His expression in the moonlight was beyond sullen.

Randy loosened his tie and top shirt buttons and plunked down next to him, letting his hands dangle on either side of his knees. After a moment, he asked quietly, "Son, does your mother know you're here?"

Jimmy hesitated for a long time. "She's the one who said I had to come."

Randy took in another long, deep breath and then sighed it out. He got up, held out a hand to Jimmy, and said simply, "Okay. We'll talk this out tomorrow."

Jimmy bent to pick up his backpack and guitar, relief and shame mixed in the set of his shoulders and jerky strides into the house and up to his childhood bedroom. Randy watched him go. He wiped his hand over his bristly hair and ran himself a glass of water at the tap. When he checked his messages, he listened carefully three times to what his ex-wife told him.

The other problem was Tanya.

The girl had agreed to help watch Eddy over the summer. Shelby wasn't planning to return to her former daycare business and helped out upon occasion after school. With his nephew complaining about lack of playtime with Grace and the stinky baby at Shelby's, Ted was stressed, which didn't help his health.

But if Tanya was on the other side of the hedge with Eddy, Jimmy was bound to sniff it out. After last summer's sparks, who knows what trouble they'd cook up now? One thing for sure—Jimmy needed a job of his own if he was going to stay until he went to college in September. Washing dishes in Soo might not have been the most sought-after position, but it had been steady. The boy needed to occupy his time and keep his work ethic muscle in shape.

For two weeks Jimmy sweated picking at the local cherry orchards before flatly refusing to return. Randy had been rushing around getting ready to go to work and not in the mood to discuss the situation at that particular hour of the morning.

Angered, he sputtered, "You made a commitment, Jimmy. Everyone's counting on you."

"I'm sure they're nice people, Dad." Jimmy didn't meet his eyes. "And yeah, I know everyone has to work hard. But I don't understand Spanish. And they make fun of me when I can't even defend myself."

Randy opened his mouth.

Jimmy cut in. "And I have a scholarship. I don't need more money for college. I been *saving.*"

Randy's mouth pursed. Then he sighed and contemplated his son's huge feet. "And when you fail English and have to stay another year? What then? Son, you have no idea."

Jimmy slammed open the screen door, shouting. "That's what everyone says! Why can't you just let me find out for myself? I'm supposed to be a *man* now and everyone treats me like a kid!"

Randy looked at the door, heaved a breath, and abused the work truck's transmission on the way to Co-op headquarters. What was a father to do?

East Bay was a hidebound community. It didn't take long for the stories to circulate back to Randy. He could have guessed, having nothing else to do, Jimmy would discover what days he might find Tanya not in the stuffy café uniform but in a skimpy swimsuit and playing at the park with his cousin.

They told him, the ladies at the gift shops around the square, how Jimmy and another gaggle of boys hung around, discouraging their customers. No one wanted to pass the half-dressed, dirty boys and their smoke and spit to come inside and spend money.

He needed to do something about those boys. And tell that girl to put some clothes on.

How to approach his son? Was there any way possible, Lord, Lord, to have an actual conversation with a teenaged boy who thinks he's an adult, without being treated like the Grand Inquisitor? Randy ran a stoplight on the way home. At least the crossroad had been empty, and only Madge Hardaway who watered the plants at church, stopped on the other side, saw him and honked.

Randy rolled into the driveway. Should he start the conversation with the story of his own failure? A question? A comment? Oh, God.

Pulsating music floated from behind the house. He followed it to spy his shirtless man child sprawled on a blanket, radio parked near his ear.

Randy loosened his tie and sat down. Jimmy opened one lid. Then the other.

Randy took a deep breath. "I think we should talk about girls."

Jimmy rolled over onto his stomach and didn't stop talking until the mosquitoes drove them inside.

The short version was he had dropped the ball with Tanya. He didn't know what happened, why after Christmas he wasn't all that keen on texting anymore. Not having her voice right in his ear made her seem too unreal—too far away. Jimmy was also embarrassed to tell her his mom grounded him from the phone for the big bill he incurred after Thanksgiving.

The best he could do was watch her this summer since she wouldn't talk to him. That's why he went to the park so much.

Then the guys showed up. Coulda stuck his finger in a socket and not shocked him worse. "I mean, Dad, how did they know? The first time I heard Robert say 'yo,' I knew there was going to be issues."

Randy figured he knew which boy was Robert. Hair was as shaggy as Jimmy's, but streaked. A gold circle gleamed around one earlobe and scruffy black hairs spouted from a soul patch underneath his bottom lip.

"Jason, and Paul, too."

"Which is the one who smokes?"

"Paul. Home-rolls."

"Those were the ones in your band, right?"

"Yeah, Dad. I told them I wanted to *play* music, man. I didn't want that backstage scene they were doing."

Randy shivered. Should he ask? "You were uncomfortable?"

"I just wanted the music." Jimmy rolled over. "They told me they wanted to see the dunes."

"Let me guess. You were all at the park where Tanya and Eddy were playing."

"Yeah." He put an arm across his eyes. "I told them to leave her alone."

"And that didn't go over too well."

"You could say so."

"Do you know if they're still hanging around? Or where they're staying?"

"No. Please—don't do anything, okay?" Jimmy sat up and begged him with an earnestness Randy remembered from his own youth. "I'll deal with it."

Randy nodded, certain he was going to regret it.

Chapter Sixteen

As a physician's assistant at the medical clinic Grace felt useful if unremarkable. She was still called to heal, just not be spectacular about it. There had been no "recharge" after working on little Alyssa, no sparks when she touched her patients, no rush…nothing special. Since she longed for anonymity, could she accept the special gift to perform miracles had fizzled out? The only thing it hurt was her pride, and that she could do without. She didn't have sheepskin with her credentials for nothing.

The clinic counted on steady funding from the fruit growers' co-op, for which she knew Greg was grateful. Migrant workers came in all summer, and she enjoyed learning a few phrases of whatever nationality they were.

A few bothersome annoyances persisted. Tony's eyes widened every time he saw Grace. She no longer took care of him, per his mother's request. Since Tony was a little monster, she could deal with that.

One slow afternoon at the clinic she volunteered to take inventory as Nancy wanted to put together a restock order. Grace sat on a low stool to take a breather after counting towels. A polite cough made her look up.

Greg leaned against the door frame, his legs and arms crossed. "Quarter for your thoughts?"

She laughed. "Inflation that high?"

"Are you okay? Things going all right? I know the pay can't be living wages for you, and I know you don't always—"

"I'm fine, Greg." His concern for her welfare was a surprise. They had treated each other with friendly professional deference since Christmas. "It's nice of you to be concerned, but I assure you I have no financial worries."

Greg straightened and put his hands in his pockets. "How about your house, then? I can recommend repairmen, or help out with some"— he grimaced—"ah, *simple*, work, if you need anything done. Or work on your car."

Grace smirked. "You forgot lawn-mowing. All those helpless female chores," she teased. Greg's expression sobered. She stopped smiling.

He studied his worn loafers. "I just thought I'd remind you—I care."

After setting the towels on the wire shelf she stood and faced him. "Greg." She touched his arm. "Thank you. Really. I don't mean to be one of those people who can't accept help from anyone. I appreciate your offer, and your…care. I see it all day long, and I know you're sincere."

She dropped her hand and stepped back. "People around here rely on you. They don't really understand how much you've given up to stay in East Bay to care for them."

Greg took it all in. "And you? Will you ever be able to rely on me?"

"I have, ever since I first met you."

He unfolded his arms and took a step toward her. "You know what I mean. I backed off. Since Christmas, I've sat back. I've waited and watched. Things are not getting better."

Nancy breezed in through the door, crowding the little space with her perpetual annoying cheerfulness.

"Have you got that order, Grace? MediCo is on the line and I want to save our dime if they're calling here first."

"Sure, Nancy. I'll come with you." Grace moved past Greg, asking him with her eyes to drop the matter. His own hooded expression told her he wasn't finished.

* * * *

"Let's play hooky," Ted greeted her one late June Saturday morning. "We feel like going to the beach today. Wanna come?"

Eddy wiggled at his father's side, grasping the metal cross bar of the new crutch.

How could she resist the display of unusual cheer? Ted was often morose these days, and seeing him in a good mood was worth its weight in—raspberries!

Glad she'd started working with the berries before it got too warm, she wiped her hands on her apron, wondering how Ted would manage crutches on the sand. Well, if he thought he could, who was she to spoil the party? "Hmm, sounds like a plan. I just have this last batch of jam to set up. Can you wait for a while?"

"It smells soooo good, Grace. Can I help?"

Eddy's "help" might cost the rest of the morning. His enthusiastic stirring last time spun a goodly portion of the sticky red stuff on her table, the chair, through the seams of the leaves of the table, the floor, and his shirt front. She tried to let him down gently. "Thanks, my little man, but I have to finish the cooking and stirring."

Ted caught her hesitation. "Why don't you show me what's new at the playhouse, Eddy? We'll come back when Grace is done, okay?"

She watched them amble around the corner before she went back inside to finish the batch of jam and make a picnic lunch.

Ted drove them drove north on M131 an hour later.

"You people don't seem very imaginative on naming your roads," she commented after passing signs for exiting onto 9 Mile, 14 Mile, and 22 Mile Roads. "I can see why the country folk feel at home here, though," she continued. "The hills aren't so high nor the valleys so deep, but it has the same wild and lonesome feel."

She looked over at Ted's profile. Sunglasses perched on his nose and his hair fluttered in the breeze of the open window. Intimate scents of soap mingled with warmed skin wafted in her direction.

He glanced at her. "No fighting over using family or American Indian names this way. We'll reach the tourist spots soon enough. The shoreline has gotten all built up over the few years. Industry has obviously changed from agriculture, general farming, and the like. There used to be a thriving lime works, too. That, and the mission, is what started Petoskey going, if I remember right, after the railroad went in."

"Petoskey?"

Eddy sang in the backseat. "Pitashkey, pitashkey."

"Pe-tah-sky," Ted repeated, over the sound of his son. "It was the name of an Ottawa man who owned a lot of land on the shoreline. Or, I guess, technically, the white settlers changed his name to this pronunciation and spelling."

He hummed, tapping the steering wheel. At least he seemed comfortable in the driver's seat today. Grace sat back. "How far are we going?"

"Not much farther. You need to stop?"

She laughed. "No. I was just curious. I didn't hear you say where we were headed."

"Right."

"You're kidnapping me?"

He gave a cheeky grin. "If you want to look at it that way, go ahead."

Grace stuck out her tongue. She turned to stare out the window as they came into the next city. Charlevoix perched alongside the bay, its quaint and beautiful Victorian homes lining the street.

Ted seemed intent on stuffing her full of history. "You can probably tell by the name that this part of the state was deeply influenced by the French. Fur-traders, 'way back. That's where most of the early money was made. The good old days of John Jacob Astor."

Eventually they wound around the shore to the village of Petoskey which overlooked Little Traverse Bay. Ted drove past the trendy marina, tidy buildings, and ballpark. "We'll stop at the Historical Society Museum on our way back," he told her as he pointed out the pretty blue-gray and white painted building. They traveled along the coast to the north until they came to Petoskey State Park. Ted drove in through the gate to the ranger station.

"It's usually best to come here in the morning, early in the season after the ice is off, but that doesn't mean you can't find them anytime."

Grace didn't have a clue what he meant. This time she refused to ask for clarification. She began to leaf through the brochures Ted handed her after showing their park tag.

"Petoskey stones," she read aloud, "are Michigan's state fossil."

For a petty second she was pleased at hunting up this answer for herself. "So, we're hunting for rocks?"

"Not just any rocks. These are special. They were part of an ancient reef off the coast of Lake Michigan, and break off due to wave action, washing in toward shore. They're gray, anonymous-looking things, actually. The pieces are all sizes. It's easiest to see the pattern of the reef when they're wet. It appears like clusters of white rings, or sometimes sorta like broccoli. They're really cool when polished. People even make jewelry out of them."

"Oh! I think I've seen some at an antique store."

They drove in toward the beach through the dunes and parked the car.

"Are we gonna find one today?" Eddy asked his father.

"They're not always easy to spot, remember? Especially with all these people around, looking, too. But we'll have fun checking out the beach, won't we?"

Grace admired the way Ted left hope for his son, but also did not promise something he couldn't be sure of.

They walked along the narrow waterfront, moving at a slow pace. Eddy skipped among the waves on the sandy beach which was filled with people wading up to their knees, eagerly searching in the breakers for the special fossils. After struggling across the deeper gravel to get to the water's edge, Ted had fairly easy walking where the wet sand gave him smoother ground. Using only one crutch, he held Grace's hand. Support, she could give.

The sun and whoosh of the waves washed contentment over her. High-pitched squawking of boisterous seagulls lent an otherworldly atmosphere. When they reached some tall beach grass they stopped to watch the little sandpipers *cheep* and run up to and away from waves rolling inland.

Ted gazed out into the open water. He seemed mesmerized by the scene until he turned to Grace. "You must have felt alone a lot after your husband died, and your parents, too." He didn't add her son Sean's name to the list. She turned to seek out Eddy, a few paces away.

Ted looked lake-ward again. "Do you ever wonder if humans are alone in the universe? With all of the space exploration going on, and everything, it seems so strange to think about."

She wondered at his mood today. Ted started out cheerful, although he was obviously in some pain shown by his white-knuckled grip on the crutch and how he kept his weight off his left hip as much as possible. He draped himself over the crutch as he swung his head around toward her, black hair falling across one eye, waiting for her to answer.

She brushed a blowing curl from her lips and stared back into his ocean blue eyes, at the crinkled lines around his nose and mouth, the wind ruffling his loose white shirt. Did he feel alone? Should she tell him now how she felt? But where would that conversation lead? Better stick with his question.

She bent her head to stare at the grains of sand and the crawling critters she could pick out. "Do you think those sand lions realize we're here?" She pointed to the ant lions, insects commonly called "sand lions" around that part of the state. Delicately winged creatures usually an inch or so long, they made pits in the sand and awaited for the unwary prey to come close enough to be captured and eaten.

Ted frowned at her return question. "So you think there's something, someone, bigger than us in the universe, and we simply don't realize it? Come on."

She didn't back down. "I know there's *Someone* bigger than us in the universe. In fact, this Someone made the universe."

Ted heaved a sigh. He lifted and set down the crutch. "God. Of course. Everyone knows that."

"Everyone does, indeed. But very few people know God."

"You can't know God any more than your sand lions know you." Ted squashed a few of them with his crutch.

How quickly her gentle love turned to angry pity. "Unlike you, Ted monster, the God of the universe would never crush you without warning and for no reason."

Ted shifted on the sand, the muscles of his forearm flexing as he resettled the crutch. "What about the wars, and heart attacks, and-and all that other stuff that happens, lots of times without warning? What about me? I deserve at least some answers."

"What makes you think God causes that to happen? Honestly, that's such a lame blame." She set her hand on top of his, inviting him to face her. "People don't want to admit *we're* the problem. We think we do everything right, and then the Almighty can't stand it, so he throws us for a loop just to see us dance, and that's not true at all. No one does everything right. All of us have selfish desires at one time or another."

She stroked his knuckles to take some of the sting of her words. "So, the answer to your question, Ted, is 'all of the above.' Yes, I've felt lonely at times, but never completely alone. I don't know if humans are the only creatures with a soul God created in the universe, but no, we're not alone."

She removed her hand and faced the breakers, shielding her eyes from the sun and wind.

"Ha! I knew it! You do believe in aliens from outer space!"

Ted changed the subject, as she suspected he would. He was good at starting a conversation, but when things got dicey, or uncomfortable, he ran as fast as she did. And she was perfectly willing to go along with him, not willing to break the bubble of trust developing between them.

"Well, of course. Don't you? Please don't tell Eddy, or we'll never hear the end of it."

Steamy wisps of bubbly gray fog began to billow in across the waves. The air cooled in a moment, and Eddy came back to them, shivering.

"Let's go," Ted said.

"B-but I haven't found the right s-stone, Daddy!"

Ted didn't, or couldn't respond, but stood stiffly, his lips pressed into a narrow line.

Grace offered her hand. "We'll come back. Pretty soon you won't be able to see through the fog, anyway. You can hunt as we walk." She pointed back toward the parking lot. "Look, we have a long way to go." Eddy dubiously stared at their trail along the beach. He shivered harder and puckered his lips. She pulled a towel and shirt from the beach bag slung over her shoulder and rubbed him dry before she tugged the shirt over his head. All the while he stared intently at the waves crashing up next to them, carefully watching each ebb and flow tickle her toes.

She eyed Ted, hoping he had the strength to walk back. He was breathing hard, but otherwise looked all right. He nodded at her. "I can make it."

Eddy brought a bit of greenish stone for them to look at. "Is this one?"

Ted smiled. "Maybe. We can take it home and look at it better."

"Yippee!" Eddy skipped ahead.

"I have a stone my mother gave me, when I was about his age," Ted said quietly as they wandered in the child's erratic trail. "My dad found and polished it when he was young. You can't put them in a rock tumbler because they're so soft. You have to rub them very carefully by hand with different grits of paper."

They trudged on, stepping in tandem. "Anyway, my dad gave the stone he spent so much time on as a boy to my mother when they were dating." He stopped for a moment to catch his breath. "He told me it was a symbol of how much he believed she was the right one. Permanent, yet fragile." Ted seemed to be quoting, eyes half-closed. "She passed away a few years after she gave it to me. I take it out and look at it when Eddy and I talk about his grandma and grandpa." He watched his little boy scamper back from a bold seagull. "I even make up stories sometimes," he confessed, "about what she might have been like if she had lived."

He cleared his throat, blinked, and stared out over the lake. "I guess it's time to pass that stone on to Eddy."

Grace said nothing, but pretended the breeze blew something into her eye to make it tear.

* * * *

Grace relaxed on her porch swing later, idly pushing herself with her bare foot against the wide painted boards. The sunset rioted in front of her, bathing the yard with psychedelic oranges and mauves. Misty shrouds hung in low clouds out over the lake, which she couldn't see, but knew was there. Greg Evans's familiar car nosed up the driveway and the engine cut off.

She stopped her swinging and sat up, wary as a moth around a security light. What now?

"Alone? Really?" Greg got out of the car and challenged her from the walkway. "The Marshalls give you some time off or will one of them show up any second?"

She sighed, composed herself, and slumped back into the seat, toeing the floor to set the swing back in motion. The best way to confront a bully is to ignore him.

Greg sat, uninvited, on her front step. He stared at the remains of the color show in the west, clasping his knee and watching the path through the hedge to the main house, as if considering an attack on anything that crossed over. The sky grew dark.

"I'm sorry, Grace. I wanted to continue our conversation from the other day, and this was not a good way to start. I've never, well, at least not since second grade, had this intense experience of dislike for another person."

She still did not acknowledge his presence.

"All right, Grace. I deserve this. May I humbly request your attention?"

"You're sounding like a jealous lover. You're my boss. I don't want to jeopardize that. I don't want anything between us but a friendly professional working relationship right now." She was glad the gathering dark hid much of his expression, as well as her own.

Greg sat up straight and stared at her. "Can I at least be concerned about you? Everyone who sees Marshall knows he doesn't have much longer. What will happen when he dies? Have you thought about that? I want you to know I'm here for you."

She rocked the swing a little harder. "Thank you." She sniffed and rubbed her nose, then stopped the swing altogether and stood. "I'm going in now. Goodnight."

"Wait."

At his quiet command, she stopped but didn't turn around.

"I am jealous," he said. "I admit it. Marshall had the opportunity to know you first, and needs you—sees you—in a way I hope I never will.

But I'm whole, Grace, healthy and able to give you what you'll never get from him. I speak your language and I understand you have needs, too, needs I can meet, if you'll please give me a chance."

"Don't beg," she said over her shoulder. "It's unbecoming."

His body heat reached through her shirt when he walked up and stood directly behind her. His hands settled on her shoulders, but she resisted turning in his arms.

"I can't pretend you don't appeal to me," she said, speaking toward the empty doorway. "And it's nice having someone to talk to at the end of the day, someone who can appreciate what you've tried to do, anyway." Grace let her head droop. "We both owe Ted a lot of leeway here. He's been good to me when I needed it. There's still something important I have to do yet, something I don't completely understand. But I know that I have to wait."

Greg's hands gripped her shoulders convulsively as he pulled her back to rest against his chest. His voice ruffled her hair. "Okay," he managed in a slightly choked voice. And then he was gone.

Chapter Seventeen

Matty filled in the place of a mother figure for Grace, the one person on earth she could talk to about these troubling personal issues. Yet it was risky to talk to her about the men in her life, as she was her co-worker as well as friend.

"I hoped I read more into it last week at the clinic when Greg told me he'd been waiting for me since Christmas," Grace said as they walked around the chicken yard the next day. Under Harold's watchful attention, Eddy scrambled after the latest litter of puppies.

"But last night, when he came over and said those things to me… I just don't know what to think. He's such a good man. I'd be a fool to throw away a chance at a normal relationship with someone like him, wouldn't I? Especially since…since I'm beginning to think Ted might not get better."

"I've never known the doctor to be so smitten," Matty admitted.

Grace drew in a breath, stopped, and held a hand up to shade her eyes from the glare of the sun. "Smitten? With me? You don't mean others think that… That?"

"Well, only if they know him so well."

"Nancy?"

"Yup, prob'ly!" Matty said cheerfully. "He's not exactly been a lady's man about town. Nancy, too, she can see it, I'm certain."

"Oh, Lord. I can hear it now. They think I'm a man-eater."

Matty grinned. "I think they're still taking bets about the poor man being gay."

Grace rolled her eyes.

"Always the whispers. You have feelings for young Marshall, yes? And only this year now since losing your beloved. Tch, tch." She shook her head. "People jus' don't understand. You help Mr. Marshall to face God with dignity now. That is the greater need, I think. Greg—well, he is waiting to be convinced that God has meaning in this place. He has waited many years for the right mate. He can wait a little longer, yes? Perhaps even the watching you with young Mr. Marshall will help him. So."

She grasped Grace's waist and pulled her close in a motherly hug. "We trust in the good Lord to sort things out in His time."

Grace nodded and soaked in the comfort. Even if Matty and Greg believed Ted had no chance to live she was not ready to abandon him to terrifying indignity of wasting pain. Routine care could help him for now. Maybe that's what she was supposed to do.

Wait, wait, wait, the breeze carried the whispers through the leaves on the big willow tree. *Wait on me.*

* * * *

Mrs. Vanden Heuvel finally caught on. Grace had conjured a record number of excuses to dodge her turn to lead devotional for the ladies' society at First Covenant Church. The ten women who met enjoyed each other's company, and Grace gradually developed a comfortable if not close relationship with many of them. She probably would never have gone if Shelby wasn't a regular. But she had successfully avoided taking a turn to lead. Baked goods—yes; helping at the annual "used but nice" yard sale in the church's parking lot—yes; Eddy had loved it helping the customers find things they absolutely needed.

She had come regularly to worship with the Marshalls, and while it wasn't anything like the dynamic experience of practicing faith at her home church, God was everywhere, even in the quiet contemplation and slightly dry but quaint liturgical readings. She taught Eddy the words to the Apostle's Creed, earning his uncle's praise.

When Mrs. Vanden Heuvel made a loud comment about how

much the group looked forward to her leadership the next month, Grace had to give in. The assigned passage was from the letter to the Hebrews, chapter six. "Hope is an anchor for the soul, firm and secure."

The other women simply read out of the book they used at prior meetings. But hope was something Grace experienced daily. She didn't need to read someone else's experience. There didn't seem to be any reason to hide anymore, to keep secrets like Sean, to worry about not being accepted if they knew her past. At least, the parts she was ready to share. On the day, she was surprised not to be afraid and spoke from her heart.

"I want to share with you a little about how I feel about hope, instead of reading out of the book," she told the women after cake and coffee. "You can read the message yourselves, anyway, right? I like to think hope is secure and firm. Sometimes that's all we have, you know, when we're hanging on by our toenails, watching the next giant wave heading our way."

A couple of the stylish gray-haired ladies nodded and encouraged her with self-conscious smiles, encouraging her. Shelby beamed.

"'Hope does not disappoint us.' That's from the book of Romans, you know. But I think it refers to our hope of salvation, of seeing God when it's the right time and right place. Those are the things we shouldn't be afraid of. Like sickness and death."

This time the ladies exchanged a few puzzled looks. Mrs. Wolver tapped the cover the devotional book in front of her.

"Here's another verse we should all know: 'perfect love casts out fear.' I'm only just beginning to realize what that means. I've never really had to hope before, you see, and I've never had to be afraid. I wrapped myself in my own little perfect world, doing perfect things. Nothing really went wrong, until—well, until everything went wrong. Even then I didn't understand I should have been afraid—I didn't have the proper fear of the Lord. You see, I went one day from being a daughter, wife, and mother, having the perfect career, being popular and well-known with several friends, to having nothing."

She went on in a rush to get the next part in without crying. "My parents were killed, my little boy, too, and then my husband got sick and died. I could do nothing—nothing—to stop any of it." She bowed her head. "It was a wake-up call that has forever changed me."

Mrs. Vanden Heuvel gasped. She put a hand over her mouth, eyes wide.

Grace hadn't meant to shock anyone. "I'm not going to make this a dragged-out feel-sorry-for-Grace story, but I want to let you know I've survived some pretty rough times because of the hope I have to reach for. Just because God holds things out for us, like salvation, faith, and every good thing, doesn't make it automatically ours. We actually have to take hold of it. And hope is like that, too. It's the foundation of all we want after our time on earth is done. What else can we hope for but to see heaven?"

She ignored Reverend Mattisse's sour expression. He was automatically invited to all church functions where he gave the opening prayers, ate, and left soon afterward. Today he stayed. This was as close to teaching as a woman could come in his church—though it was only to other women. He didn't join in the burst of applause Shelby started.

Mrs. Ten Boldt timidly approached after most of the others had gone home. "That was a wonderful message, Grace. I didn't know some of those things about you, and let me tell you now how terribly sorry I am for your losses. And with…" Her voice trailed off, sympathy in her posture. "Well, with your work and life now, here with us, I want you to know we are grateful to have you with us. Especially for all you do for the Marshall boys. We're cousins, you know, on their mother's side. I never thought about hope the way you talked about it before. We'll all pray harder, I'm sure…harder for young Ted. Thank you."

Grace clasped her hand. "Thank you, too," she whispered back.

"How is he doing? He didn't come to church last Sunday, I noticed."

"He's in some pain. He works hard during harvest."

"Yes, yes, that's right. All that business in the past…such a shame."

"You mean with his ex-wife?" Grace wad done with innuendo. "She's been gone for years now. Surely it's time to forgive and forget."

Mrs. Ten Boldt patted her shoulder. "Much easier said than done."

Chapter Eighteen

Near the end of July the lake breeze blew in a mixture of cold from the perpetually icy water and steam from the heated air. Grace worked evening hours at the clinic so Greg could take a couple of days off.

Lost in the land of reporting near closing, the crash of the front doors surprised her. Randy barreled in, half-carrying Jimmy whose ashen face and rolled-back eyes bore mute witness to the extent of his fear and pain. The boy cradled his left in beach towels. Grace fought the gag reaction at the whiff of charred flesh, gunpowder, and urine.

"Idiots blowing off firecrackers at the beach," Ted growled as he shuffled in after them. Grace motioned for Ted and Eddy to wait in the chairs in the darkened lobby area while she hustled the others down the hall into an examining cubicle and helped settle the young man on a gurney. Jimmy was nearly unconscious, but alert enough to fight her, and she didn't want to hurt him any more than he already had been.

She locked eyes with Randy, steel on steel. "I need to look."

Randy reached for the wrappings. "We'll check your wound, now, son."

Jimmy passed right out at that point, and Grace lifted the towel to look.

Terrycloth fibers and sand stuck in the mangled remains of the hand. She took in a breath and hoped her best professional voice was steady. "Randy, could you please go join Ted now? We have to keep it clean in here." She was grateful when he obeyed without protest.

After a full examination she flushed the area in warm saline. She injected painkiller then placed the boy's hand on a sterile field while she speed dialed Greg on his cell and let him know of the situation.

"Do you need me?" His detached voice echoed his obvious reluctance to come out of vacation mode.

"It's a bad one, Greg, but I'll get it cleaned and dressed, then have Rutgers at Bay View take a look if it doesn't look right tomorrow."

"Good, keep me posted."

She hung up, pleased at the "I trust you," in his voice.

"Okay, Jimmy, let's see what we can do for you."

He had regained consciousness and watched her with dark, suspicious eyes, keeping his lips clamped tight. She straightened his damp clothing, covering his stained shorts with a sheet and eased his head and neck into a more comfortable position. "You can change clothes soon. Don't worry, and don't be embarrassed. Happens all the time."

She talked to him quietly and soothingly about what she was planning to do to treat his wound while she went about methodically gathering supplies. Unlike the last few months of routine care without that spark, she knew tonight was the night. Rushing in like dammed up waters through a breach, her gift charged almost painfully through her, begging to be used.

Grace had worked with a few burns in Tennessee, mindful of the dreaded agony of the damaged nerve endings and internal hurt she experienced with the victims. She knew infection was a terrible, terrible threat to the healing. She kept her breathing steady and deep while she prepared herself, intuitively expecting this one to cause her as much pain as the patient.

Dousing her bare hands with antiseptic, she scrubbed as if for surgery. Only later would she put on gloves, as their protective shield would not serve either of them now.

She prayed, checked that the curtains were pulled tight, and went to work. Jimmy did not struggle as he had earlier, and she kept careful watch for signs of shock. She leaned in under the light and began the task of healing.

Several metacarpal bones were blasted out of alignment. Ow.

"I hope you're a righty, Jimmy Boy," she said, glad she was right-handed.

Jimmy gasped, gagging, and turned his head away while she probed, debriding dead tissue.

"Remind me to tell people not to ever wrap up burns." After picking out terry towel fuzz with tweezers, she began to flush the area with more saline in an attempt to remove fine grains of gunpowder, paper, and sand the force of the blast had driven deeply into the hand. Jimmy moaned, and Grace held her breath.

"Okay, babe, here we go. It'll be better soon. Promise." She leaned forward, gently placing his damaged hand on top of her left palm, inwardly hissing with him.

She began with the misaligned fingers, forcing them straight, wincing, and watched with never ceasing amazement as the miracle began. Past experience taught her that pre-dosing herself with analgesics would not deaden the pain as it was drawn into her own body. The pain sharpened her and increased her compassion—as long as she could keep it compartmentalized.

Bones snapped into place in his hand even they came apart briefly in hers. She cringed and bit her lip. Jimmy's legs moved restlessly but thankfully he kept his face turned.

Her left hand began to redden and ooze beneath his, cracks appearing in the sites where Jimmy's hurts were worse.

"So then, wanna tell me what made you pull this crazy stunt," Grace asked him, more as a distraction than actually wanting to know.

"Ow! Man, that hurts."

"No kidding."

"Okay, I was, uh, you know… Well, Tanya came to the beach with us. We were just goofing around, playing music and stuff, and I wanted to, well…after last summer, she was hardly payin' any notice… Then, she finally sees me. I only, you know, wanted to impress her."

"Yeah, well, I doubt she was highly impressed by this stunt. Okay, here's the tough part, Jimmy. Hang on. I thank you, Lord," Grace gasped out, "you have made me wonderfully," while she gently and firmly stroked along the damaged phalanges ,watching the fine muscles and sinew snake and plump before the ruined flesh could be restored.

Jimmy must have recalled the words from some distant memory of Sunday School and he began to recite with her. "I shall not want… He makes me…"

Jimmy's eyes grew wide when he finally looked down at what she had been doing with his hand. This, the reaction, she could not hide as she'd not hung a sterile drape.

Ted's voice outside of the curtain startled her. "Grace! Grace, how are things going? How is Jimmy?"

She carefully twisted her back to the curtain and kept their hands out of view, an unwelcome adrenalin rush of fear making her shake. "Go tell Randy Jimmy's going to be fine. We're—he's—in a bit of pain now, but that's to be expected. He'll need time to heal completely. Maybe therapy."

Her voice cracked as she struggled to contain her pain. "He'll have to see the burn doctor at Bay Bridge in a few days...to make sure things are going...well."

Ted opened the curtain and popped his head in.

"No—Ted, we... can't risk any more infection! No people in here before I get him wrapped...you need to go. Now."

* * * *

Ted withdrew with an apology but stayed by the curtain, leaning on his crutches. She sounded upset, and he wasn't sure what to do. He trusted her, but hurt physically at the pain in her tone. He called softly, "Grace, is there anything you need? Someone else to call, or anything I can do?"

"Pray now, okay? For us both. I need another half hour or so to wrap this right. It's tricky with the bones of the fingers needing to be set, yet the flesh around them being too damaged to support… Jimmy will be fine. Please, Ted, could you just—go sit with the others? I'm sorry, but I have to concentrate here."

"Sure." He turned painfully to manoeuvre himself back down the hallway. Something didn't seem right. Not with her medical ability, but something else—something inside of her. Maybe her soul, if that was the right word. Pray, she told him, for both Jimmy and herself.

What good was that? Prayer? He didn't even know how. But Randy did.

He shuffled back into the waiting room to find Eddy curled up against Randy, asleep over Randy's lap. Randy stroked the boy's hair, his face a craggy mask of sorrow. Ted stopped at the doorway, forcing his breathing to calm before entering the room.

"You wonder if I'll be able to care for your boy, when I can't for my own," Randy's quiet voice met him.

Ted stopped up short.

"You'd be right, thinkin' that."

"Grace says Jimmy will be fine. Sore, fingers maybe a little crooked, but will keep his hand fine." But he couldn't deny his brother's sentiments about caring for Eddy.

"Randy?"

"Yeah?"

"She also said to pray, for Jimmy and for her…um, I don't know how…I don't know the right things to say. What should we do?"

Randy's face was wet. Ted blinked. Randy never cried.

Ted lowered himself in a nearby seat, shaken. He bowed his head when he saw Randy lower his.

"I'll pray for all of us," Randy said.

* * * *

Jimmy's flesh did not instantly become smooth and pain-free again at Grace's healing touch, but it did lose the angry look. Much of the pain of healing would not affect him now. His hand would be restored to the way it had been before, more quickly than normal and without scarring, if things went as usual.

There was no reason to think anything wasn't usual. She even welcomed the dragging through broken glass feeling ebbing through her veins as the gift worked through her.

Grace casually flipped one of the sterile towels over her own hand to hide the strange effect. In a little while, she could tend to herself. *Hang on, girl.*

"Okay, Jimmy. Let's check the circulation, motion, and sensation in your fingers. Can you feel this?" She pressed the exposed tips of his fingers with the fingers of her right hand.

He jerked at her touch. "Yeah, that hurts," he hissed.

"Now wiggle your fingers a little."

He moaned. "I can't!"

"Yes you can—a little. Hurting is a good sign, really. Now, how about something for the pain? I can give you a couple of samples." She looked at the color of the skin, satisfied it had pinked up nicely.

"Let's just shoot a little picture, here, for posterity sake. You'll be famous." Grace led him over to the X-ray machine, towel over her left hand like a waiter, and took a couple of images. It might be a little unusual to take the X-ray afterward, but it would mean less explanation about the rate of healing.

"There, some reporting, instructions about keeping the wrapping clean, then you can take your dad home."

"Grace? Thanks—thanks a lot," Jimmy told her. "I'm sorry I was so—um, you know."

She waited, knowing it would be good for him to get the words out.

"Um, well, when I came in, I wasn't so sure about things. But you were terrific, Grace, really cool and all." His smile wavered.

She gave him a tired one of her own, her strength sapped. Standing still was a chore. "Sure, Jimmy. Just don't do it again, okay? You have a lot of other talents to impress us all."

She stopped him before they reached the waiting room. "Jimmy, your dad, well, it's only that we all care about you." She looked him in the eyes. "You've heard this before, but it's true. The things you do now will be with you always. Please think about the kind of person you want to be, and the kind of people you hang out with."

Jimmy swallowed and slowly nodded. They walked to the entrance of the waiting room. She'd make an appointment for him at Bay Bridge for the next morning she told them while pretending to wipe her hands on the towel.

"I'll come back later and pick you up, okay?" Ted said.

"No, don't worry. But it's sweet of you to offer. Just stay home once you get there." She edged away from him, all but jumping out of her skin with the effects of deep exhaustion. "I have my car. I'll get the paperwork done and then go home. Thank you. Good night."

It was no one's business but hers what happened next. She certainly couldn't allow anyone to see what her own hand looked like. It would remain broken and red for a few days until the marks slowly faded. The miracle didn't happen every time, this transferring of her patient's hurts. No one, not even Reverend Edwards, could explain why it happened one time and not another. She couldn't tell when her sacrifice was required and when it was not. For Jimmy, tonight it was a small price to pay.

She'd take a couple of days off when Greg got back. Just hide out until she was better and no one would be the wiser. Sinking to the stool in the darkened exam room, she allowed herself a few moments of pity, to moan and rock over her hand before wrapping it with her special aloe salve and clean gauze. She bit her lip and drove back to her house, cradling her hurt hand in her lap.

* * * *

Randy took Jimmy to a second follow-up visit. After the nurse was through, they waited for the specialist to take a look.

"When did you say this happened, again?" Doctor Rutgers at Bay Bridge Hospital pinched his nose between his fingers. Frown lines furrowed either side of his mouth as he examined the health of the skin and bones. He continually switched between the images Grace had shot with the X-ray unit at the clinic and the boy's hand, and shook his head. "I just saw this a couple of days ago, correct?"

"It's not right?" Randy tried to keep the fear from his voice. "Where else should we—"

"Remarkable! You are one lucky young man to have this clean a hand after what you told me. It looks as if the incident happened weeks ago. There's no sign of infection."

"So it's going to be okay?" Randy asked. "She did everything right?"

Jimmy looked at him, pursed his mouth, and rolled his eyes in the way he hated. "Da-ad, of course she did. Grace is good."

Rutgers continued to stare and twist Jimmy's hand.

Jimmy let them know he wasn't thrilled. "Ouch, man, do you really gotta do that?"

"Firecracker, you said?" Rutgers shook his head again. "On the beach? Sand and dirt. Remarkable. Excuse me, I have to make a phone call. Wait right here, please."

* * * *

Greg accepted the call from Rutgers. On his first day back from the solitary vacation he'd taken in three years he was dizzy with catching up.

"I want to talk to you about one of your cases," Rutgers said.

Greg sighed. Rutgers's tone contained that little something in between professional courtesy and professional complaint. He was pretty sure he knew which case Rutgers meant.

"Burn accident—teenager—came in to see your PA."

Just as he figured, and though he liked the thought of Grace being "his" he had to keep to the topic at hand. "Did my PA do anything inappropriate?"

"Unless filing misleading paperwork is considered appropriate now at your clinic. That wound could not have taken place only four days ago."

"And what would my PA have to gain by filing misleading paperwork, Rutgers?" Greg picked up the file on his desk and began to page through it again. Arrogant SOB. He switched over to his computer monitor to check the images of the healing hand sent by Rutgers's office, taken the day after and today.

Rutgers had a point, but Greg would defend Grace if it meant his license. Good thing the complaint was Grace had done too good of a job rather than the other way around. He switched the intercom of the phone unit on, and swiveled in his chair, hands behind his head.

"You tell me, Evans. I don't know why anyone would do this—"

"My PA has, ah, some special talents—in the medical field," Greg broke into the tirade. "Matty even says she has a gift. There's this salve she brought back from the hills of Tennessee where she was before—"

"Mumbo-jumbo hillbilly stuff! Really! Did she do a dance, too? I'm afraid I'm going to have to report this."

Greg sat up straight and leaned into the telephone as if he were staring into his unhappy colleague's eyes. "Doctor, with enough witnesses to report the incident happened just the way they said it did, you don't have much of a case. That would solve nothing and bring unwarranted and unwanted attention on both our clinics and the hospital. Do you really want that? Runyon did nothing wrong! In fact, she did more than right by her patient, as you attested to yourself."

He didn't know what Grace did other than what she wrote in her report and he didn't care. He wasn't going to lose her because Rutgers was jealous.

He grasped at straws with his next statement, but he had to deter Rutgers.

"I had this salve analyzed when she first started using it, and there's nothing more than aloe gel and vitamin D, and jojoba oil, she says she sometimes adds. Capsaicin for arthritis which, believe me, does do wonders for some of my patients. I use it myself, but not with the kind of success she has," he told Rutgers. "Come on, man. She's been here nearly a year now. I'm not going to question this, and I urge you not to, either."

"I'm still keeping a close eye on this. If I find so much as—"

Greg punched off the intercom and picked up the handset after a suitable pause.

"Thanks for checking up. If you'll excuse me, now, I have patients. Good day."

* * * *

Randy couldn't stop time. He knew that. But if he could, he would have made August last another month so he had more time making things right with his son before the boy went to college. Jimmy had so much to learn about life, about making choices. But first…

"You have to pay the consequences. Not only did you get hurt doing a stupid, dangerous illegal act," Randy said, trying not to notice he had to look *up* into Jimmy's face, "you could have had your life changed forever. What if you'd lost your hand? How impressed would this young lady be then?"

They stood outside the back screen door of Kaye's Café. Jimmy leaned against the wall, hunched, serious and not sullen for once. The white bandages around his hand were in stark contrast from the tan of his skin.

Tanya was on her break, in her white serving apron with her hair pulled back severely from her face. "It's really my fault, Mr. Marshall," she mumbled.

Randy couldn't help it—he stared at her, making an effort to keep his jaw tight.

"You see, Jimmy was just trying to, um, well…" Apparently flustered, she bent her head and mumbled, "to, um, impress me, I guess."

Jimmy nodded.

Somewhere inside glassware clinked. A dishwasher started gurgling. Used french fry grease mingled unpleasantly with a strong disinfectant.

"He stopped texting me right before Christmas and I was, well, mad about it."

Jimmy went pale under his tan at Tanya's confession and closed his eyes.

Randy remembered the feeling, nearly nineteen years ago, when a relationship went south. "So you didn't hear from Jimmy, and for that you write him off? Sounds like an excuse to dump him, if you ask me."

Jimmy cut in. "No, Dad. I don't know if you knew this, but Mom stopped Internet service at home in January 'cause the company changed, and so did the rates and stuff."

Randy took a deep breath. "For the love of a stamp, you get yourselves in this kind of trouble." Then he laughed. "I can't be the one throwing stones here."

"Dad…"

"Oh, for Pete's sake, work something out, you two, before you blow up something bigger."

Randy started to walk away. "Oh, yeah. Jimmy, you're not allowed to play with matches for the rest of the summer, and of course, those fellows from Soo—well, they're not welcome here anymore." He thought some more. "And your dates have to be supervised by me or Kaye." He frowned and walked on, and then turned back. "One more thing. The fine for the fireworks on the beach without a permit? You have to pay half."

"Okay, Dad." With a little backward glance at Tanya, Jimmy stumbled over to him. "Dad—just, thanks."

"Sure." He nodded at Tanya who stood watching them with an anxious expression; one foot crooked to her knee, ponytail wrapped neatly in a bun. Kids.

He'd been no different. He rubbed the bristly new buzz cut of his hair and turned away. He'd been that young, that self-assured mixed with terror about the future; so stupid he'd never thought about any consequences. Certainly not parenthood. Would he be any different at this stage of life? Be a better dad, for instance, if he'd done things in the right order and waited for the right person… Water under the bridge.

The sound of Kaye's laughter drifted out the screen door. She did a good job, parenting her niece. She should have married, had kids of her own. She still could, of course. But not with his brother.

Chapter Nineteen

Ted wondered again if he was doing the right thing.

Kaye swore she'd seen Grace at the Seagull Inn. He wanted to respect her privacy, but concern overrode his senses.

She'd disappeared nearly a week ago, just after Jimmy's accident. There'd been a note, sure—something about taking a little vacation for a few days. She planned to drive up the coast. "Don't forget to feed Trigger and the kittens."

Memories of her white, drawn face at the clinic that night made him feel selfish and rude, mean. Last year he had simply expected her to step into his life and make it easier for him to go on dying while taking care of his child, and now his nephew, without thinking about her needs. He mentally kicked himself when he recalled the harsh words over her getting a job in the first place. Fighting like a married couple who'd thought they knew all the secrets and were shocked to find they were wrong. Something he'd been good at once.

What about him? Not for the first time, he wondered if he could ask her to help Randy with Eddy when he had passed on, or maybe even take him. Randy was out of town so much, and not the best parenting material as this episode with Jimmy showed. Be fair—he'd hardly gotten to know his own child. Jimmy grew up in a different household. The main thing was to ensure Jilly would not get her hands on Eddy—ever. A blood relative would go far making sure that never happened. If somehow Grace and Randy got together…

Eddy loved her. She had to be all right. It didn't matter that he loved her, too. If he was going to die in peace, he needed to know his son would be safe.

He stopped in the parking lot of the inn, next to her car. Slumped in the seat, he felt like a stalker as he waited. The breeze off Lake Michigan cooled his face. The sun lulled him while he wrestled with his decision to go in and confront her or leave her alone. A half-hour later he decided to go. As he turned around ready to pull onto the road he saw her sitting on a dune facing the water. She brushed hair off of her face. He waited until she did it again, tucking her flying hair back around her left ear. Yes—something white like a bandage wrapped around her hand.

Why wouldn't she want anyone to know she'd been hurt—obviously while working on Jimmy? Unless there was something he didn't know about Jimmy —didn't want to know. Young man, loose in Sault Ste. Marie, tattoo parlors with all the sailors coming through; anything could happen. Ted hurried out of the parking lot back to his brother's house.

Jimmy was playing a one-handed game of catch with Eddy in the backyard. Ted sent his son into the house for Popsicles and then confronted his nephew.

"You been sick lately? You have hepatitis, or AIDS?" Ted took a menacing step closer and grabbed the boy's shirt. "Been a user, Jimmy? Did the deed with any of your friends who got sick?"

Jimmy's face turned white and then red. He peeled Ted's fist away and backed up, shouting. "Hey, man! What are you talking about? I'm not like that—I'm clean!"

"Then you want to tell me about the night Grace fixed you up at the hospital? If you hurt her in any way…"

Jimmy shook his head and drew his brows together. He bent to pick up the ball. "She helped me—she was good, and she was all right when she walked me out."

Ted shook his head in denial. "Where would she have gotten hurt?" He turned, gathering himself for a lunge, but betrayed by a leg that wouldn't obey him quickly enough, fell heavily on the lawn. Jimmy hunched down close, though not close enough to get within arm reach.

Ted painfully heaved himself into a sitting position. Eddy, trailing red Popsicle juice like blood dripping over his arms and bare legs, came barreling out the door and pushed Jimmy away.

"Whoa!" Ted called out. Eddy crawled into his lap, glaring up at his big cousin. "Enough."

Jimmy rolled over and threw his arm over his eyes.

Ted took a deep breath, rallying his strength for the effort to rise. "Hey, Eds, isn't that one of the kittens?" Eddy slipped away to investigate.

Jimmy spoke, low and quick. "Something's weird, man, when Grace was helpin' me I swear I saw her hand and it looked as bad as my own. I must have been hallucinatin', though. She held my hand in hers—no gloves. I thought it was kind of strange, but I've never been in that kind of situation before, so I didn't know, it coulda been the right thing. It must have been my blood on her hand…"

"Okay, okay. I believe you." He'd always figured there were secrets she hadn't shared, something she had to hide about what happened back in Tennessee. He hadn't cared. It hadn't affected him before. But this… Randy needed to know. They deserved to know. But he would have to wait until she came back.

* * * *

Ted watched Grace's return and limped over to confront her as she opened her car door.

"What's wrong with your hand? Why did you go away?"

"It's none of your business, Ted."

"You're wrong." Ted stared into her eyes as if he could pull the answers out of her. "I need it to be. Did you hurt yourself working on Jimmy? Is there a problem I should know about? It's been over a year since you came into my-my life, and I can't help it Grace—I just want to… I don't want to see you hurt—for any reason. I can't stand for me or my family to cause you any more pain."

"I needed a break, Ted. That's all. A vacation, because, like you said, it's been over a year. Why would you think I'd been hurt?"

Ted was uncomfortable knowing she could see him struggle for words. Had he become a stalker? He turned to stare at the dead apple orchard. "I care. About you. And my son and Randy's. If there's something you're keeping from us, anything else that could interfere with…my family," he gritted out, shaking his head. "I have no right to feel this way."

"Feelings don't have prerequisites of 'rights' to them. And I don't know what you're talking about. I just needed to get away for a couple of days, that's all. Or can't I have a vacation?"

"A person doesn't simply go a few miles away for a vacation. And I saw you with a bandage."

"Ted."

He eyed the fine lines around her gray eyes, the soft hair framing her face, her pretty mouth. "I'm sorry. I'm not proud of it, but Kaye saw you and told me. I have to know. Did you hurt yourself?"

"I did not hurt myself."

He closed his eyes when he felt the warmth of her hand on his shoulder.

"There's more to this, isn't there? Ted, I don't presume to know how much longer you are given—or for that matter, any of us. If I've learned anything it's to expect the unexpected."

She moved away to sit on the top step. "Join me." She waved to a spot beside her, and then wrapped her hands around her knees.

Late afternoon sun picked up the golden highlights of a few strands of hair that had escaped her barrette. He ignored her invitation to sit. Her left hand looked chapped. He knew how often she needed to wash at work, so he couldn't make an issue of whether or not it was unusual.

"I had no break—no vacation—while I nursed my husband through two years of terrible illness and death." She put her cheek against her knee. "It doesn't seem like anyone really knows for sure what will happen to you, right? I mean, you look pretty good to me."

Ted smiled when she flushed.

"What I'm trying to say is"—she turned her face into her knees at Ted's chuckle—"I don't see death in you." He lowered himself to sit clumsily two steps beneath her, at eye level. Her eyes had flecks of black and hazel speckled among the pewter of the iris. He wanted to believe her. "What do you see?"

"I see a man with a past, who wants to be more than the sum of what's gone on before. I think you're worried about something worse than dying." She pursed her lips and wiggled her toes. "And I guess I wonder where I fit in here, my real purpose."

"What could be worse than dying?"

"Not being sure of what happens next. After death." She sighed and shook her head. "Sometimes it's so nice to think this life is all there is. But it's not. And you know it."

"Shelby says you have some special talent for knowing people from the inside."

Grace's dimple appeared. "You could call it that. You know I can—help—people sometimes, more than just with—medicine."

"Yes." Ted nodded. "I guess I've had that feeling for a long time—even before Jimmy's accident."

She shrugged. "Okay. It's a hillbilly thing. My granny had the 'sight.'"

Ted picked up on her change in tone and honored it. "I love my son. I want to know he'll be cared for, after I'm gone." He swallowed. "Randy is good with him. But you...together, maybe we could talk…"

He was distracted when Eddy clumped up the steps with his hands reverently cupped around a butterfly. "Look!" he whispered, awed as only a small boy could be. He plopped down between them. Ted looked down across his son's ruffled sun-kissed head at the insect, treasured between the little boy's palms. Ted wrapped his arms about Eddy and looked at Grace, making and answering a wordless promise.

* * * *

Summer was ending, along with a great many other things Grace took for granted. She walked over to the Marshall house one morning after Eddy made a very rare phone call.

"Daddy didn't get up," Eddy told her. "I dressed myself all everything."

Ted had lost more ground every day, health-wise. His short rally had ended and no treatment seemed to stop the degenerative effects of the illness.

Grace was not ready to give up.

Eddy reacted to his father's illness with surly, uncooperative impatience, unusual for the normally contented five-year-old. Oops! Make that "almost six, Grace," she could hear him rebuke her. He didn't like breakfast anymore. He didn't want to go the library story time. And Uncle Randy was mean when he told him to turn off the television.

She let herself into the house and greeted Eddy who wore blue shorts and green-striped shirt, no socks, and sailor hat.

"Looks like you're ready for the beach, Eddy," Grace said to his squirming delight. "Should we stop in and see your dad?"

Eddy's shoulders slumped and he clutched his stuffed tiger under his chin. "Yeah, okay."

Ted's room smelled dank. A mister spurted in one corner. It seemed to help his labored breathing but made the atmosphere sweaty. The shades were pulled, for light seemed to make his constant headaches worse.

She paused inside the doorway to listen. Ted beckoned to his son. "Have a good day, okay, sport? I'll be up when you come back, I promise," he rasped.

Grace bent to pick up a used drinking glass and crumpled napkins.

"Just leave it." Ted rolled over and pulled the sheet over his face.

It was hard, but she did. She drove them to the dunes for a romp in the waves and a picnic lunch. She ran harder than ever on the beach, chasing Eddy and the waves and birds and the little fish that swam near the shoreline until they were both exhausted. Ted's white face haunted Grace and she pretended the bright sunlight made her eyes water underneath her sunglasses whenever Eddy came close.

* * * *

Randy pulled up to the front lobby of the clinic to wait for Grace after work. She had her car in the shop and Randy agreed to pick her up on his way home. Ted had seemed overly delighted by the news, and that, topped with a couple of sly comments about how well he and Grace got along lately, poked his suspicious button.

He hesitated in the empty parking lot before exiting the car. When he saw her through the glass of the clinic doors, he turned off the engine but waited. Evans followed her into the small vestibule.

Randy felt like a voyeur but he couldn't look away. Like some kind of TV melodrama he watched the doctor stand in front of the door, peel her hands from the grab bar and put his arms around her.

Randy opened the car door to…do what? Help her? Did she need him? Grace held up her arms to push against his chest before she let her forehead rest between her hands against him, a move he recognized as defiant and submissive.

Ashamed, he pulled the door shut and turned away, mind going a mile a minute.

He knew how his brother felt about Grace. He thought she returned the feelings, although he couldn't call himself much of an expert on that sort of thing. A dying man loves a woman who obviously—what—loves him back? But the woman also wants to be with other men? Healthy men? Men who don't die? Randy shook his head and tapped the steering wheel, trying hard to find fault. He should stay out of it. Ted didn't need to know any of this—whatever he thought he saw.

The passenger door opened and shut. Grace sat silent before clicking her seatbelt and wiping her face. She fished a hanky out of her pocket and blew her nose. "Sorry to keep you waiting. I had to—"

"You don't owe me any explanation."

Grace's hands shook. She laughed a little—high-pitched and hysterical. "I could tell you it wasn't what it seemed but I'm not sure you would understand."

Randy shifted his legs on the seat. "It's none of my business. And I'm not planning to say anything to Ted."

"Ted knows."

"I doubt that! Ted loves you. And he deserves better." Randy started the car and drove off with a squeal of the tires. They didn't exchange a word all the way home. He didn't know if he was angry at Grace, Evans, Ted, or himself. End of season business would set him on the road for the next several days. With Ted's obvious decline, he was going to have to face some tough decisions when he got back.

* * * *

The next phone call from Eddy made Grace call in late to work. She went to check on Ted and found him sitting on a straight chair next to his bed, breathing hard. He had managed to pull on some clothes that did not hide the fact he was wasting away. Grace's mouth trembled at the sight of his bony shoulders. What should she say?

He brushed at his dark hair with his hands, flushing.

Grace shook her head. "I'll call the clinic and take a day off. Let's get this room aired, and the mister cleaned up." She bent to tug the sheets from his bed.

He caught feebly at her hand as she passed. "Randy said you two had an argument before he left. What happened?"

She sat on the edge of the bed, twining her fingers in her lap. "I wouldn't call it an argument, and why was he talking about me, anyway?"

"He wasn't, but I was. I just said he should take you out when he got back."

Grace narrowed her eyes. "All right, buster. Now it's your turn to tell me what's going on."

Ted took her hand in his thin, cold, white one. "Look at me. It's all right, Grace. We never—" He hesitated. "I know you need someone to lean on, someone strong, who can care for you. I'm not that person. I can't be. I just thought maybe, after…you know…it would be good for you and Randy…"

"You're kidding. We don't have anything in common. I can't believe you're trying to play matchmaker between me and your brother! Don't you have a clue?"

"You don't need to explain anything to me." She let him touch her temple, then her hair. "It won't be much longer. This has to be harder on you than on me, after all you were through before, with your husband."

"Listen, Ted. When Randy came to pick me up the other night after work, he saw me crying and Greg…comforting me."

His fist clenched around hers. "Oh."

She withdrew her hands. "Please. I don't want to talk about this today."

She rose slowly and walked Ted into the bathroom. Upon her return she continued to strip the bed with short professional motions. When Grace finished, she helped Ted to the kitchen.

She left when Jimmy came back. At home, the first thing she did was call Randy.

He picked up the car phone after four rings.

"Randy? Randy? Are you there?" She heard the squeal of car tires and took in an alarmed breath. Before she could speak, Randy answered.

"Hi, sorry about that. Yes, Grace, I'm here. What do you need?"

"Are you driving? I'll call later."

"No—wait! Grace, it's all right. What's the matter?"

"I've been over to help Ted out a bit, after Eddy told me he was having trouble getting up. I just, well, I wondered if you thought yet about—well, maybe it's time to think about, you know—"

"Yes. I have thought about it."

"I'm sorry, Randy, but surely you've noticed Ted is having more and more trouble getting around. It's just not enough for you and Jimmy and Eddy to help him anymore. He needs some professional care. And I can't—"

"I know. I wouldn't ask you to." He was silent for a moment. "I planned to talk about it when I got home. I'll take care of it."

At the click of the phone, Grace felt her heart rip.

Chapter Twenty

Grace sat in her favorite place on the wide front porch surrounded by flowerpots of yellow and pink impatiens and cascading striped petunias. The drone of bees searching among the blossoms made the little hairs by her ears feel ticklish. She brushed a callused heel against the smooth floorboards, pushing herself in the swing. Eddy alternately dug in the sandbox and scampered after Trigger who stalked something amongst the waving cosmos.

Ted had told her that morning about the arrangements with the lawyer—his plans for Eddy, the trust he set up after the sale of the house out of which he paid her salary and the other childcare providers.

She cupped her chin in her hand. Randy would make a good guardian. Eddy would always know he was wanted and loved. How hard it would be to live here—after. Could she watch Eddy grow up and not be a part of his life if Randy didn't want her help?

Eddy whooped as he picked up a growing kitten, a striped tiger that bared its tiny fangs and unsheathed miniature claws. Eddy dropped it as it hissed and spat and then chased it down again. He wasn't being cruel to the kittens. He had listened very carefully when she explained and showed him how to pick them up and handle them.

Spiraling down the drain with Ted was her career. Although Jimmy tried to play down the extent of the injury, rumors he'd blown off his hand but had it magically fixed created a ripple of unease through East Bay. People were staring at her again, and Tony Vander

Groot's mother had never let up on the botched blood draw last spring. She managed to bring up the subject at every social gathering and in every store aisle. Several children complained they didn't feel well after seeing her for their routine school physicals, and Greg had taken to observing Grace again. They concluded it was no more than playground tales and a quick summer bug that blew over in a couple of weeks, but she was becoming apprehensive about treating children. After Jimmy, other little accidents happened, broken vials, a missed spider bite, a rash and fever that soared at midnight after she'd sent a little one home.

For the first time since Christmas she summoned the memory of her house in Tennessee—the color of the carpets and drapes, the placement of pictures and furnishings. She felt like a virtual visitor on a real estate web site. When she couldn't remember which side of the door the light switch for the entry hall and formal living room was on, she forced herself to stop and think of something else, like the bizarre turn of recent events and Eddy's upcoming birthday party.

Kaye Smits had apparently decided Randy Marshall was optimum husband material. Grace thought maybe a ticking biological clock came into the computation somewhere, too, besides Ted's rather clumsy attempts to pair them off, but she reminded herself to be kind. She'd been picking up an order of tea when Kaye confided in her and sort of apologized at the checkout.

"I assumed after Jilly left that Ted would turn to me. I mean, there aren't many eligible singles in town." She took Grace's money and sighed. "All these years. I should have known. Randy was the one I always turned to when I needed help. Everyone in town really relied on Randy to make their business profitable." The register jingled. Kaye slammed in shut. "And this…emotion on my part now, it's not only because Ted is so sick, you know. I'm just glad he has you."

Grace understood.

Randy was a good person. They'd never be more than neighbors, but things were moving on the right track. Kaye might never like her, but Grace could live with that.

Kaye had then asked if she could host Eddy's birthday party. Their chat ended with a few details on the upcoming birthday party. The woman acted jittery, Must be the recent excitement. Or caffeine.

* * * *

Randy Marshall whistled through his teeth. Not even the wind whisked off the lake or the gray and dirty white clouds billowing and flattening as they rolled in shook his exuberant mood. Love truly did color everything even brighter than peaches and apples. He swung open the door of the café and returned the general greeting from Kaye's breakfast crowd.

As always, he stopped up short at the sight of the owner. Kaye looked up and smiled back. Unfortunately for Mr. Jeffries, she was in mid-pour.

The planet started spinning again at Mr. Jeffries's loud call. "Hey there, young lady!"

He chuckled and sauntered over to his regular booth with a grin. Yup, it would be a great day. An even better evening when they discussed their future.

He took her over to Traverse City since Jimmy was staying in that night and agreed to take care of Eddy. And Ted. Randy sat across the table from Kaye, too far in his opinion, but the ride over had been nice. She wore a flowered dress he'd never seen before and smelled of something subtle, some exotic flower, perhaps; nothing like the fruit blossoms he knew. Her hair was all curls for a change and fell loose around her face. Her lips were Cortland red and all he could think about was kissing them. He forced himself to look at her face and be content to hold her hand.

"Thanks for hosting Eddy's birthday party," he said over coffee.

"Oh, it will be so much fun. I used to have parties for Tanya and her friends. When she reminded me, what else could we think about? It's really Tanya who had a blast planning it."

Randy loved the sparkle in her eyes, her enthusiasm. But he couldn't help wonder if this would be the last birthday Ted would share with his son.

"You'll get custody, I assume," Kaye stated quietly, neither of them making any pretense of not understanding what she meant.

"Ted wanted me to adopt Eddy already last year. When he seemed to recover over the winter we didn't pursue it."

"We all had such high hopes for him. Everyone could see how well he did. I thought he would really get better. Does the doctor have any explanation? Eddy's always had a special place in my heart. I can't bear to think of him without his father." She reached for his hand again. "Not, of course, that you wouldn't make a great father."

She cleared her throat and closed her eyes. "I mean, you are a great father already and would be good for Eddy." She opened her eyes to gaze into his. "I love him, too."

Randy smiled. "I never had any doubt."

* * * *

Eddy's birthday took place during the third weekend of August. Besides children, Tanya had invited business associates and neighbors, along with Matty, Shelby, Dave, and little Alyssa, who cooed and smiled obligingly at everyone.

Eddy reigned supreme from his favorite red leather and chrome stool at the main counter. He leaned in to blow out the six candles on his oversize apple and cherry cake made especially for the occasion. Having extinguished them, he twirled on the stool and waved to the applause of the gathered crowd, delighted.

Grace took a step back from the counter. Eddy leaned over and wrapped his arms around her neck before she could move away. He forced her to bend low to his sticky little face to hear his whisper, "You wanna know what I wished for?" Hot breath tickled the hair near Grace's ear. "I wished you were my—"

His eyes slid past her to a shadow darkening the door to the restaurant. The bloom rushed from his cheeks leaving them paper white underneath his tan and red drink stains.

"—Mama!"

Chapter Twenty-One

A blast of searing outside air accompanied the jeans-and-leather-clad woman who sauntered in. She stood, hands on hips in a defiant pose, surveying the party scene, a smirk across her wide, chapped lips.

With cruel certainty, Grace knew she faced the past. She didn't need the steel in Ted's eyes, Tanya's gasp, or Eddy's declaration to know Jilly Marshall had come to town.

Eddy sat like stone on the seat, wrapping his arms tighter around Grace's neck, threatening to choke her. He was only six years old, and hadn't seen Jilly since he had turned two. He wouldn't have known her but Grace had seen the grainy snapshot he kept by his bed. It was still a stretch; Jilly had changed in the four years since that picture. She had kept herself tiny, but was somehow hardened with harsh lines alongside her mouth. Her lips looked like they could no longer form a real smile. Perhaps it had been little more than instinct caused Eddy to call out to her.

Grace closed her eyes. She realized her rather compromising situation, and started to untangle the child's arms from their chokehold. She sought Matty's face for help and the mixture of sympathy and encouragement in the other woman's eyes comforted her.

Kaye moved first. She stepped out hesitantly from Randy's shadow. "Why, if it isn't Jilly. This is a surprise." She faltered. "Well, maybe not. You're just in time for a piece of birthday cake."

Jilly's eyebrows came together under the red kerchief tied around her head. Another blast of hot air from the opening door hit them as a greasy-looking heavyset man in motorcycle leathers and sunglasses strode in. He claimed Jilly by wrapping a beefy hand around her right shoulder and giving her a proprietary shake which nearly lifted her from the floor.

"Jilly." Ted Marshall's voice matched the aloofness of the expression. "What brings you back to East Bay?" He did not move from his position, leaning against the side of a booth. Strain showed in the lines beside his mouth and the tremor of his left hand, which Grace noticed he kept carefully out of his ex-wife's line of sight.

Jilly nodded at her former husband, but turned her gaze to the crowd of children as if searching. Her eyes finally settled on Eddy. Grace had separated from his death grip, but let his hand stay in hers, slippery with nerves and fear. If, somehow, Sean could be restored to her now, she might feel the same way. She squeezed Eddy's hand, then urged him forward, praying his mother would not squander this precious moment.

Jilly glared daggers at Grace before bending down to sweep Eddy into a frantic hug. "My baby!"

Eddy squirmed. "I'm six. I'm not a baby. Mom?" His mouth puckered and he inhaled, making a face.

The biker man stayed attached to Jilly. Grace wrinkled her nose and noticed others doing the same. Oil and sweat on stained leather did not blend well with punch and cake. Eddy focused on his dad, sensing the tenseness of the atmosphere, and squirmed in Jilly's embrace. She let go, and he scampered close to his father, touching his legs and staring back in frightened fascination.

Shelby gave Alyssa to Dave and came to Grace, settling an arm around her waist.

"Ted." Jilly's voice was well modulated and suave for such a tiny woman. She was short, not fat, but solid, and after she removed the scarf, fluffed up the blond spikes of hair dyed red and blue at the tips. She zeroed in on Randy and Kaye.

"Well, well, well." Jilly walked toward them, biker man towed by an invisible leash.

"You shouldn't be so surprised, Kaye Smits," Jilly purred. "After all, you invited me here, remember?"

Grace felt as though a giant vacuum sucked the air from her lungs. This explained why Kaye had been so nervous. At Randy's hissed intake, she stepped away from him. "That was a long time ago."

"So? I didn't know invitations had statutes of limitations. Anyway, how could I miss my boy's birthday?"

Biker man grinned, baring a mouthful of chiseled, silver-capped teeth.

"You never bothered for any of the other ones," Randy inserted.

Jilly sized him up before she turned to Kaye. "You couldn't have my Marshall, so you settled for second best, I see."

Biker man stopped grinning.

Grace was not about to step into the fray but the kids were starting to get restless so she signaled for Tanya to finish cutting the cake and dish it out.

Kaye's chin rose. "It's not like that. And Randy is not second best, you...uh." She looked around as if remembering where they were. "Won't you and your friend sit? Over there?" She pointed to a far booth.

"Please, please, don't spoil his birthday," Grace whispered under her breath as Jilly and her biker sauntered past and sat. Shelby glided around the room, helping the children settle in front of paper plates of cake and ice cream. A balloon popped, resulting in quickly hushed giggles. Alyssa shrieked.

Grace shivered at the unnatural gleam in Jilly's eyes as she stared at Ted who remained motionless, as if mesmerized by a cobra.

The party fizzled, and after most of the guests had departed, Grace stayed to help clean up. She introduced herself warily to biker man, who, unthreatened and uninterested, told her his name was Gus. He took her hand in his great paw and wrung it gently. "Mechanic. From Spearfish." His wealth of information exhausted, he lapsed back into his fourth tall glass of iced tea, apparently fascinated by the patterns light made through the ice cubes.

Grace smiled and went back to picking up plates and glasses and putting them in a gray plastic tub. At the swinging door she stopped, momentarily unsure what to do when she heard the exchange of low, angry voices from the kitchen.

"It was four months ago—four *months!*—since I contacted you! How could you just show up like this?"

"Hey! It takes a while to get here. Lighten up! I'm here now. Yeah, I can see why you wanted me to come. Ted's in rough shape, isn't he? And who is that b—"

"Jilly! And put that out. You can't smoke those stupid cigars in here."

Grace didn't want to be eavesdropping, much less be caught doing it, so she left the tub on the counter and quietly let herself out the front door. The last thing she saw was Gus holding up his glass to the light as the door closed behind her with a gentle tinkle of bells.

She almost ran into Matty who paced the sidewalk obviously waiting for her outside the café.

"So! You jus' gonna lay down like a rug and let that wooman valk on you?" she demanded in her typical no-pussyfooting-around-the-issue fashion.

"Why are you still here?" Grace jammed her floppy green hat on her head.

Matty hissed like a wet cat. "Dat wooman!" Her Dutch accent grew thicker, proving how upset she was. "No one liked her before. What is she here for now, I say?"

"It's Eddy's birthday. A mother can spend time with her son on his birthday, can't she?" Grace was not going to share with anyone the partially overheard conversation in the kitchen.

"There's no gud in the air, mark my vords," Matty replied darkly. She veered off toward her parking spot while Grace went around the block to her own hot car and the drive back home.

Home. Where was home?

* * * *

Randy stood with Kaye in her backyard at dusk. A stiff breeze kept mosquitoes at bay. Heartsick, he listened to her repeated apologies, but he had no doubt she couldn't possibly imagine the trouble she caused, especially if she truly understood how bad things were with Ted. The legal issues were still somewhat in flux.

She squeezed his hands. "I wrote to her a long time ago, last spring, Randy, when I was upset about—just when things weren't going so well. How was I to know that she'd show up now? She never replied. Took me a while to track her down, too. It was for Eddy. I did it for him."

Kaye collapsed against Randy, leaning her forehead against his chest. "At least, that's what I thought. Ted… I didn't know what to think. A child should be with a parent, you know? I can't believe how much she changed." She sighed. "But I should have realized that a mother who didn't want her child before wouldn't change her mind now."

He swallowed a bitter taste in his mouth. "You know having her here will be trouble."

"I see that now," Kaye said, her chin wobbly. "I'd undo it if I could. I swear, I'll make this right. I'll do whatever I can—go to court, whatever."

Randy pulled her into his arms. "When she finds out about Grace…"

"She already knows," Kaye said, her words muffled against Randy's shoulder.

"Oh, Lord," Randy breathed out. *What next?*

Four days later Randy came home to find his brother, white-faced, holding an official-looking letter. "What is that?"

"She went and did it."

"Did what?" Randy reached for the letter, which Ted surrendered.

"I can't believe it."

"You'd better believe it, man," Randy replied after skimming through the official language. "But she doesn't stand a chance. How could she? She abandoned her child." He looked up at Ted. "I can't understand how she thinks she could get away with this, but we'd better call Alvin to have him start the paperwork."

* * * *

They sat at a round table in attorney Alvin Marlby's meeting room where he and Ted had worked out the trust and guardianship arrangements months earlier. Jilly wore a softly feminine beige tailored suit, though Ted caught a whiff of burnt tobacco. Stupid. She'd started in college, puffing on cheap cigars, to convince herself she could keep up in a man's business world. Apparently there was still a lot of business to capture in biker world. Her hair, devoid of garish colors, lay close and smooth around her face. Gus was not in evidence. Ted couldn't help but remember earlier years when he thought he and Jilly were happily married. She had been pretty and enthusiastic, smart, charming. It had all been a sham.

Jilly's lawyer leaned over the table now, whispering to her while Marlby took his time thumbing through the proffered documentation. Ted and Randy both sported button pins Eddy's teacher presented to them with a knowing smile. She'd made them in time for the open house so parents and teachers could become acquainted before school started. "They're for all the parents," she explained. "I'd like you to have yours early, if that's all right." A digital camera image of each student, with the message, "I love Daddy," and "I love Mommy," or in Eddy's case, "I love Uncle Randy."

East Bay helped its own. It had been unfortunate, but all the local inns and rooming houses were full, so Jilly and Gus had to find a motel room forty-five minutes away. Gas stations mysteriously were closed or out of fuel when their motorcycle roared up, and Kaye seemed to run out of precious many menu items whenever the pair came to eat.

After a suitable pause, Jilly's counselor began. "My client, Mrs. Marshall—"

"*Ex*-Mrs. Marshall," Marlby inserted calmly.

The man went on with hardly a pause. "Is asking for custody of her son due to the obvious ill health of the boy's father. It is only natural and right the boy go to live with her."

Ted's attorney sported his best poker face as he slid their written response to the suit across the table.

Gus had let slip his financial state to Grace when he asked for advice on his backache. While she worked on him, he obligingly mentioned his dismay Jilly had run through the money from the sale of the house. "So quick! Man, just an investment tip turned squat." He'd pressed a thick thumbpad and forefinger together. She turned around and spilled the beans to Ted who felt obligated to share the news with his attorney.

Ted watched emotionlessly as his ex-wife's lawyer whispered in her ear and gestured at the paperwork. Her eyes widened slightly, and he could tell she held a tight rein on her emotions by the firm set of her lips and clenched jaw. She skimmed the papers her lawyer shoved under her nose. Jilly was smart. She could read the bottom line as well as anyone.

Ted now smiled and recited to himself, as if he could read the counselor's lips, "You see, my dear, when you run a business into the ground, it can't earn any income for you." She had ruined the Marshalls' orchard. Ted stared at her. She glared back. The only property they owned jointly had been the house. After Jilly took her half of the sale and ran, Ted put his share, as well as all his remaining assets and business income, into an irrevocable trust for his son. Randall Marshall was the executor, with the Brouwers as secondary executors. The trust wouldn't even buy a decent house in larger markets, but it was enough to ensure, with careful handling, it would take care of Eddy's needs during childhood and see him through college at one of the state schools.

Jilly's eyes shifted to Randy. Ted read the attempt to challenge his brother as she jabbed, looking for a weak spot, trying out scenarios of what it might take to gain control of the trust. Then her eyes dropped to the button pin of Eddy.

Yes, my dear, you'd still be stuck with our kid when the money runs out again.

The last of his limited patience fled. "You never sent any pictures, Jilly—how was he to know what you looked like now? I hardly recall what you looked like."

"Ted!"

"Mr. Marshall!"

Both lawyers warned him to stop.

Ted raged on. "You didn't know what day it was when you came in. It was your son's birthday. I never even heard you wish him a happy birthday, let alone bring anything for him. One thing I'm sure of, you will never, ever get your hands on my son when I'm gone."

Jilly played her trump card. "That woman you hired to babysit. The witch—the one from the hills down south—you gave our home to. Who is she? How can you let her near our son? It's all over town how she hurts other children with her mumbo-jumbo and magic potions."

Ted struggled to his feet. "How dare you? I had to beg Grace to help us out when…" Too late Ted realized how he sounded.

Jilly smiled.

* * * *

Randy sniffed it first at Kaye's not long afterward. The smell of blood and venom in the air. The mood of East Bay shifted and washed with the mention of Grace Runyon, the woman with the mysterious past who hurt their children. The care applied to the Marshalls did not extend to outsiders. The battle began.

Randy was right to believe no judge in the world would give a child to a mother who demonstrated as little maternal care as Jilly Marshall. The suit had been dropped.

Gus had made no secret of his opinion. Randy had been informed of the loud discussion right on the street.

"I heard him," Mrs. Woolver said. "Shouting in front of the shop. Shameful, it was. He told her, plain as day, since poor Ted, your brother, is done for—what an ugly turn of phrase, 'done for,'—and the little boy doesn't know her, they should leave. But, how could it be true? A child not like his own mother? And, Mr. Marshall, it's not true about the money is it? That you have none?"

But Jilly exacted her own brand of revenge. She had always wounded the best way she knew how. And Randy was afraid for them all.

At the park, at the community pool, and the playground, Jilly spread her poisonous whispers which were dutifully repeated at Kaye's and the co-op. The ex-Mrs. Marshall might not have left any friends in East Bay, but there were plenty of ears willing to gobble up the latest gossip and pass it around. Then she disappeared as quickly as she'd come, no good byes, not a word to Eddy or Ted.

Randy's heart burned with the horrible accusations. "Witch" had been the one used most often. "Adulterer" had been mentioned more than once.

Tanya interrupted him in the office about a month after school had started. "Did you hear? Hear what they're saying now about Grace?"

"Yes. Just rumors, Tanya. The best thing you can do is not pass them around."

"But what about her job?"

Randy pushed himself up from his desk. "What do you mean?"

"Some of the kids have accused her of hurting them on purpose. What are we going to do? I heard them talking about a petition to get her fired."

"Okay, thanks. I'll look into it." Randy started to sweat. He rubbed his hand across his head and escorted Tanya outside. "Don't worry. It's nothing. The clinic isn't run by committee. Doctor Evans is in charge and he knows how to handle this."

If only he believed it.

Chapter Twenty-Two

When Nancy gently let the two families in the clinic waiting room know there was an emergency and they needed to reschedule, they were not happy. Grace glimpsed their narrow looks when she flew past to meet Jimmy in the parking lot, Greg on her heels.

Jimmy had called and Grace still wasn't sure how serious he was until she saw the amount of blood on the towel wrapped around Tanya's hand. Greg hustled the unconscious girl inside, ordering Grace to stay and find out what happened.

"I was waiting for her to get off work, and I was early," Jimmy said. "She was slicing the next day's order for deli meats with that big, noisy meat cutter in the kitchen. I just stood there at the back door."

Grace nodded, encouraging him while keeping an eye on the exam room door.

"'So, what's up?' she asks me, looking over her shoulder," Jimmy went on. "That's when it happened. It was so fast. I didn't really see anything. I ran inside, fast as I could.

"I reached past her to shut off of the machine. She looks down. I could tell the moment she figured out what happened when she saw the blood."

Jimmy swallowed. "I tell you, I nearly lost my lunch. The whole tip of her finger was gone, down to the bone. The blood—it kept coming. So I ask Tanya, 'where's Kaye?' I'm trying to keep calm. 'She's gone,' Tanya says, and starts to giggle. 'She went out buying.'

So I yell 'be quiet!' and grab a towel. It wasn't exactly clean, but by then I didn't care. I start to call 9-1-1, but then I realize we can get here quicker than waiting around for an ambulance."

He swallowed convulsively. Grace reached out to steady him as he swayed. "You did good, Jimmy. She'll be just fine, I'm sure." What was taking so long? She looked at the exam room again, wondering if she should go in.

Jimmy kept talking. "I heard somewhere that sometimes they can sew your finger back on, so I looked for it. I tried not to gag at the sight of all the blood. How do you do it, Grace? How do you not throw up?"

She shook her head. "Practice."

"You can help her, right? Like you did for me?" Jimmy's eyes bored into her, bold, frightened, and confused all at once.

"It's not the same kind of hurt, Jimmy, you know that." She turned away. "Did you call Kaye?"

"She's out, Tanya said. Tanya didn't say whether she'd taken her phone."

"Well, keep trying, okay? Wait—never mind. We'll have Nancy leave a message, and try a couple of the places she usually goes."

"But you can help, right? Go, now, go back there and help her. We both want you to."

"Doctor Evans knows what to do."

"Please, Grace, go back there. She needs you."

Grace looked at the blood drops on Jimmy's sleeveless gray tee. She looked at the exam room again. With a pat on Jimmy's shoulder, she got up and went down the hall, fright and determination vying. She could help Tanya in a way Greg could not.

Greg looked up as she opened the door. He didn't acknowledge her. Matty soothed Tanya's other arm, talking calmly, urging the girl to look away.

"I think we might need to take a little ride over to the hospital," he said. "I wonder if, ah, the missing piece might yet be salvaged. It's unlikely there's enough to reattach, but it's a good clean cut. Deli cutter, the girl said. Do you think… Anyway, nail bed's probably shot."

Tanya gasped. "My nail bed? You mean, I won't have a fingernail anymore? Please, Grace, you have to do something! I don't want to be a freak!"

Grace leaned over Matty to assess the damage for herself. Much of the bleeding had already stopped. She agreed with Greg's assessment. The sterile matrix was neatly sliced lengthwise at an angle, a large subungual hematoma already forming. She looked at Matty, saw the concern and compassion not just for Tanya in her expression. There was also sympathy and a desire to allow Grace a chance to work.

Matty spoke matter-of-factly to Doctor Evans, her brogue thicker than usual. "Let's leave these two for a moment, Doctor. We should speak to young Mr. Marshall, and help Nancy find Kaye, yes?"

"Grace?"

She nodded, not meeting his eyes. He frowned. He looked at Matty again, and then abruptly turned around and left with her.

Grace, grateful for Greg's silent trust, watched Tanya carefully for a moment, and then sat beside her. "Jimmy's accident was different than yours, you know."

Tanya shivered, but nodded. Grace took the girl's hand in both of hers and turned so that she would not see her actions.

"I'm just going to look a little closer, and touch it some, okay? It will probably hurt. Matty gave you a shot, didn't she?"

"Yes."

"Okay, then, here we go. Try to stay still."

Grace could not recall a single prayer. The air felt dry, the atmosphere gone, and it hurt to take a breath. She stared at Tanya's wounded finger while trying to gather the courage to touch her, fearful nothing at all would happen.

And nothing did, at first. Gradually Tanya stopped trembling. Grace inhaled deeply, holding the breath while she let the pad of her finger caress Tanya's. The blood darkening the remaining portion of the girl's nail bed turned bright red and began to flow freely again, draining the hematoma.

Tanya gasped. The blood gradually cleared away and the edge of her finger looked pink.

Grace waited for the pain.

Nothing.

"It doesn't look like we'll need to stitch it," she said. "We will need to take a picture, Tanya, to make sure nothing is wrong that we can't see, okay? It won't hurt."

When the healthy nail bed was clearly visible, she carefully applied petroleum, so a new nail plate could grow underneath. She put on an Alumafoam splint and then wrapped the finger in clean gauze and taped it gently.

She wasn't sure if the entire pad would come back, but the nail shouldn't grow abnormally.

"There, Tanya. You'll be all right. It may not look exactly look the same, but you won't be a freak. The nail will grow back soon. The splint is just for a couple of days so that if you bump it, it won't hurt worse. It will take as long as two to three weeks to start looking better, okay? Let's go see if anyone got in touch with your aunt."

Greg pretended to look at files at the reception desk. Nancy and Matty simply waited. Jimmy hovered nervously.

"Did anyone find her aunt yet?"

"No," Nancy said.

Jimmy studied Grace's hands. So he had seen and guessed during his own accident. She fought the urge to slide them into her pockets. She watched him narrow his eyes when he saw her hands were fine.

She pursed her lips before pulling the computer monitor toward her to chart. Filling in the proper spaces, she told the others in her clinical voice what she had done. "I applied some petroleum to protect the nail bed, as the original plate was too badly damaged and missing. It looks clean and healthy and should heal normally. I explained to Tanya it will probably not grow back exactly like before."

Greg watched her unblinkingly. She finished woodenly. "I reduced the hematoma under the bed. She should come back but not tomorrow, I think."

Nancy nodded and checked through the book and they set the time, automatically filled out the little appointment reminder, and with a page of instructions of what to watch for, Jimmy drove Tanya home, the question still on his face.

* * * *

Old Elvira Brown died in her sleep, after a blue moon had set. No matter how well and long a life, it was still a shock; one Mrs. Brown's granddaughter was not willing to accept.

Grace took it hard.

Greg told her what happened. "They called you a witch, for crying out loud. Said you'd burned and poisoned her in the past. She wasn't that old and shouldn't have died."

"But she was," Grace whispered. "She had a long life, a pretty good one. I'm not a witch."

Greg snorted. "Of course not." He still had an autopsy done. It was expensive and revealed nothing out of the ordinary.

The story grew at the funeral which Grace attended. They didn't bother to whisper though she stood nearby, flushed, dizzy with hurt and confusion. "Burned with stuff the witch used on her. Died screaming in agony, Elvira did. Poor soul."

"The witch was there with her, you know—as she lay dying."

"Really! She took care of my niece's child, you know. At that clinic in town. Hurt her something dreadful."

"They're talking about me?" she asked Greg. The numbness was back around her heart, gripping it, squeezing, like that last day she'd sat with Jonathan, willing each tortured breath to be his last. Please, God, let him die…please, God, take me too.

Greg took her home.

* * * *

Randy paused on the threshold of Kaye's, debating whether to stay. The atmosphere felt so tense. Although the place was half-full of customers, the conversation was sporadic and carried out in tone outside of comfortable range, whiny like a mosquito in the dark.

Tanya slammed her pitcher down with a crash on the lunch counter.

"How dare you?"

The background hum came to an abrupt halt, customer's mouths open in mid-gossip, hands gesticulating in mid-point. Even Randy jumped.

"You heard me!" She yelled, her voice echoing through the sunny room. "How dare you people act like this? Are we back in seventeenth century Salem here? Granny died of natural causes. Doc Reuwarts said so. Natural. Causes. She liked Grace. You can all guess how the clinic got paid."

Kaye walked out of the kitchen, wiping her hands on a white towel and stood next to her niece. With an apologetic glance at Randy, she squeezed Tanya's shoulder and added her voice.

"Tanya's right. You ought to be ashamed of yourselves. How many of you folks has she done right by? Without asking a lot of questions?

"You, there, Gil Winters. I can guess what you been seeing her for. Most everyone knows what you do when you go off on one of your weekends. How did she hurt you any? Huh?

"And you, Maryann. Your girl would repeat anything anyone told her, truth or no. You know that. Everybody knows that."

Randy felt helpless to move, awed by their rage. Kaye quivered. Maryann got up quickly and took her daughter out of the café. No one stopped her or asked for her check.

He watched in slow motion as this amazing woman studied her remaining customers.

"We'll be closing up for the day, folks. We've just run out of…everything."

Tanya held up her heavily bandaged hand. "Grace saved my finger. I believe she helps people, not hurts them." She drew herself up, proudly. "You all better just think about what you're doing to…to my friend, Grace, and to each other. I don't believe any of you can prove she's hurt you on purpose, either. I'm ashamed you would turn on her so quickly."

Kaye added, "Especially if you believe Jilly, the one who really did almost destroy the town's business and hurt all of you for real."

Wow. Randy watched Tanya turn the door sign to "Closed" and lock up. He shook his head, grateful they were on the same side. He'd better do something quick to make sure he didn't lose Kaye this time.

* * * *

Restless after their meal one evening at the big house, Ted asked Grace to join him for a walk. Her cheeks had hollowed over the past month. Her eyes lost their sparkle and even her hair looked dull. He ached for her, knowing only the passage of time would work against the foolish and shameful attitude in town. He hoped he would be around long enough to see them sorry for what they had done.

Maybe he would make it to the first snow. He would miss outside most of everything he would have to surrender to death. Heaven must be something else if it was better than watching the seasons of a fruit tree. Ted hated the fact that his brother could effortlessly pick him up these days and carry him to bed when he couldn't drag one foot in front of the other. Jean, the home health aide, was a necessary evil.

"I'm tired of being tired. Take me for a walk, would you?"

They wouldn't go very far, obviously. He simply wanted an excuse to be alone with her. Ted shuffled his feet along the furrows of the old orchard. Stumps and straggly growth made an eerie backdrop that was the perfect foil for his attitude. The sun was just below the horizon so they could not go far. Twilight and chill cocooned him. She matched his ponderous pace, as silent as he was. They had become comfortable in their unspoken places, which only made the thought of leaving her ache more deeply. They had become the walking wounded.

"Dad was ready to start cherry trees," Ted said, his words spurting out in gasps. "He loved this place so much. It was his life, after Mom passed away. I wonder if Eddy will want to stay here, work with the land."

Grace stopped. Ted leaned on the crutches, trying to breathe evenly.

"Eddy has a great future ahead of him, with a wealth of opportunity," she said. "I'm sure he'll make good choices."

"Sometimes I wonder if I was wrong, denying him his mother. Or any mother. I could have married someone else."

Grace stared at the ground and said softly, "I have no doubt at all you're doing the best you can by your son. Eddy deserves only love and joy in his life. You were careful not to show him how to hate his mother, but to let him know she couldn't take care of him the way

Randy can. Eddy will always have a family who will be honest with him, remind him of how much you…" She started to sniffle. "How much you love him."

Ted closed his eyes before he reached across the crutch to take her hand. With the other, he gently caressed her cheek. She took the step closer he needed in order to wrap her as tightly as he could against him. Drawing emotional support from her revitalized his dread-filled heart. When their mouths met, he felt the strength of her love flowing into him. Hungry for an intimacy he could not claim, he kissed her deeply, wanting her to know how much he would regret letting her go. She tasted of the mulled cherry cider they had with the pork. He detected a hint of the garlic from the potatoes. Sweet and sour—just like life.

When he was able to pull away, she stayed close, turning to lean her back against him and wrapping her hand around his biceps. They stood, locked together, facing the direction where the sun had gone down.

Before it was completely dark, they returned to the house.

She stopped at the stoop. "I have to go home, Ted."

He couldn't let her go without returning some of the courage she had infused in him. He felt her withdrawal and did not blame her for wanting to physically distance herself from this place and the people who had grieved her. He hoped she would stay until… But she had the right to do what was best for herself.

"I know things have been pretty rough these last few weeks. Thank you for not giving up on us. At least, not yet. No one's holding on to you here, and you certainly have good cause to leave us. But people will calm down. Things will get better, really, if you wait a little longer. Randy told me how Kaye and Tanya stood up for you the other day, and I think more will follow suit. They'll remember your care."

He shifted a little around his crutches, lifting his head with some effort, rotating it to ease the muscle strain. "I can't apologize for my ex-wife. There's simply no excuse for her maliciousness. I'm sorry you were hurt. I'd give anything to make everything all right again."

Grace smiled in the glow of the porch light. "I know. It's all right, Ted." She drew her finger down his nose. "It's all right," she whispered again and lightly brushed her lips against his.

He shivered with the ache of being forced to keep on breathing, thinking, listening, and responding when he felt as though he was already halfway to the other side. "Would you at least come in for dessert? Tanya brought something. It would make her feel good if we ate it."

"All right. For a little while." She smiled. "For Tanya."

Dessert was cherry cobbler warm from the oven with ice cream. Grandpa and Grandma Marshall stories were told freely, all the dreams and hopes included.

Ted jumped when Eddy ground on something hard and shrilled. "Ouch!"

"Oh, there, now—I'm so sorry, sweetie. I must have missed a stone," Tanya said.

Ted watched him reach into his mouth to remove the little round cherry pit, curious to see what the boy would do.

He looked at it, puzzled, and then a wondrous smile slathered his face. He bolted out of his chair. "It's the cherry first tree! Mrs. Webb says trees come from seeds! I'm gonna plant this one! I'm gonna have an orchard when I grow up, and take care of it like Grandpa."

Chapter Twenty-Three

Randy felt the change as fall slowly cooled the atmosphere of East Bay. It was a relief to watch the change of summer children to winter children. No more time for petty stories to circulate on the city playgrounds, no whispered fears to fuel the fire against his family and friends. The harvest kept them busy. Talk turned to prices and packing and shipping and finding good help.

Shortly before leaving for college, Jimmy had allowed Tanya to cut off some of his hair. Randy thought it made his son look more mature. On the day the dorms had opened, Randy left him after they'd built the loft for his bed. Jimmy's smile had been shaky, but so had his.

He'd soon be raising another boy. What had he done right with Jimmy, what had he done wrong? This time he'd have Kaye to help.

* * * *

Grace agreed to pick up Shelby's lesson plans from church on her way home from work one afternoon. Walking down to the basement classrooms, she paused and cocked her head toward an odd scratching sound. She hoped it wasn't mice and decided to investigate.

Twitching feet stuck out of the janitor's room.

"Oh! Mr. Jeffries! What's the matter? No! Don't move! Just..." She hesitated only a second at the fear on the old man's face. "Don't be ridiculous! You know I won't hurt you. Can you speak?"

His eyes rolled back in his head. She went into action, clearing his breathing passages and wadding up her sweater for a pillow underneath his head.

"Help! Reverend Mattisse! Mrs. Rush!"

Once she determined the gathered phlegm was his only obstruction and had his head turned so he wouldn't gag and choke, she wondered why no one had answered her call. His eyes opened. She had no choice but to leave him so she could call the ambulance. "I have to run for help. I promise—I'll be right back."

At his whimper she almost turned back. She ran all the faster.

* * * *

"Massive stroke," Greg shared with Grace the next day when she went in for the few appointments on her docket. Despite the formal privacy act he told her anyway. "You deserve to know you caught him in good time. It was pure luck you happened to be there just then. The old man would have died—with the pastor and secretary in the office all the time, totally oblivious."

She knew better than to refute Greg's "luck" theory when he was complimenting her, so she simply nodded thanks.

"Just so you know," Nancy whispered at lunch, "I said to everyone that you were the one who was there and saved his life. I don't care what anyone else says. It's time those busybodies quit."

"I—"

"And I don't care what you say, either! You've been the greatest. When Brian's mom died, I know you didn't want anyone to know what you did for us, but, honestly, Grace, I don't know what we would have done without you there to help with the kids."

* * * *

Mrs. Jeffries surprised the congregation the next Sunday.

As soon as Reverend Mattisse's "amen" finished bouncing around the cold sanctuary, and before the organist could slam the first chords of the response, petite, powdered and rouged Mrs. Jeffries stood up.

"Reverend! I have to say something!"

"Mrs. Jeffries! Excuse me. I'm not—"

"Oh, I'll only take a second to update the good folks here."

Mrs. Jeffries turned around and pointed at Grace.

A hole in the floor could not open fast enough to swallow me, Lord, Grace prayed frantically.

She checked Reverend Mattisse's expression from between the fingers of the hand she held in front of her face. Oh, man, oh, man. Red cheeks. She listened to Mrs. Jeffries, whose voice seemed peculiarly magnified.

"As many of you already know, last week my husband Earl, the church's janitor, had a stroke. Who knows how long he laid there on the cold floor near the furnace without anyone noticing."

A thump came from the direction of the pulpit. The microphone squealed.

Mrs. Jeffries's tone grew louder. "Grace Runyon happened to come along and find him. If not for her, he would probably have died. But thanks to her quick action, not only is Earl alive, but he's going to make a good recovery. I simply wanted you all to know. Thank you for your attention."

She folded under the tweed skirt of her usual summer suit and retook her seat, but not before nodding firmly at Grace.

No one moved.

Mrs. Jeffries jumped up again. "And he's able to receive visitors." She sat.

The Reverend wiped his mouth with a striped hanky. "Ah, thank you." He gestured vigorously at the organist, who began a creaky rendition of the Doxology, normally played after the offering.

Ted squeezed Grace's hand. She felt Randy shivering on her other side. Worried, she looked at him out of the corner of her eye. His shoulders were shaking. He covered his mouth with his right hand and had his eyes squeezed shut.

She glanced at Ted, who shrugged.

Mrs. Jeffries was the center of attention after the service. The woman repeated her story over and over, clutching Grace's elbow in a vice grip.

"We're so grateful to Grace," Mrs. Jeffries said. "East Bay could not get along without her help at the clinic, or in the Ladies Guild. And you know how she dotes on that boy, and the Brouwer baby."

* * * *

Grace and Shelby took Alyssa out for long walks in the stroller on days they plucked like lilies from their calendars. Shelby had decided to stay home with her daughter instead of going back to the daycare center. "I know. I should be an advocate of daycare with my credentials, but I just couldn't do it, Grace. I couldn't put my little one in with all the other kids all day long even though I would actually be there with her."

"It's the right thing for your family. And you're fortunate you can afford to do that. Not everyone has that choice."

"But though I'm glad to be home with her, I tend to go stir-crazy some days. I can't tell you how glad I am to have you here, willing to take time for me and the girl."

"Hey, I keep telling you. It's really you doing me the favor. You stuck by me, helped me. Listened to me, too." Grace butted Shelby with her shoulder as they walked along. "Friends like us—it's mutual."

"Don't you miss your friends from Tennessee? I know you still keep in touch with some of them."

"A little. Lena, well, she's the Shelby of Woodside." Grace grinned. "I keep in touch with her, of course. In fact, she's coming to visit for Thanksgiving this year so you'll have a chance to meet her."

"What did you do—I mean, can I ask you about, well, about what you did with—"

"Sean? My son? You mean, did I keep working after I had him?"

"Yeah. Do you mind?"

"No, not at all. It's getting easier to talk about him. I guess since you know about him, too. Well, I did keep on working as much as I could, usually only till two or three in the afternoon, though. I had been working as a midwife, which I loved. But I gave it up, due to the unpredictability of our schedules. I couldn't just leave in the middle of the night any more, with him to think about. My parents..." She swallowed and stopped, her throat tight. "I had my parents there. They helped a lot. So did Jonathan's parents."

Wafts of memory whirled around her. Shelby stayed silent.

"I really had it all back then, or thought I did," Grace mused.

"Sounds like it. Would you have been different, done things differently if you'd, well, if you knew what was going to happen?"

"How do you love them more? Wish they were back? Spend more minutes with them holding them close or watching them sleep? You can't. You can't ever get that back. But I make sure those memories stay with me. Most importantly, I know with all my being I will be with them again"—she gestured all around them—"when all of this doesn't matter anymore."

They nodded and greeted Mrs. Ten Boldt, who stood outside her shop soaking up the last sunny warm days of fall. Grace smiled and remembered the woman's help when she had been so new in town she had not had a change of clothes.

Back at Shelby's, Grace lifted the baby out of the stroller to take her inside. Once Alyssa had settled in for her nap, and they each had a cup of steaming tea, Shelby pounced on Grace. "How can you forgive them like nothing happened?"

Grace looked at her glass, swirling the tea. "You're forgetting nothing really ever happened," she said, finally.

"How can you say that? They spread rumors, lies, about you. Accused you of hurting their children, and for heaven's sake, of killing that old mountain woman, not to mention starting a petition to get you fired."

"Sticks and stones…"

"It wasn't a childish prank. Slander is a criminal offense."

"What would that prove? Forgiveness is personal. They may have thought I hurt them and if they thought it, didn't I actually do it? That's how they felt and we can't dismiss it. Even if I did nothing wrong, they thought I did. It's subjective. It doesn't matter an investigation of clinic records turned up nothing. At least it was done, so they can't whisper about it. Practicing any kind of medicine is like depending on how the mad king feels from day to day. Some days you do everything exactly the way he wants and other days, well, there's nothing that can make him happy. People in general act like that. Rumors and lies a person can get over—especially when they're unsubstantiated. They didn't make me leave town or run away, which, believe me, I was tempted to do."

Grace took a sip of her drink. "I have to go along with their mood and act pleasantly. The forgiving will take a little longer in my heart," she admitted. But it was not like what she'd deserved in Woodside, after Jonathan died. She hadn't deserved their vitriol this time; had no need to forgive herself for doing nothing wrong. Still, the feeling festered.

* * * *

In the evening, Grace served dinner to Ted and Eddy, a simple cassoulet of tomatoes and beans, spices and beef to eat with chunks of bread. Afterward, Eddy was allowed to watch one of his videos on her computer while she and Ted sat outside, no need to fill the quiet spaces. On the front porch swing, she relaxed in Ted's arms. Fall had nipped the edges of the trees and sent them huddling for warmth. She watched the interplay of their entwined hands. His skin felt dry and cool. Their fingers caught and caressed each other.

Patient care had resumed to a more normal level at the clinic. Greg had said little about the problems, telling her not to worry, he'd handle things. He'd never cut back her hours, though she went home more than once when there was nothing for her to do. She no longer felt too tired to think, although she knew she hesitated way too much before making a decision at work or when answering one of Eddy's interminable questions.

The flash of healing touch never returned after she'd healed Tanya. Had God left her? Was she no longer following his good and perfect will after what had happened with Jilly? She doubted herself and her courses of treatment more and more. What could bring it back?

Maybe in this good and peaceful moment she could call upon the gift for Ted. She released his hand. He looked at her, questioning. She inhaled and closed her eyes, remembering the accusation in Jimmy's face when he'd seen her after treating Tanya. She reached around Ted and slipped her hands up under his shirt to carefully nudge along his spine.

Now? Can I use your power to heal this man?

She felt nothing but his flesh. No heat, no spark of energy, only the familiar bumps and ridges of the vertebrae through his skin. Hurt and afraid, she opened her eyes, the fragment of mystery broken.

Ted pulled back to look at her. "Something you want?"

She shook her head. "No. Just…checking."

He laughed and nuzzled her neck, threading his fingers through her hair. "Hmm, you smell so good. What were you doing?"

Heaving a sigh, she tugged his face away. "I wondered if I could feel it."

"Feel it? You mean, what's wrong? It's not in my spine, the doctor said." He took her hand and put his lips against her palm. "I didn't mind, you know. That's about the only thing that works."

She leaned toward his mouth and let their lips touch, teasing, questioning, exploring. It would be so easy to give in. Back down, girl. You have no right.

"You made me wonder something," Ted said.

"Wonder? What about?"

"What it's like, you know, when you're truly in love. I realize I never had that before."

"You were married, Ted."

"Not in the right way. Not like you and Jonathan."

Grace went silent. What could she say?

"I'm sorry. I shouldn't be talking like that."

"No. You shouldn't." She twisted in his arms so she could rest her head on Ted's shoulder and still feel the rumble of his voice under her cheek.

"Don't you ever wish we—"

She put her hand up over his mouth. "I just showed up one day, bought your house, and helped you out when you needed it. I don't want to talk about anything else."

Ted pulled her hand away. "What if I asked you—"

The screen door creaked and bounced twice when Eddy poured out of the house like a glass of spilled milk. "Will somebody listen to me? I hafta read my story out loud. Mrs. Webb says it's important homework. She gives us a checkmark when we do it. Then you sign this paper."

Grace sat up and slid away from Ted to make room for him on the swing. Eddy snuggled up onto the seat. He leaned against his father, eyes dark and solemn with impossibly long lashes.

"Who will sign my paper? Mrs. Webb says for my mom or dad to sign it."

It seemed important to Eddy they discuss this business of signing before reading.

"I will," Ted said immediately.

"But Daddy, I want Grace to sign it." He leaned over and stage whispered to his father, "I wished she was my mama, you remember, at my birthday cake. I asked God about it in Sunday School, too. Then she can sign."

Grace went very still. A tremble started in her elbows and worked upward. She tried not to look at Ted but could not turn away from the sight of gleaming moisture gathering in his eyes. In slow motion she watched his lips part and heard his words.

"That…well, Eddy. We love Grace very much. But she can't…" He looked helpless.

Grace turned away and bit the inside of her cheek.

"Eddy, you know I won't always be here for you, remember? We talked about it. And Uncle Randy will take care of you then. You have your own room and everything and won't have to move. Kaye will always be here, and…"

Ted choked and gathered his son tight, his tears streaming into the boy's hair.

Eddy turned demonic. He hit back, beating his little fists on his father's side and back and arm. "I want Grace! I don't want Kaye! I don't want Unca Randy!"

Pent-up confusion and helplessness fueled a rage only the very young can know. His cries were barely short of hysterical and he gasped. "Grace! Grace! I want Grace!"

She reached for Eddy, angry and so sad she felt her heart creaking. Eddy clung so tightly she could not take a deep breath. Why were the only emotions she was allowed despair and pain? She turned away from Ted, who huddled on the swing. Eddy swung his legs tightly around Grace and rocked hard, almost pulling her over in his wild grief. She walked unsteadily to the other edge of the porch, where she leaned him on the railing and clung to him. "Shh, shh," she whispered, "it will be all right."

It was the classic mother's lie. Nothing would ever be all right for this little boy. She rocked to the side so she could look at Ted who sat, forehead on his arms, hands clenched in his hair, rocking in his own agony.

"Why, God? Please, let me do something," she prayed to her silent Lord. "Don't deny me the gift now. It's not fair to ask this of me—to watch helplessly. You let me help others recover from their ailments—wasn't I doing what you wanted? Why are this man and his child so unimportant you don't help them? Or is it me, Lord? Are you punishing me because I hesitated to obey when I first came here? Are you punishing everyone around me to make me suffer? It's not fair!"

* * * *

Randy, alarmed at the shriek from next door, came hustling across the yard. He stood, silent, at the foot of the steps, his hands and jaws clenched. His prayers joined Grace's.

"What do I live for? What do you want from me? What can I do so that you will spare my brother? I will gladly give you myself."

* * * *

Eddy's sobs gradually calmed. Grace continued to pray, trying to regulate her breathing. "When will it be? When will you let me know when you'll let me work the gift you bestowed upon me? When he's dead and gone? Why did you bring me here, put this in my face, and then deny me, Lord?"

* * * *

"It's not time yet." Randy heard the voice and looked heavenward.

* * * *

It's not time yet. Peace." Grace heard the whisper and breathed it in.

* * * *

"Shhh. Be still." Ted had never heard the wind sound so much like a voice speaking to him. Shh…shh. *Be still, my son. I love you.*

* * * *

Randy appeared at the clinic one afternoon when Grace's shift was over. He held his hat in his hands, twisting it around and around while he waited for her to finish logging her reports.

"I hoped to talk to you privately. Can you—would you mind going for a little drive with me if you have time now? I promise we'll be back before school is out."

"Sure, Randy." She checked out and walked with him to his vehicle. Randy drove to the edge of East Bay to the turnout at the Lake Michigan shore. This time of day they had the little space to themselves. Randy let down his window before turning off the engine. They listened to the waves and gulls for a few minutes in companionable silence.

"I heard from Jimmy today," Randy said.

"Oh? How is he?"

"He sounded good. Says he liked your package. Thanks for thinking of him, Grace."

"You're welcome. He's a fine young man."

"You did more for him in an hour than I did his whole life."

"Randy, I don't think so. This can't be the reason you wanted to talk to me."

Randy fiddled with the keys. "I found myself judging you awhile back. I guess I've been doing it ever since you came to town, when you never deserved that from me. I've always had that tendency, to put people I meet in a particular box, and it hasn't done anyone around me any good. Certainly not my son. It's been good this summer, getting to know him in a way I never took the chance to before. You've been helpful in that regard."

Grace laid her head against the comfortable seat and closed her eyes.

"The thing is, I know you have some sort of special thing you can do with people's hurts and I even know it's because of the kind of faith you have." He tapped the steering wheel in helpless gesture. "When I think of how I accused you of not being a church-going woman at first…"

"You also accused me of being unfaithful to your brother. What do you want, Randy?"

"I wanted to tell you I'm sorry."

"I don't know how much longer I can stay in East Bay. It doesn't matter how sorry everyone is. The damage is done. I don't trust myself."

"But Ted—can't you help him?" Randy asked. "Can't you do anything for him, like you did for Jimmy? Or Tanya? They told me, you know, in Woodside, that you helped people there. They were afraid when you left things would change, that no one could get better again."

He looked at his hands clasped tightly before him. "This one man, he said that when your boy and your husband died, they were afraid you would be angry with them, that you wouldn't be able to help them anymore. But you helped people when you came here, didn't you? Even when you didn't like me?"

The plaintive note in Randy's voice convulsed Grace's heart into an angry lump. She brought her elbows up over her ears. "I don't know. I don't know. I don't think I can." Grace leaned over and let the tears flow. "God doesn't hear me these days." When she felt more in control she took his proffered handkerchief and rubbed her eyes and nose.

"I hadn't cried for so long, not since I, well, before I lost my husband."

"Maybe I don't really know… No, that's not right." He shook his head. "I hope I never know what it feels like to go through what you have over the last few years, Grace. I also want you to know Kaye and I are getting married after Thanksgiving."

Tears welled again and Grace turned her head away. "I'm so glad for both of you," she said. "I apologize for this crying jag. I'm happy for you. You know Ted tried to set us up."

He laughed. "Yeah, that lasted all of two seconds, didn't it?" He cleared his throat. "The thing is...we don't want you to leave, Grace. Not Kaye, or me, or Eddy."

"I don't know." She shook her head and sniffed.

"It will be so hard for Eddy after, well, afterward. The other night was a small sample of what he'll—we'll all go through, after…"

"My whole life is like some big sacrifice. I'm just supposed to go and watch people I love die slow painful deaths. What about me?" She shoved the car door open and strode to the railing surrounding the overlook.

She paced along the shore for several minutes, her jacket billowing around her in the breeze, her hair flying all over her face and shoulders. She had not had it cut since she moved to Michigan. It was longer than she was used to, falling down between her shoulder blades. The gulls squawked above, turning in aimless circles hoping to spot a speck of dinner that hadn't been there on the last pass. Cold, steely waves broke and foamed white, inward toward the shore. The breeze blew chill fingers under her jacket and up her sleeves. She glanced over her shoulder at the car to see Randy watching through the windshield. She turned to climb back in beside him.

They said nothing at all as Randy returned her to the clinic parking lot to pick up her car.

Chapter Twenty-Four

Grace's cell phone rang from its charging cradle on her nightstand. She rolled over and checked the screen. She squinted at the too bright display. Shelby? "Hi, what's up?"

"I'm so sorry, Grace. I didn't know what else to do. I know I can't just call for antibiotics anymore, but she's so little. I don't know what to do to take away her pain."

"And yours, too, right?" Grace rolled over to look at her alarm clock's illuminated green dial. Two thirty in the morning. Yeah, morning.

She yawned. Shelby's little girl wailed in the background. "Davy's away, fishing, isn't he? Okay, I'll be right over. You can make a washcloth warm by soaking it in hot water, but only hot enough you can hold it comfortably in your hand for several seconds, and hold it against her ear. You probably know about that. Sometimes it helps or at least distracts them a little. I'll get dressed and come over, okay? Hang on."

She realized she was repeating herself and hoped Shelby wouldn't notice.

After pulling on some jeans and a shirt, she shoved her feet into tennies, grabbed a windbreaker, and headed out to her car, brushing feebly at her head. The brisk air woke her up a little more and she looked up at the brilliant diamond night sky. There must have hardly been any moonlight to interfere with the starshine. She almost hated to put on her headlights as she drove.

Shelby met her at the door. Alyssa bounced in her baby seat on the living room floor, flapping her arms and throwing her little body backward against the restraints with all her might. Her little face was puckered and red and her hair was sweaty ringlets.

"What's her temp?" Grace asked first.

"Oh! How could I…? Um, give me a moment."

Shelby was so flustered Grace pushed her down on the couch. "Never mind. I know where it is. Hang out, relax."

"She's so little," her friend said helplessly. "I just, I just—how much baby pain medicine can I give her? She had a few drops already but she screams so hard she throws up."

Grace came back into the living room in time to hear the last part of the lament. "If she's throwing up, she'll become dehydrated. Are you giving her water, too? Here, let's check your temp." Grace picked up the baby and slid the strip inside the baby's gown under her arm, holding her firmly a few seconds for the sensitive tape to register the temperature.

Alyssa's mom paced nearby. "How high is it? Should we take her to Bay Bridge?"

"She's sweaty. The fever isn't very high. I don't think we need to take her anywhere at this point."

"Oh. Well, sweating is good, isn't it?"

Grace had no doubt Shelby knew all about children's temperatures and was simply exhausted and panicked. She'd sometimes felt the same with Sean, although she'd had Jonathan for back up.

She drew a lukewarm bath for the baby and took her into the bathroom, ordering Shelby to lie down on the couch and close her eyes for a little.

The water distracted Alyssa enough for Grace to encourage her to take some baby drops of medicine and keep them down. A couple of hours later both mother and daughter were relaxed enough that Grace felt comfortable leaving them again.

"Call me any time yet tonight if you need anything," she whispered on her way out. "But definitely check in with me tomorrow and let me know how she is, okay?"

She left them cuddled on the sofa under Shelby's favorite granny square afghan.

* * * *

Later in the afternoon Grace and Ted sprawled on a blanket in her backyard. Meager fall sunlight made it pleasant enough to be outside with a couple of sweatshirts for warmth. Eddy played with his basketball and hoop, two curious kittens prancing around exploring whenever Eddy dropped the ball.

"I couldn't sleep last night. I saw you leave," Ted remarked.

"Oh? Checking up on me?" She laughed. "Shelby called. You know Davy's gone."

"Yeah. We usually go fishing. Another thing I miss."

Grace studied his expression, wondering if he meant now, or forever. She yawned. "Alyssa had an earache, and I only went for moral support."

Ted turned on his side. He bent his elbow and made a fist to rest his cheek on.

"I'm sure she was glad to see you." He touched her hand.

"She was. That's what friends are for, or so I've been told."

"Ah, I wondered about —what we're here for, that is."

Grace felt muzzy-headed with missing sleep and couldn't tell if he was making idle talk or if he really wanted an answer. "I think we're here for each other. To cherish each other and help each other be brave when things get rough."

He gripped her hand with convulsive strength but turned his face away. "I'm not brave, Grace. Sometimes I'm so afraid." He spoke so quietly she had to lean in close to catch it.

"Afraid of what?"

"I guess of dying. Of being so lonely without Eddy and you and Randy… How can anyone bear it?"

She took a deep breath, debating whether to keep their conversation light or delve deeper. "What do you think will happen?"

"I'm not sure." He twitched as his leg spasmed. He sat up and kneaded the taut muscle above his shin. His expression softened when he looked at his son.

"That it might hurt." He shivered. "Is that what happened to you? That you couldn't bear it, alone, after your husband died? Is that why you ran?"

Grace touched his cheek. He had shaved that morning, and his skin was still smooth. How much more alone would she feel without this man? Why had she run in the first place, anyway?

"In a way, Jonathan left me long before he died. When he—we—both knew nothing could be done to preserve his life, it seemed like he…turned off." She looked at him carefully to see if he understood. He nodded.

"You see, I was afraid, too," she said. "Afraid they would hate me, think I didn't try hard enough to help him and blame me for his death. Everyone loved him."

"Did they act like that? Like…like some of them did, here? Say anything?"

She shook her head. To buy time, she plucked a few blades of grass and rolled them between her fingers. The moist scent of sweet summer lulled her, though the crackle of dried, dead leaves whispered around her. Summer was over. "No. How I reacted to what happened was all in my own head. I think I needed to learn more about who *I* was. I only knew the parts everyone else claimed. Daughter, wife, mother, PA. I ran away so I could figure out what part of me was the most important. I still don't know."

Ted set his hand on hers again. "I know. And it isn't what you are to everyone. It's who you are inside that's important. To me, and to Eddy. That's what I treasure most. That's what I want to hold on to forever."

"Forever only starts when our life on earth is over."

"Maybe." Ted rolled onto his back, keeping her hand close to his chest, so she had to lean across him to talk. It put her in a vulnerable position. Maybe Ted needed her to feel that way.

She wouldn't let him stop her. "Remember when we talked at the beach at Petoskey? You've been running away from this conversation. Maybe it's time to stop running."

"Okay. Tell me."

"We each have something we're born with that makes us unique beings. We all bring something special into the mix of humanity, and when it's gone, there's a gap."

"You mean, when I'm gone, someone might notice."

"Death is temporary. Your soul, Ted, is what goes on, not your beat-up body. You have the head-knowledge of faith as so many people do, but the hardest thing now is letting go of your misconceptions. To believe the impossible—there is an afterlife, heaven, is—well, difficult."

Ted jerked her closer.

Grace resisted him for one last try at his soul. "Our miserable little lives are such a flash in the pan compared to what's real."

"What's real?"

"None of this means anything compared to the promise of heaven, of having all our tears wiped away. That's a sure thing."

"How can you know? And heaven always sounds boring." He tugged her the rest of the way so she flopped across his torso. He put a hand behind her neck and pressed his lips against hers ungently, nipping. "Does heaven have that?"

"Something better."

"Really?" His leered and squeezed her shoulder.

"Better than that, too."

He let his head fall back. "Hmm. Do you really believe this stuff? I mean, I'm not sure even Righteous Randy has that part down—about knowing for sure."

"I do know it. And I believe it with all my heart. I'd like to be with you again in heaven."

"What about Jonathan? Will he be there?"

"I'm pretty sure he will."

"Then what about us?"

Grace twisted her lips. "What about Jilly?"

"I'm pretty sure she won't be there," Ted said, tongue in cheek.

"Ted!"

He laughed and fended off her smack at his chest.

"I can tell you there's no more tears, no jealousy, no pain in heaven," she said.

"I'd like to spend eternity with you, Grace. And with Eddy, and

Randy, and Mom and Dad, and Sean…but I'll have to think about Jonathan."

Back in playful mode he sat up. Grace pushed him over again. "You!"

He closed his eyes against the sun. "It would be nice. I'll think about it."

"Don't think too long. Promise," she demanded, leaning across his face so her head shielded him from the glare.

"Cross my heart," Ted said, feebly attempting the gesture.

Grace caught his hand and held it tight.

"And hope to live," he joined her whisper.

* * * *

Shelby called Grace at suppertime—from Bay Bridge Hospital.

"Honestly, everything was fine until she woke up from a nap this afternoon. I was going to call you," she said miserably, "but I was so tired, too, and I fell asleep when she did. Her cries were different when she woke up and I just panicked."

"Oh, Shelby. I'm so sorry."

"I'm sure it's not your fault, or anything," Shelby mumbled into the phone.

Grace pressed the instrument closer to her head in order to hear.

"I hesitated to call even now. I knew you'd feel bad and there isn't anything we can do. Her fever went high and they have… they have…" Shelby's voice faltered. "They're giving her IV antibiotics. She's strapped d-down."

"Oh, honey. Did you get hold of Davy?"

"Yes. He's on his way back now."

"I'll be right there."

"No, Grace, please. Don't come, okay? I'll call you later."

Grace pressed the button that terminated the connection, more stunned Shelby did not want her company until Davy arrived, than disappointed her friend thought she might have hurt Alyssa the night before.

She brushed at her face, surprised her cheeks were damp. This episode was the last straw. Her career in medicine was definitely over. There was only one more thing to do. She grabbed her handbag and car keys and drove over to the clinic.

Grace ignored the four patients in the waiting room and Nancy at reception and marched past them all down the hallway into Greg's office. She slammed the door and sat down blindly in front of the computer terminal at his desk. Setting her purse on the floor, she gave the mouse a little shake to bring the screen back up from Greg's screensaver of Jamaican beaches. Hesitating only a moment, she rapidly clicked out a terse resignation letter, double checked for embarrassing typos, printed it off, and signed it with a flourish. She tossed it toward Greg's desk where it breezed back and forth on its way down to the red blotter. As she watched it flutter, the doctor strode into the room. He snatched up the paper just before it settled, barely giving it a glance before tearing it to shreds.

Grace watched him, thoroughly irked. "That doesn't change anything. I should have resigned months ago when…when the garbage talk started," she hissed.

Greg's face remained impassive. He said nothing. For whatever reason, his silence made her more upset. He sat on the edge of his desk, swinging his foot, and calmly watched her composure unravel. He smiled a little, which threw her into a fury. She raised her purse over her head and dashed it to the floor and began looking around for something else to throw.

Greg handed her his Gray's Anatomy. She had to take it in both hands as the volume was so large. By the time she recovered from its weight, her anger changed to frustration. She hefted the familiar book. Pages of illustrations flashed behind her eyes, memories crept out of her determination to learn all she could before even graduating from high school.

She plopped into Greg's guest chair with the book on her lap and let her head fall forward.

"I talked to Maddux, the Brouwers' pediatrician," Greg said. "The baby is fine. She happened to be one of the few cases that actually needed an antibiotic, something I wouldn't have prescribed until the afternoon." He wadded and tossed the shredded resignation letter in the garbage can. "So, what's this really about?"

"What if I hurt her? What if I can't help people anymore? I've lost my—"

Greg put his hands over his ears. "I don't want to hear this! Mrs. Brouwer was worried you might overreact like this. That's why she wanted me to talk to you. I was on my way out to your place when I noticed your car already here."

He stood. "Look, Grace. I don't know exactly under what auspices you work. You know I don't go for that faith healer stuff, but you have some special ability in treating patients. I know what happened with the Marshall boy and I'm not kidding myself there wasn't something, ah, out of the ordinary that you did to make it heal clean and fast, but I'm willing to give you the benefit of the doubt. Tony Vander Groot is a little demon and I'm certain he jerked or did something to hurt himself during that accident last summer and I simply don't care about the rest."

Greg folded his arms and stared at her. "Now with this—well, you've never been a coward."

She shook her head, drained.

"I think you've been coddled, admired, even worshiped, for what you can do for people and haven't run into much opposition before," he said mercilessly.

His sharp darts thrust into the fabric of her pride. Grace jumped out of the chair and stalked to the door.

Greg stepped in front of her, and held out his hand, palm facing her. "Now, wait. Isn't that just a little bit true?"

She halted and nodded reluctantly, not meeting his question.

"So, a little character definition doesn't hurt."

Grace crossed her arms and turned her cheek. "I want to be someplace where hard things don't happen all of the time. Why can't I just work, eat, sleep, and be happy?"

Greg wandered over to his louvered window and looked out. He put his hands in his pockets and rocked on his feet. After a few minutes he said, "I think that's a rhetorical question. At least I hope it is."

He jingled the loose coins in his pocket and then turned to face her. "But in case it isn't, my answer is, sometimes you can just work, eat, sleep, and be happy. And you have to keep those moments close, so when you can't please everybody all the time, you haul out those happy moments and relive them until the unhappy people crawl back into their own little lives and leave yours alone. And, of course, you chose one of the worst careers to meet those conditions," he concluded. "Now. I have you scheduled—"

"I'm not kidding, Greg. I can't work here anymore."

He sighed and sat in his chair behind the desk, looking much like the first day Grace met him when he was weary and ill with flu. He leaned back and closed his eyes briefly before opening them and leaning across his desk. "I think I can only remember one time when you ever took a vacation, which was in July, right?"

Grace saw the direction of the discussion and began to shake her head.

Greg reached across the desk and grabbed her hand. "Listen to me," he said in his no-nonsense voice. "I want you to take some time off. There are extenuating circumstances"—*Ted*—"that necessitate your care being given elsewhere for the time being."

He cocked his head and squeezed her knuckles painfully. "Two months' leave for now. Middle of December I'll expect you back here, bright and eager."

Conveniently after Randy and Kaye's wedding.

"I'll keep in touch," he promised.

Or threatened.

She understood that was all the time he was giving Ted Marshall to live.

Chapter Twenty-Five

Grace walked aimlessly toward the few scraggly apple trees behind her house. Hurting her best friend's baby was horrifying, but having a date stamp on Ted's life gutted her. For the first time she knew for sure he was going to die and nothing she did could make any difference. God wasn't going to give her the chance to try. How could he do this? He had left her gaping and wounded, bereft.

Wasps buzzed lazily around the late summer fruit, its fermenting juice filling her nostrils. Tall grasses waved in the breeze and she stopped to watch a blackbird land nearby and tilt its shiny head at her. A wasp landed on her jacket sleeve and she wondered if she should shake it off. She put one foot in front of the other until she walked right up the cement steps leading to the Marshalls' stoop. Ted stood braced against the door, waiting, arms open and shoulder available. It was the first time Grace had gone to him. She felt his chest heave even as she fitted so smoothly into his arms it was as if the two of them were two halves of the same mold.

Sharing her grief made it only a little less frightening.

* * * *

Ted breathed in her scent, the familiar aloe mingled with the freshness of outdoors. Grace's nose felt like ice buried in the side of his neck. She trembled. He jiggled her shoulders a little when he knew he could no longer stand comfortably.

"Hey." He held her away. "I need to sit. Come." Ted turned and led her into the house.

The ticking of the grandfather clock tried to drown out his worried thoughts. Ted smoothed her hair and cheek, running his finger around the rim of her ear while they sat on the couch. He whispered, "Grace. Look at me." Her eyes were blank, shocked, as if she were just waking up in a strange bed. She looked around and slowly settled her gaze on his face.

"Shelby called here. She's so worried." He gave Grace another little shake. "You're not supposed to be the one to make people worry."

She didn't respond.

"People talk, you know—it's not mean or anything, or accusing, or strange. You have a special talent—the ability to make people better." He babbled to fill the silence. "But sometimes things happen. Not even a doctor can save his patient every time. Germs find their way in. Shelby and Davy understand. It's okay with me. You can't always simply fix everyone…"

He was stunned at her reaction. She thrust herself away from him, getting to her wobbly feet. Two spots burned on her cheeks and her eyes shone unnaturally bright.

"Like I can't fix you, you mean? It's supposed to work. That's why I have it, that's why I was called to be a healer." She paced strangely off-course as a blind woman might have been. She put out a hand as if to fend off the wall at the far end of the room. Ted wondered for a moment if she had taken something or had a drink. He pursed his lip and sniffed. No booze on her breath.

What to do next. She had come to him—for what? He went carefully over the sketchy information he knew. Shelby had asked Grace to come and check out Alyssa but later took the baby to the hospital. Alyssa was sick but not that sick and recovering nicely. Grace wanted to quit her job but instead was on leave.

Why was Grace so upset? She had not reacted this strongly back when everyone was talking about her last summer.

Ted thought back to their conversation of the previous afternoon.

"Death is temporary," she had told him. She was so sure of herself he had no choice but to consider over and over what she said. He thought of her until he saw her through the window as if he had wished her to appear.

She stood before him, agitated. "Randy said…Randy told me…" She stopped, looking as confused as he was at the words coming out of her mouth. He watched her crinkle her forehead, before swiveling to face the window. She started pacing again. "Randy asked me to help you. But I can't," she whispered.

Ted stared, fascinated at the tears rolling down her face. She couldn't be going through all this for him, could she?

"He knows. He found out when he went there. They told him…he knew I couldn't then, and I can't now." She shuddered.

He had no idea what she was talking about. He wondered if she were in the midst of a mental breakdown. What should he do? "What does Randy have to do with anything?" Ted asked. "You're talking about last spring when he went to Woodside? I realize he had no business checking out your credentials and background but it's not like you have anything to hide, is it? Your husband died of cancer. Your child was in a car accident far away from you. People die all the time. You didn't want to stay in that place and came here to start new. Believe me, if I could I would have left, too—just taken Eddy and gone somewhere else."

She wandered away from him, shaking her head. "No, no, no." She slumped on the sofa.

He followed her. "Grace."

"I'm so tired, Ted. I just need to lie down, okay? A little nap."

"Grace!" He shook her shoulders. "Wait! You didn't, um, take anything did you? Some aspirin, or…" He tried to think. "Or anything from the clinic, did you?"

Grace looked at him, smiling dreamily. "Of course not." She patted the seat beside her. "Come, be here with me. It won't be always, you know." Her smile turned sweetly nostalgic. "We were talking about something important this afternoon. Before Shelby and Greg. It was important," she said. "Ah, yes, about it not being always." She frowned. A woozy, bemused little line appeared between her brows. "Some things are temporary, though, aren't they?"

Ted sat beside Grace and pulled her close again, smoothing her hair and rocking her gently.

"But some things are always."

And it occurred to him it was true.

* * * *

Eddy thought it was the coolest thing in the world to have Grace sleeping over on his couch. Eds anxiously waited for her to wake up in the morning and kept going to check, tiptoeing with exaggerated care. He sounded like a herd of elephants on roller skates. Ted was surprised she slept through it. He caught his son breathing practically into her ear at one point and made him stay in the kitchen to give her some privacy.

* * * *

Grace woke all at once right before ten o'clock. What she was doing on Ted's couch? And why was he standing there?

"What happened?" She felt sick to her stomach and combed her hair with shaky fingers.

"We talked. Then you fell asleep, nothing more. Let me get you something to eat."

Ted fixed her tea and Eddy brought her toast, walking carefully still on tiptoes with his precious burden. The child tipped the plate at the last minute and a few crumbs landed in her lap along with the plate.

"Whoops!" Eddy opened his eyes wide and dropped his chin.

"My lap isn't that hungry," Grace told him. He giggled. She looked closely to see that all the sadness of the last week and the anxiety of who would sign his reading paper had gone.

When Eddy was satisfied she had eaten every crumb of toast, the little guy went off to dress. Ted joined her, lowering himself stiffly in a nearby rocker with the aid of his crutch. Grace watched.

"I don't remember anything from the time I left the clinic until this morning. The last time that happened was when I first came here to East Bay. I woke up in the motel with a paper that said I checked in two days earlier and I had no recollection of it. Or of much of the trip before."

She put the empty plate and mug on the coffee table and leaned back.

"I think you were really stressed out."

"How's the baby?"

"Alyssa went home with her parents about a half an hour ago. Davy called. She'll be fine. I could hear her cooing in the background on their car phone when they called. They tried here when you didn't answer. Shelby was worried."

Grace squeezed her eyes shut in relief. She opened them and sat forward, thinking it was time she left. She glanced around, trying to pick out any of her belongings. Shoes would be good. She put them on and stood up.

Ted awkwardly pulled himself out of the rocker.

"I guess I'd better go. Thanks for the couch. And the shoulder." She followed his slow walk.

At the kitchen door, Ted stopped her. "You came to me, Grace. I'd like to think that means you trust me."

"I always have. Somehow I've always felt that way, that I could trust you even when we both know… Well, anyway, I'll be going now." She couldn't look at him, embarrassed in her vulnerability. "Thanks for breakfast, too. Say so long to Eddy, okay? And thanks for making me toast just the way I like it." She twitched her shoulders and slipped out before he could touch her.

* * * *

Grace opened her door to Shelby later that afternoon. "Davy's staying with the baby," Shelby answered her friend's voiceless question. "I needed to come over and talk to you, see if you were all right."

"Me?" Grace pushed the front door back tight against the frame after Shelby walked right in and plopped herself down on the sofa.

"It's not that I didn't trust your medical expertise at the hospital, Grace. I trust you with the life of my child above my own," she said. "You know that."

Grace was still silent. She slowly closed the door and turned around, leaning her back against it. She knew nothing, nothing. Why would Shelby come to torment her like this?

"I don't know how I can say this right. You showed me the face of Christ. And honestly, every time I see you in action I see that look you have, the face of God imposed on you."

Shelby jumped up and grabbed her hand. "Oh, please don't doubt. I don't know why things happen."

Grace allowed Shelby to tug her toward the sofa. "Here, sit down. You look awful. This is not coming out right. I don't want you to think I'm not grateful, because I am—truly. And you can't leave us. You just can't."

Grace shook her head. A headache started to pound behind her eyeballs. She pressed her fingers against her lids. "I don't know what to say. It's not quite the same as a year ago when I was terrified—overwhelmed—and had to leave Woodside. Well, maybe I'm overwhelmed, yes, but not frightened. Even after what happened last summer. I'm worried I've lost my…my faith, my ability to help people."

She searched for answers in Shelby, who had only sympathy to give. "I guess it's safe to say now I really have lost it. What if I'd hurt Alyssa more than I did? How could we ever forgive each other?"

"Don't be silly. I panicked. You helped her a lot actually, by bringing her fever out earlier and getting her to take some medicine. The doctor said what we thought. He wouldn't have given her anything, either, at the time."

"But you ended up doing what you wanted to do all along, which was take Alyssa to the hospital. If I had listened the first time…"

"We'd have been sent home like a couple of broody hens and you know it. I still would have had to go back later in the day, just like I did."

Grace listened to the clock's gears measure out the seconds.

Shelby broke the silence. "Maybe it's a good thing, though, to take some time away from work for yourself and Ted right now. You've been going and going since practically the moment you moved in. I don't think you stopped long enough to let yourself grieve your husband properly. We're all kind of tired. It's been a hectic summer. With the wedding coming up and the holiday season—all of that—I'm telling you, for all I've missed working, it's been awful nice being able to be around home to do some yard work, pick fruit and stuff without having to try fitting it all in around another job. It will be good for you to take some time off. You'll see. Everything will work out."

For all Shelby believed, Grace knew it could not be true for her.

Chapter Twenty-Six

Grace's hands were numb. She felt clumsy, inept, had little energy and often stayed in bed on her days off. She'd only made an appearance at the door for Eddy's trick or treat costume. Took a picture, smiled, and waved. Then went back to bed.

Shelby brought the baby over to show they were fine. Her voice buzzed.

Alyssa cooed and waved her arms. Grace raised her heavy head, hoping Shelby wasn't going to stay much longer. She was so tired. In fact, she shouldn't be around them. What if she was coming down with something and was contagious?

"Have you eaten today?" Shelby asked.

"Yes, sure." She had, right? She just couldn't remember what.

Shelby's cool hand rested on her forehead for a moment. "You don't have a fever."

"I think I should just go home to Woodside."

"You are home." Shelby knelt by the sofa. "Please, everything is so much better. The worst of the gossip is over. We need you. I know it. I'll keep talking to people, and so will Dave, and Matty. Please, don't leave now."

"I'm tired, Shel."

"A vacation. Come on. I'll help you plan it."

"I can't."

"Promise you'll tell me if you go anywhere. We all need you."

"Maybe once you did. But I can't help you like I did before. How can you ever trust me again?"

"I never stopped trusting you."

Her words meant nothing. "But you don't understand. I've always had a special ability. It was a gift, to be able to help people in a special way. You knew that."

Shelby looked blank. "Well, that's what you do. Who you are."

Grace groaned. No one understood. "But it's gone now. It's more than gone. It's like it's turning against me."

* * * *

Lena was of little support, either, when Grace called her.

"You went to medical school for a reason," Lena reminded her. "Use that knowledge like you always have."

"But, what about… I mean, why would God take away—"

"Grace." Lena sounded hesitant, reluctant to speak of Woodside even over the telephone. "You know I love you, right? You know I would never, ever say anything hurtful, but I only want to help you." A gusty sigh apologetically crossed the communication lines. "You sometimes treated the gift like a magic touch, or something."

"What?" Grace choked against the tears. How could Lena turn on her?

"Not in a bad way, though. I mean, we all respected how the Lord blessed you with the healing touch, and we stood in awe of you, too."

"Until they all died, you mean," Grace said slowly, enunciating each word. The numbness in her hands traveled toward her lips. "Until I couldn't help those who were closest to me, and they died."

"I wish you had never gone away like that, after Jonathan," Lena said. "A vacation or something, yes. But you hurt us when you left. We cared about you. You were family."

"I'm sorry," Grace whispered, the tears starting again. Self-pity. Didn't she deserve that much? Why could she cry and not feel it? She touched her face and stared at her hand.

"I'm sorry, too," Lena told her. "Look, why don't I come up there, visit a while?"

"I don't know, maybe. That would be nice. Maybe—can I call you in a couple of weeks?"

"Sure."

It took both hands to press the off button. A visit? Was that all Tennessee was anymore? A place to visit?

Surely her mother-in-law wouldn't feel the same. Grace reached for a piece of paper and pen and started a letter. She'd start with the niceties, facts, observations.

Eddy is in First Grade, putting the letters together, forming sentences. Addition and soon, subtraction. Things Sean would have been learning about now. I can't believe I have a chance to see it happening, even with someone else's child. That's truly a blessing for me.

She could see that, now. She was getting another chance to make it up to Sean. Eddy was the gift she needed to redeem herself back in Woodside. She would show them she wasn't a failure in everything she tried. She tapped the pen against the page. She looked out of the living room window where leaves curled and skittered across the yard and road.

I'm glad I came back to visit last spring. It was time to put some of those bitter and frightened feelings to rest, to see you again. I look back at that time, over a year ago, and wonder what I was so afraid of. Anyhow, it's been good to experience a different part of the country. Though Jonathan and I got to travel some on vacations and meetings, and went to school over in Greenville, it's not like staying somewhere long enough to soak up the culture.

Yes, it gets really cold and yes, there's a ton of snow and rain in Michigan, but you'd love all the marvelous fruit we pick. I know I've said it before, but you can hardly believe it! And the fresh fish here on the Bay is indescribable.

Elizabeth would understand how she felt. Michigan was nice. But it wasn't like Woodside. If anyone would welcome her back, it would be Elizabeth.

Ted's not doing so well. I guess I've told you about him. No one can fix on a particular diagnosis, and I think it's past the time where an effective medical cure can be found. I've taken a leave from the clinic.

But I'm so unsure of my purpose. I thought God wanted me to heal him, but my touch, well, it doesn't work anymore. Now I'm hanging on doing death watch like the rest of the people around here who know the Marshalls.

Maybe she could still help people, even if she couldn't touch them and help their physical wounds to heal. She could try when she returned to Tennessee. Would they understand? Would Eddy? Eddy needed her. But Jonathan had taken her heart to the grave. Who did she think she was kidding when she thought she could love Ted? It wasn't fair. Not fair to Jonathan. He wouldn't like that. She would tell Ted it had all been a mistake. He could not love her, either. Next time he said it, she'd tell him so.

So, fall comes more quickly up in the north. The leaves change colors so spectacularly. It's true, that's why people go on tours to see the fall colors—the maples they have up here really do look like they're on fire. I dread the snow again on one hand, but on the other, it's beautiful in its own way. It makes you appreciate having a snug house and a cup of tea to warm yourself by.

Oh, maybe I forgot to tell you. Ted's brother is getting married soon. To his high school sweetheart, of all people! They've known each other all their lives, and lived in the same town. But I guess Kaye, his fiancée, never appreciated what a great guy he is until his son was hurt in an accident, and she saw how he handled the whole thing.

That accident had started her downward spiral. She'd used up everything she'd had in Jimmy's healing. Maybe her gift only worked long term when she lived in Woodside, where it came from.

No, that wasn't true. The gift didn't grow from the ground on Woodside, or live in the water. It came from the Spirit, who lived all around. Everywhere. No matter where you went or how far you ran. No matter what you'd done or hadn't done.

So, at least we have that happy event to look forward to. I think I may come back sometime during the winter when things calm down. I would like to be home when the dogwood are in bloom, definitely. I miss that.

Love, Grace.

Home, home, home. A blast of wind flung ice crystals pinging against the window. Cold, they felt. She shivered. *I'm so cold, so cold, so cold.*

* * * *

Grace telephoned Ted in the morning. "Eddy can't come here today, Ted. I'm sorry."

She heard him clear his throat. "Grace? Are you all right? You mean, Eddy can't come after school today?"

"After school. I don't know, Ted. I think I may be coming down with something. It's better. Better for all of us if he's not here."

"What's the matter?"

The matter? Matter with who? Why couldn't he stop talking and listen for a change? "Nothing, really. It's silly. I don't usually have… I haven't been sleeping all that well lately."

Whoops. Didn't feel that one coming.

"Since you stopped working at the clinic, you mean."

"I talked to Kaye already," she went on, as if he hadn't said anything. "Tanya will drive out. She'll watch for Eddy by the time his bus comes in, okay? I'm really sorry about this."

"Don't give it another thought. I'll stop in and check on you later."

"No, please. I'm all right. Just lazy today." She hung up.

After a dopey, overly long morning in which Grace wandered aimlessly with a dust rag around her house, she opened the front door and walked out onto the porch. Chilly as the air was, she still felt the most peace out there. The sleet of yesterday had melted and gone. She went back inside to grab her fluffy multi-colored afghan from the sofa and took it out to curl up with on the swing.

Finches and juncos pecked at her bird feeder. Dried nut brown centers of the brown-eyed susans swayed. A few purple asters peeped out of the graveyard of a flowerbed. With a stockinged toe on the floorboards, Grace pushed the swing until it matched the dance of the dried flower stems. She had planted a border of small annuals around the outside edge of the garden this year.

Jonathan's irises were bachelor button blue. She brought his memory out of long hiding, faded, but comfortable. She closed her eyes and pushed the swing.

Jonathan reached out to her with wasted white arms and a razor thin face dark with stubble. His touch would burn if he caught her.

"Grace, help me! For the love of Jesus, help me! Or kill me. Why can't you help me? You can touch everyone else and heal them."

Grace was terrified of this Jonathan. The Jonathan she knew never said even once he wanted Grace to help him, never hinted he felt Grace should do something for him.

Her stomach churned with sick acid. She held her gut and put a hand over her mouth. She wanted to run but she could not feel her feet. When she looked down, she saw they were attached to the brown brush welcome mat at their kitchen door in Woodside. The kitchen door had no handle. Grace lost her balance. Had someone pushed her? She pitched forward, sliding against the door, slamming her head and scraping her fingernails against the screen.

"Owww…no…wait…"

* * * *

When Tanya came over to their house to put dinner together, Ted slipped out, saying he wanted to check in with Grace next door and would be right back. "No, Eddy, you stay here. Daddy will be only a moment."

Ted slowly made his way up her front walk, pushing the hated walker, feeling like he trudged through molasses when he wanted to hurry. She needed him. She had not said that to him, but he knew. He spied her immediately in her favorite place, in the swing on the front porch, which they had not yet put away for the winter. She was wrapped up in her afghan, hair and nose the only things visible. Something wasn't quite right. One of her legs dangled off the swing. Shoeless. She must be cold.

* * * *

Jonathan was on the other side of the kitchen door, peering through the mesh. She pushed away from the door. She felt her head. Was there blood? Why couldn't she move her feet? She tried to jump. Her arms windmilled as she crashed into the door again.

Jonathan reached through the screen, tearing it with his hand. If he touched her, something bad would happen. She could not let him touch her.

With a gigantic effort, Grace flung herself away from the door, only to fall at someone else's feet. Elizabeth Runyon's. "Everyone has been given a gift, Grace," she said. Her tone was lyrical, hypnotic. "We all know yours. Go on, help my son now. You're the only one. It doesn't matter what happens to you, as long as you help him."

"No! I can't! You know I can't do anything. It's too much. You ask too much. He's the one who has to…"

Elizabeth's face melted and remolded as Ted Marshall. Ted laughed and nuzzled at her neck when she set her hands on his bare back under his shirt, touching him like a lover might. What was she trying to do?

His skin became hotter and hotter and she tugged her hand away, burned. She tried to run again. There he was! Jonathan reached through the opening at the kitchen door, grabbing for her arm. "Now! Touch me now. Give me everything. Make me all better!"

* * * *

Ted reached the swing barely in time to fling himself down to soften Grace's landing as she fell from the swing. She felt warm to him, and his arms automatically folded around her to keep her from rolling away. She had that same confused look as when she awoke on the sofa at his place.

"What? Where's Jonathan?"

Ted cleared his throat, involuntarily squeezing her shoulders. "It's Ted, Grace."

Her pupils were dilated. From this close he could see the matting stuck in her eyelashes and the blue veins in the thin skin under her eyes. He watched her pupils shrink as she focused on him.

"He never asked me. I just realized. All during his illness, he never asked me to help him. Why now?"

Ted did not understand what she meant and simply waited for her to sort herself out. He gently pulled her over so they could sit up. "Here. Are you cold? It's freezing out." He tugged at the afghan and pulled it around her. He took a deep calming breath and gazed at the setting sun.

Grace shook her head. "You haven't either. Why not?"

It was an accusation for which he had no defense. He looked at her, hoping for a clue.

She put her hand on his sleeve. "Randy asked me to."

Randy again. What did Randy know about Grace he did not?

"While Jonathan was alive I tried so hard. I begged God to take the illness from him, but he didn't. I never realized until now that Jonathan never once asked me to help him," she repeated.

She crawled away from him in slow motion. "Do you think he didn't want to be healed?"

Ted felt a chill that had nothing to do with the outside temperature. *She's really lost it. Oh, Lord, what do I need to do? Who do I call?* He pushed against the step, trying to stand.

Grace knelt on the top step above him. She gripped his ears and pulled his face against her. "Oh, Ted, I'm so sorry."

Me too. "Grace, try and relax. It was a dream. Help me—"

"I couldn't help him—or you. I tried, but…"

"Shhh." Ted put his hand to her lips. "It's not your fault. Sometimes people simply can't be helped."

"But dreams mean something. I know it. Jonathan never believed he could be healed. Maybe that's why he died. I've been so stupid! I blamed myself all this time."

"Come on, let's go inside, where it's warmer."

"Warmer? You're cold? Of course. How thoughtless. Yes. Here, grab my hand."

He allowed her to tug him up the steps. She chattered the whole time.

"You believe in me though, don't you? You believe I could help you, right?"

"It's too late, Grace. No one can help me now." At the door, he held her back. He leaned down to rest his forehead against hers and gripped her face with shaky hands. "I'm the one who's sorry. I should never have yanked you into my life. I just don't know how I'm going to let go. Eddy, and now you."

Grace feverishly ran her hands over his cheeks and hands. Ted mourned for her, frightened he would lose her first. "Come on. Let's get you inside."

"I know this is right!" she exclaimed, once they were both on the other side of the door. Ted, winded from his exertions, sat on the couch trying to catch his breath.

"I don't know why it never occurred to me before." She plopped down next to him, turned to the side, one knee pulled up underneath her. Her hair was tangled and her cheeks rosy. Her energy level felt maniacal. He had only known one other person who was manic depressive, one of the students in his dorm. Had he completely missed that about her? Or could the symptoms start out of nowhere?

She jumped up and paced. "I have to think this through. It's possible this is the clue I've been missing."

Ted feared Grace was still in the midst of a breakdown. Had he brought his cell phone? He poked through his pockets. Nope.

Grace stopped in front of him, frowning. "Ted, what are you doing here? Are you all right? I told you I was fine, earlier. But this dream…" She turned away again, striding across the living room and back, hand at her throat.

She faced him again. "You must know someone locally who can help me, Ted. Don't you know anyone who does dream therapy?" She turned away again, speaking to herself. "Of course he doesn't know anyone. Why would he? But Greg probably does, or Davy. Yeah, I'll call one of them."

Ted watched helplessly as Grace went from one activity to the next talking to herself, stopping to write something on a pad of paper, to fix them something to drink, but thankfully, not making any phone calls. Once he got her to sit down, he turned on the radio to her favorite evening program and she seemed to relax and doze. He covered her up and left quietly, locking the door behind him. He had to go home and figure out what to do. He'd ask Shelby. Even Evans if he had to.

* * * *

Lena's telephone rang about one thirty in the morning. Accustomed to emergencies, she was immediately alert and answered professionally.

"He never asked me," a familiar voice said.

"Grace, is that you?" Why was she calling in the middle of night? "Never asked you what?" Lena said.

"I had a dream," Grace said slowly, deliberately. "I was dreaming about Jonathan. I realized never during his whole illness did he ask me to heal him. I tried, yes," she went on, almost cheerily. "You all know I did. But he never did come right out and ask to be healed."

"So," Lena said, starting to be peeved. Grace could have called about this anytime.

"So it means he never believed I could. Don't you see? If he never believed then of course I couldn't help him! It wasn't my fault!"

"Grace, of course it wasn't your fault."

Now Lena felt the prickle of alarm. She sat up and reached for the light next to her bed, pulled on her glasses, and reached for a notepad.

"Don't you get it?" Grace's overly excited voice rushed on in her ear.

"I think you're the one who doesn't get it. You know what happens when you work with the difficult cases. Jonathan never wanted you to suffer and possibly die if you took on his illness. He loved you. You listen to me." Lena leaned desperately toward the telephone, as if she could make her friend hear her better. "You have to calm down. It's the middle of the night. Have you slept at all? Did you just wake up from this dream?"

"No, I had it this afternoon. On my porch. But I didn't understand it until now. It's the missing piece, I know it. But that still doesn't explain why he never asked me. I would have done anything for him, Lena. I tried. Everyone knew that. You believe me, don't you?"

"We always believed you. And Jonathan knew that, Grace. We all did. No one blamed you—you felt that for yourself. You're the only one who thought you should have been able to fix him." Lena tried desperately to think of what she could do long distance. She didn't know anyone else in East Bay except the Marshalls. She wondered if she could find that doctor for whom Grace worked. There'd been a friend, too, who had a baby.

"Grace, are you okay, honey? Are you still there?"

"But what about Ted? He won't ask me. He doesn't know. How can he ask me if he doesn't know what I can do for him?" Her voice came back quieter, less intense.

"Grace! You can't say anything to anyone. You know what happens. You called me before, afraid you lost the gift, remember? What's going on?" Lena tried to keep her talking.

"But what if it wants for someone to ask? To need it enough? Maybe that's what I'm missing. Then it will come back, and I can make them all better."

She was definitely not all right. "Grace? I need to see you. Someone needs to be with you now. Are you alone? Who can I call to come and stay with you until I can get there? I'll leave right away." Lena began to pull some clothes out of her dresser and make a quick list of people to contact.

"No! Really, it's okay. You don't have to interrupt your life."

"Grace, you cannot, absolutely under any circumstances, tell Ted Marshall or anyone else, about the gifts of the Spirit. You know how outsiders think it's all hocus-pocus or some sort of magic spell. Honey, I'm worried. I'm coming. Give me the number for, ah, that friend of yours—Shelby, right? Just tell me her phone number, okay?"

"No! You can't come! You're right." Grace sounded panicky. "You're right, Lena, I won't tell. They don't understand, here. No one does."

"I do. I understand." Lena sat back down on the bed, half-dressed, closed her eyes and made a helpless fist.

"Yes, you always have. I-I think I'm better now. I'll be okay. I'm sorry I called you like this. I just, just couldn't tell anyone else."

Grace did seem quieter. "You were right to call me. I'm always here for you. Hey, babe. You're sure, now? You'll be okay?"

A little hysterical snort. "Some day. Yes, everything will work out. Shelby said that. She said, 'everything will work out.'"

Grace was quiet, breathing into the phone. Lena was comforted by the even tones of her voice.

"Grace," Lena said after a moment.

"Yes?"

"I love you, you know. I want to come."

"I know," Grace said. "But not now, okay? In a little while, like we planned."

She seemed calmer, back in her right mind. Maybe it had only been the dream. Lena decided to talk it over with Reverend Edwards to hear what he thought.

"We're all praying, Grace, for you and for—everyone there. Elizabeth, Jeremiah, everyone here who knows you."

"Thank you," Grace whispered. "That's the right thing right now. I'm sorry I woke you."

"Don't be. I'm glad to hear your voice. I miss you."

"I miss you, too. Goodnight."

* * * *

Matty's soul pinched her awake every time she tried to rest. After Ted Marshall called her three days ago, asking her advice, she had gone right over to see Grace. Other than exuberance, she seemed well enough. She made sense when they talked, but Matty had not stayed long. Something did not feel right, but she wasn't sure what to do.

She called Ted on her lunch break. "How is she today, Ted?"

"She wouldn't let me in. She answered the phone once this morning. Said she was busy. I don't know what to do. Would Doctor Evans—"

"No. I must think on this. If we can't prove she is a danger to herself or others, there is nothing to be gained by attempting to draw in authorities. I, too, have been so worried. This is not the Grace we have come to know and love, is it? Do you know what happened?"

"It started with a dream, a nightmare, I think, about her husband's death. She kept talking about not being able to help him. That he never asked her to help him. And then, Randy asked her to help me. You must have seen her at the clinic, Matty. Did she ever act like this? Or can you find out if she's been treated for problems like this?"

"That would have been revealed in her records. No. I'll visit again today. Perhaps Grace simply needed to work this out. All that business from the summer took a toll, yes?"

"Yes."

"Just wait. I will try and have her come here to us, so I can see. And Harold will see, also. I think you are too close to her."

"You may be right. I'm sorry."

"Tsk, now. Sometimes too much emotion overloads a soul—like a circuit, no? We find a way to help her release. You cannot be sorry for love. Or for living."

* * * *

Matty spent two long days trying to contact Grace by telephone before she finally went over to her house after work and forced her to accept an invitation to Saturday dinner at the farm. "If you don't arrive on time, Harold will come and pick you up."

Saturday was cloudy and gray with surprise cold rain showers. Matty felt on edge. Maybe she should have had Harold get her. Should she be driving?

Matty winced when Grace squealed the tires turning into their gravel drive. She stopped the engine only a couple of inches from their new maple tree.

She had obviously not washed her hair, or even brushed it, for the past couple of days. There were dark circles under her eyes, and her sweater was buttoned wrong. Grace smiled, but her expression seemed childishly blank. Matty shivered.

"Harold! Here's our Grace, now," she called to her husband, who was right then walking in from the barn. He took one look, and calmly said, "We're going for a little walk around the yard before it grows dark. We'll let you alone to finish up dinner. I'll get to talk with my favorite Tennessee gal before you girls start to chatter up a storm. How's that?"

Matty simply nodded, too upset to speak. She knew he would take care of her. Maybe he could do something to help. Grace gave him a dazzling, if dopey, smile and followed meekly in his wake.

* * * *

Harold turned the light on once back inside the barn. He led the girl over to where the latest litter of kittens mewled in their nest of hay bales. He wasn't sure why, but seeing new life often seemed to bring on some kind of healing for those in trouble. That Grace was in a heap of trouble was an understatement. He had seen a few of the boys from his unit in Nam go bonkers like this. Post Traumatic Stress. Yeah. And no wonder. Death upon death with no time in between to recover. Helplessness. Poor girl. Could they bring her back? He watched her carefully. She had been so good with the boy whenever she brought him out here. If they weren't too late, if she wasn't too far gone, maybe he could reach in there, dig it out and help her deal with it. He would wait and see which direction the spirit guided him.

Grace poked her finger at the kittens. A tear rolled down her cheek.

The little fluffballs were only a day old, blind and helpless. They wandered, crying piteously for their mother. Mother was actually close by taking a cat bath breather before returning to her duties.

When he saw Grace look at the mother cat as if she was angry it ignored its babies, he knew what to say. "Even the most devoted cat mothers need to stop and gather their wits about them before getting back on track," he said gently. He picked one of the babies up to put into Grace's palm.

She took the precious handful of fur and sharp nails, cuddling it close, rocking. She held it to her cheek when it started a wheezy purr. "I don't know what's the matter with me, Harold. Lately I feel like I'm losing my mind. Sometimes I feel I can do anything, and sometimes like I can do nothing."

Harold nodded. "I know what you mean. I thought I had my life all mopped up, a good career, nice pension plan. Then when retirement came closer, I began to panic."

Grace looked at him. He was glad to note she appeared more focused.

"I thought I had worked everything out so Matty and me, we could do pretty much anything we wanted to for the rest of our lives and have no worries. Not money-wise, leastways. So then I went and did something really dumb."

"Oh?" Grace knit her brows.

Harold nodded. "I wanted to show Matty I was so smart, I could make us some easy money so she wouldn't have to worry about working any more. I took our biggest retirement account and put it in stocks— you know a few years back when things were so good for everyone? I got a tip from someone I knew and trusted. And at first things were pretty good."

The cat came back, sniffing about for her lost baby. Grace set it back down next to its mother, where it stretched its tiny body and immediately began to nurse.

"What happened then?" she asked.

"Same as most everyone else, I suspect. I trusted the wrong person. And when the panic set in, so many of us lost the whole thing. Me too."

"What did Matty say?"

"You know, that Matty. She's pretty special. She knows a lot about what to say and when to say it, when she can fix something, when to ask for help." Harold looked at Grace. "She told me she never had any intention of retiring when I did, anyway."

He leaned down and gave her a hand up. "We're both concerned about you, Grace. Won't you tell us what we can do to help?"

Grace closed her eyes and swayed. Harold tightened his grip. She shook her head and looked down toward the floor. She must have realized her sweater was buttoned up in the wrong holes, for she let go of his hand and started to fix them.

"From my experience in the army, Grace, I think you might be suffering from PTSD."

She looked up at him, frowning. "Post Traumatic Stress Disorder? That fits, I suppose."

"You've been through a lot of turmoil, many personal losses and all that ruckus of the summer. Maybe you should think about letting others help you for a change."

"Maybe. I guess I have to learn who I can trust around here, Harold. Thank you."

She took his arm and leaned against him affectionately back to the house where he and Matty showered her with all the love and healing they could provide.

Chapter Twenty-Seven

Matty sought out Greg at the clinic the next day. "All my years before I came to you, I worked in the mental health unit."

"Yeah, it was great practice for coming to me."

She didn't smile at her boss's flat joke, and went on as if he never spoke. "Harold thinks Grace might have PTSD."

"Well, until she goes through the next big trauma, there's nothing we can do. We just have to wait. Then, maybe…I have someone in mind she can see. If she wants to."

Matty grew furious with him. "Wait? Until when? The Marshall boy dies?"

"That's inevitable. After, we can see she receives the help she needs."

"You can help her, you mean. I've never understood you to be so-so pig-headed…"

"There's nothing else we can do. Unless she goes off the deep end and hurts herself, or someone else."

"We can pray," she said.

And to her surprise, Greg reached for her hand, his expression strangely brittle and hooded. "Yes. Maybe we can try that."

* * * *

Grace's healing continued with the prayers of her friends, and a phone call. The card of the counselor Greg recommended sat on her dresser. Thoughtful, but not necessary. She needed to remember who she was. That would be the best treatment. Pull out and examine each stressor, deal with it, and bury it.

Mrs. Webb, Eddy's first grade teacher, invited Grace to speak to the class when they reached their Good Health unit. Grace stalled for three days before she pulled herself together and decided she could do it. Most of the children's talk after Eddy's birthday party had blown over. They no longer acted afraid of her when they saw her in the shops and at church. The past few days had seemed like gelled blobs of time during which she could not recall eating or sleeping or talking to anyone. Mrs. Webb's call seemed to pull the plug of a stopped up vat of rendered emotion.

Grace washed her hair and did her laundry. Those simple chores reminded her of the routine tasks to perform to keep functioning. Eddy! Had someone else been taking care of him, when she could not care for herself?

She waited for his bus that afternoon. He barreled into her arms when he saw her. Eddy was back. She waved to Ted, who watched them from his door. She was not ready to talk to him yet. Soon, though.

She visited Eddy's class at school. Their mesmerized little faces reflected every emotion when she explained about germs, blowing noses and washing hands and covering your mouth when you cough. She showed them pictures of Germaine Germ at work and hoped they wouldn't provoke angry calls from parents accusing her of causing nightmares.

The fifth grade teachers invited her, too. Grace returned to Wind Point School and spoke to the older children. She was more prepared with slides of real organisms and a couple of medical books. She also talked about the kind of education they would need to be doctors or nurses.

Tony Vander Groot had undergone a dramatic personality change, the bleeding incident of the summer now forgotten.

"This is my doctor," he introduced her, having beat out any classmates for the honor.

Neither Grace nor the teacher corrected him in front of his peers. Instead, Grace asked him to tell about some of the things that happened to necessitate a visit to the clinic.

He made the most of a dramatic pause up in front of his class. "Well, I had some broken bones," he said, pulling his shirt collar aside to indicate his collarbone. "Grace put a, a…" He turned to her. "Whad'ya call it?"

"Sling."

"Sling on me, first time I met her. And she told me I couldn't roller blade. But that's okay. I got better quick. Then I busted my knee…" He rattled off his many grievous wounds. Grace hid a smile when she saw the teacher mouthing something alongside his recital.

Tony never once said anything about almost bleeding to death, for which Grace was grateful.

She joined some of the children for lunch and recess, talking to a couple of sincere little girls who wanted to become doctors. Not nurses. Grace wasn't sure whether she grew or dropped in their esteem when she explained she was something in between a doctor and a nurse.

But a measure of confidence returned with that small success.

* * * *

Randy and Kaye stopped over at Grace's house one afternoon before Eddy came in from school. She had not cleaned for weeks and was glad she had at least the living room picked up when she answered the door.

Grace met them with a self-conscious smile, knowing everyone around her had been given good cause to worry. Yes, stressed-out made sense. Figuring out the nightmares were a result of not dealing with Jonathan's illness, or even Sean's death was a major revelation. Harold had been a better sounding board than she deserved. She'd treasure forever their long talks and walks around the little farm, a kitten cradled in her hand and the promise of carrot cake and strong coffee afterward. She felt as though she had gone through a terrible dark, cold place but could now feel the warmth at the end.

"It must be something like Alzheimer's patients go through—missing whole chunks of their lives," she told them when they asked how she was. "I guess I know I had some bad spells, there." She reached to return Kaye's embrace. "Thank you—you and Tanya—for helping out more than usual with Eddy." She sat back. "I suppose you want to know what my plans are, after…after your wedding."

Randy and Kaye exchanged looks.

"This is your home, Grace," Randy said. "We care about you. But I guess we can't pretend there aren't going to be a lot of changes for all of us this winter." The deep sadness of his whole being reminded Grace and Kaye of the loss he could not prevent.

Kaye smiled at Grace. "I want you to be one of our witnesses." She glanced at Randy. "The wedding isn't very big or formal, you know, and I didn't want bridesmaids." She paused. "It's hard, making choices, you know. Tanya and Jimmy will stand with us, as will my brother, of course. But Tanya is a minor and we need adults to sign the license and such. We want it to be you and Ted."

Grace stared at their twined hands, held white-knuckled tight. Who would hold hers? Greg? Matty? She should have loved Greg, not Ted. How do you turn it off and on, forget one man and then another and another? Decide who is best, who might be healthy enough to stay for the long haul or who will be taken away? Stop!

"I'm so touched, Kaye. And deeply honored," she said. "I would be so happy. Thank you."

"I don't have any particular clothing requests, so please yourself," Kaye told her, getting into the juicy part of the wedding plans. "We're having a small reception afterward."

Randy excused himself as the bus drew up. "I'll go say hello to Eddy. Gotta check on Ted."

Eddy leaped into the room, his backpack making him look like a little gnome. Grace pulled it off and helped him peel out of his coat. He gave Kaye a big hug. "What're you doing here?"

"I needed to talk to Grace about the wedding."

"Yuck! Girl stuff!"

"Well, I was hoping you would help me pick out the wedding cake," she said and turned her mouth down and looked at him with puppy eyes that twinkled.

"Awesome!"

They would be all right. Maybe Kaye would have a child of her own, if she and Randy wanted that. They made a sweet little family. Grace brought them a piece of coffee cake fresh from the oven and her usual cup of mint tea to share.

* * * *

Ted's team of doctors recommended the insertion of a pump to deliver a steady flow of medication they hoped would alleviate some of his constant pain. While he was at the hospital, Eddy moved in to stay with Grace. It was easier all around, rather than dividing his time and interrupting the school schedule.

Having someone else to care for helped Grace battle back to face life…and death. She saved up as many precious moments of sleeping, eating, and caring for Eddy as she could for the rough times to come.

Shelby's visits made life seem more neighborly, more normal.

"I can't stop thinking about Ted," Shelby told her during one of them. "Even listening to his voice this morning on the phone. I can't imagine he's not going to be around. Anyone else I've known who died, well, it was expected. I know we've had time to prepare and all, but it never will seem like enough. He's been such a good friend, always. No one else from our class has died, except Frank Reynolds in that farm accident eight years ago. We've been through a lot together. I just can't imagine…I can't believe…he'll really be gone."

She laid her head on Grace's shoulder. "How can that be fair? Why would God let that happen? What can we do to make God change his mind?"

Clarity returned in a rush. Without a doubt, she did have the courage to see this crisis through. Make God change his mind? Who knew what God had in mind in the first place?

"I'm not giving up yet," she told her friend. "I don't know what the final outcome in all of this is supposed to be, but it's not over yet. I can feel it."

While she patted Shelby's shoulder and stroked her friend's soft hair, she imagined taking her faith out, shaking it hard. She mentally wrapped it around herself, knowing it would uphold her no matter how deep the water in which she landed. She was the one who left the path by giving up. "When we're at our weakest, that's when miracles happen."

"I know." Shelby sniffed. "It's hard. It seems so late for him to stop what's happening. I can't bear to think of going on without him. What about Eddy?"

"We all have each other. When we need a hand, or a pat on the back, right? That's important. I knew I had friends like that in Woodside, too, but I was so afraid people expected more from me than I had to give. God isn't like that. He never asks more than we're capable of giving, and he gives us what we need, when we need it."

"So you don't think he'll change his mind? Save Ted?"

"Honey, Ted is going to be just fine. No matter what."

Chapter Twenty-Eight

Trigger the cat refused to move to Randy's house. Since Randy was less than enthusiastic about having the cat at his place, Eddy had another reason to spend more time at Grace's. He did his homework and played after school. As long as she was on leave from work, there wasn't any need to discuss schedules.

Ted's pain was under control as much as could be expected. He described it to Grace as a burning sensation all along his spine and harsh ripples in his stomach. His hands were often numb, as were his feet, when it didn't feel like needles were probing him.

When he could muster up the strength, he made the walk across the yard. Like he did tonight, after spending the afternoon with his doctor. Grace finished washing up and settled Eddy at the kitchen table to practice his writing. She then joined Ted in the living room.

She followed his lead about discussing his brother's upcoming wedding.

"I hope I'm not putting a damper on the celebration. Really bad timing, I guess."

"I'm sure you're not, Ted. Kaye said she didn't want a huge, expensive party."

Ted sighed. "At least Eddy will have some positive female influence in his life. You know, with Kaye. Tanya will be a sort of big sister."

Grace turned up her lips when he touched her cheek. "And you."

Nothing she could say would help his peace of mind. She must not upset him now. "I had another letter from Lena today. The one intern they hoped would come to Woodside found a different position, so they're still short of help."

Ted's eyes narrowed. "They'll find someone."

"Yes."

A knock on the door startled her. She wretched her attention from Ted and went to answer it.

"Kaye! Come in."

Kaye pushed her fur-lined hood back and smiled. "I wondered if Eddy was staying over? If not, maybe I can take him home, put him to bed?"

Grace looked at the clock. Eight fifteen. She made a face at Ted. "Past bedtime. Forgive us." In the kitchen, Eddy sat on a chair with one of her cookbooks. He snapped it shut when she approached. "Find anything new?"

He grinned. "Maybe. Hi, Kaye. I suppose it's time, isn't it? The big hand is passing that eight right by."

Grace laughed at her expression. "Sometimes I think he's really here to take care of me."

"I love you, Dad," Eddy told his father. He took Kaye's hand and waved good bye.

"I'll be along in a little while," Ted told her. After they left, he explained, "Randy's always got the news or something on. I can't concentrate."

Grace sat next to him after closing the door. She handed him a section of the newspaper. "Here's your big chance to catch up on the world, then."

After rattling a few pages, he shifted restlessly again.

"Still uncomfortable? Can I get you anything?" she asked. His face was gray. His tremors must have made reading the newspaper difficult. Grace could no longer pretend Ted was not a whisper away from meeting God face to face. She wondered if he knew.

Ted coughed and jiggled his foot, grimacing. "Tell me about growing up in Tennessee. What was it like in Woodside?"

Now it comes. Forgive me. But he already knows.

"Besides college, I never lived anywhere else. Until now."

Ted's lids lowered. She helped him shift until he was lying down with his head on her lap. She forced herself to study his long eyelashes, bright in the lamplight, against his ashen cheeks. He labored somewhat to take a breath and after a moment Grace hurt, too, with the struggle of forcing herself to breathe out of sync with him.

"The hard part of living outside of Tennessee is adjusting to different customs. In Woodside there is an unwritten courtesy not to touch non-family members." She watched him for his reaction. He did not open his eyes, as if he didn't want to know this.

Finally, with lids clamped, he said, "We've hugged plenty. It's more than that, though, isn't it?" His expression was not gentle as he sat up again to look at her.

She lowered her gaze and plucked at the hem of her blouse with a shaky finger. Her earring fell across her cheek and the tear she couldn't stop flowed against it.

"Grace—Grace, please—look at me. Please, tell me about—why. Tell me about the touch. You tried it that day, didn't you? Right before you took a leave of absence? You've tried to show me before, haven't you? That you can help people—like with Jimmy? What exactly went on there, anyway?"

Grace got up, brushing at her face with an angry gesture and went to stand at the big window to look out onto the porch and yard, able only to make out the dark shapes of bushes and trees in the cold, late autumn dark.

"Tell me what the doctor said today."

* * * *

Ted shook his head, annoyed at her change of subject. He had come home that afternoon from another session at the hospital, exhausted and defeated. He was glad Kaye had taken Eddy home. Back. Whatever.

"Doctor Beardslee took the case to his teaching hospital in Philadelphia," he said, trying to make it sound like a faceless, nameless report. He felt encouraged when she nodded. Why didn't she turn around? What was she looking for, out there? It was dark.

"You know how we knew the therapy was only working a little up to this point, despite the fact I was better over summer. The pain proves it."

He wanted to get up, or ask her to come back and sit close to him. He shivered. "Beardslee and the others initially thought what I had was some kind of virus. And the stem cell thing they tried, well, now I find out it was only for experimentation. It didn't help my condition or cure me, or anything. He confirmed today he can't stop the nerve damage. Soon I'll become completely immobile. They want to do some, ah, some research—to help others with my symptoms."

Beardslee had been blunt. Ted's expected life span with the condition was up, but if Ted wanted, it could help others if he would allow them to perform experimental surgery.

"One of the students had been involved with a case sort of like mine," Ted said reluctantly. "My condition may or may not be a result of an injury"— he reached up to his temple and the scar there— "like this. Sometimes lesions form along the spine, maybe in response…or not… I didn't catch all of it. The gist is, once these things start forming on my nerves, my, ah, 'functions' are cut off and death follows pretty quick."

He watched Grace take hold of her elbows and hunch.

"He was sorry, there was nothing they could do. There were so few cases, blah, blah." Ted was cold with fear and slightly ashamed. He knew Grace would understand the medical jargon, the outcomes. Would she want him to do whatever he could to help others like him?

The hesitation on his part—would she understand? How could he not want to participate in research that might help others? But he did not want to be totally crippled and helpless for the rest of his short life. The drugs and surgery might cause him to lose complete mobility and control of his bodily functions. He would rather be dead.

He looked up at her then, not wanting to admit his fear to her but at the same time wanting nothing more than to crawl into her arms and shake and shake and have her tell him it would be okay. She faced him and held him with her gaze. He reached out. She came closer and took his hand.

He held on with both hands, now, trying not to cry.

* * * *

How could she tell him his suffering was because of her? She left Woodside, unforgiven and unforgiving. Angry, sad, militant, because God had not done what she wanted him to do.

But, now she had a chance to go back and do it over, why did he stop her? *God, I thought you brought me here to fix him!*

Jonathan and Sean were faded, fond memories. Eddy seemed the only one oblivious to her peculiar gift, even the times he needed it. She could bandage a scrape without becoming all tingly and gaga over the unnaturally quick restorative powers her fingers promoted. Eddy anchored her body and soul and did not take anything from her she wasn't willing to give.

Grace thought about her grandmother. A healer, too, Grandmother Eames had been called upon to make the ultimate sacrifice. Was she willing to pay the same price? There was always some exchange for the gift.

"Empathy," Jonathan called it. She had the touch of an empath. He studied the concept at college, though he had to go into mysticism to find anything about it. He had been fascinated by her gift, almost obsessed by watching her at work. When the cancer crept into his bones, she couldn't reach deep enough to find it and draw it out. Jonathan had never asked her to work the miracle for him, she remembered from her dream state. Had Jonathan wanted to die?

He had taken the death of Sean with a bizarre calm that obviously masked his inner grief. Maybe she had been afraid to try to heal her husband. Maybe she had been so guilt-ridden her own parents had ultimately been the instrument of his loss. Naturally, their marriage foundered afterward. Jonathan had withdrawn into a solitary shell until he was able to lose himself in his illness.

Maybe she had been a coward. *Forgive me, forgive me.*

Now what did God want of her, if she couldn't use the gift on this man? How could she be forgiven if not through healing Ted? God blocked the way, like the angels with flaming swords guarding Eden.

She put her hands over her face and talked through them, so she wouldn't have to look directly at him. "Ted, please—I need to think for awhile. I'm not putting you or your news off or anything, but I…I don't feel very well right now. Can we talk more tomorrow?"

If tomorrow comes—if tomorrow isn't too soon—if tomorrow she could still be coherent.

She only half-heard Ted's slow, defeated struggle to his feet to reach the door.

Like Jacob, she would wrestle with this angel through the night, determined not to give up until she found the answer. Would the blessing would be there, too?

Chapter Twenty-Nine

Redemption came in the palest hour; the hush just before the sun rises. The sky glimmered angry and red this morning. She watched the red ball rise as she huddle on the veranda with her steaming tea. Her soul was so cold. Her tears were frozen solid inside and could not escape.

Healing the body could never be enough. The firm touch of a clinician would never be the same as taking their suffering into your soul, cleaning it and restoring that piece of spirit to make the hurting ones whole once more. She could not escape her calling.

Grace thought of stories in her Bible. Jonah ran from God and was swallowed by the whale so he could be sent back to complete his task. Mary, the mother of God, had been asked to do the strangest thing, which resulted in people forever questioning her veracity, her sanity.

She was somewhere in between. A task unfinished, the state of soul in question.

I am not my own. And that's where the struggle ends.

Everyone is given unique talents, she had once told Ted. Understanding how to use them is the challenge. "When the time is right," Lena said. "You'll know."

The time was right. She called Shelby as soon as it was decent.

"I would like it if you could take Eddy for about a week. Ted has some special therapy and decisions to make, and I need to be with him."

"Of course. Just get him ready and have Ted write a note to Mrs.

Webb that I'll pick him up after school."

"Bless you!" Her laugh came out as a bit of an hysterical croak.

Now for the hard part. She had to convince Ted to agree to go with her. They had to go to Woodside. Now. That was the only thing she knew for sure she could do for him when she rang Ted's doorbell.

* * * *

At the Woodside cemetery in Tennessee the next morning, Grace squatted near the weathered stone, hunched against the wind and mist of the place. She was not afraid, but trembled nonetheless. She traced the dull lettering cut into the stone. "No greater love…" She grabbed its lichened edges and rested her forehead against the coldness.

She was not greatly surprised when they found her here. She knew they would come when it was time. She left Ted at the hotel after a slow and painful journey from Michigan to Woodside. She forced him to eat some beef broth and bread when they stopped, but since yesterday she had taken nothing for herself. He had slipped into the immobility that would soon affect his ability to breathe on his own.

Now she was here, doubt wrapped everything in gauze.

"Jonathan's life on earth had come to an end," Elizabeth said clearly through the rising breeze. "There was nothing you could do and we recognized that. I'm sorry you felt so guilty about it. He understood, you know, dear. He never blamed you or anyone else. It's right you come back. You need us as much as we have always needed you. You were forgiven long ago. Now it's time to accept that, and to allow yourself to be healed."

A deeper voice spoke next, less gentle and understanding than Elizabeth.

"You do not hold sway over God, Grace." Reverend Jeremiah Edwards, the town's governmental and spiritual leader, intoned. "You cannot bend God to your will."

He knew her heart then, the secret she thought she had hidden. He peeled her away from her grandmother's gravestone and tugged her upright.

Gentle fingers traced her palm. "No sign of the scars that once marked your gift," Jeremiah said. "No trace of the stigmata you received as a child in His presence. Your grandmother used her gifts as God wanted, even when it meant her own life. Grace Runyon, you are facing the ultimate test. How much do you love God? He is a jealous God, demanding you love him before all others. Have you given your love to another? Have you perverted that love by worshiping the gift and not the Giver?"

"I don't know!"

Little prickles spurted at her hairline. Liquid rolled down her forehead and caught in her brows. Something trailed the bridge of her nose across her cheek, dripped off her chin. Red. Her palms ached. She heard them pray as if at a distance. "We hold your daughter in your loving care. We commend her soul and her gift of healing unto you. It's time, now, Grace. Lena and the others helped to prepare."

"Yes, I know. Grandmother loved them, didn't she?"

"Yes, Grace," Jeremiah said. "She loved them. Come." He wiped her face, staining his white handkerchief. They lurched together across the cemetery yard, bent against the rising wind, dead leaves blowing across their path.

* * * *

Ted lay on a padded gurney at the church, unclad but for a sheet across his pelvis. He could no longer move, but he felt strangely calm. It no longer hurt to breathe, but he had to remind himself to draw in air when dots danced in his vision. Why didn't he care more about that? The peace of this place permeated his soul. If he died here, he was grateful to be surrounded by so much love, even if it came from strangers. Lena, Grace's friend, and two others who identified themselves as care workers, fetched him that afternoon from the hotel. He had not been surprised at their presence or their destination.

He had nothing to do but think while he lay here. Grace had tried to explain to him what she wanted, why they had to come here to Woodside. He agreed to try because he loved and trusted her. This was different than Beardslee's experiments.

He still was unsure of many things. One thing he knew was, if he was to die, he would rather go to heaven than hell. Grace's example of trust and faith taught him that. That much he believed. Was it enough?

Eddy was too young to understand all that was about to happen, and though he missed his son, he had said good bye in a way that hopefully did not frighten him.

The car ride had been hard. The thing that helped him get through it was Grace's story. As they exited Interstate 75 north of Knoxville and drove deep into the center of the state, she told him what her childhood had been like.

"We are a gift and an enigma, one of the oldest communities to settle here. We were a village that rose up together and came to the New World after the elders determined there was nothing left to be gained in Scotland. Eighteen families came to make a fresh start. They called their new home Woodside. They were devoutly faithful to Christ and the true and literal teachings of the Word of God. At some point, one of our priests began to speak of the Holy Spirit and the gifts given to everyone in the church. He told us that the Spirit wanted us to use these gifts in service to Him and each other, and he would show us how to recognize and develop them."

"When was this?" he asked.

"Two hundred years ago. Ever since then, families have shown certain special abilities. Mostly, outsiders would never be able to tell that people had gifts above what was normal. My in-laws have the gift of hospitality, for instance. They run the hotel and other vacation properties. People who stay with them keep the memories of the most pleasant stay they can ever recall, though they can't put their finger on exactly why. My parents were teachers."

"And your gift isn't so easy to hide. You can heal people—not just by practicing medicine."

"Yes. At one time the Holy Spirit worked healing through me."

"Those at the clinic in East Bay, who thought you were so gentle and professional, they noticed their hurts healed faster. People said so. Is that true? But why didn't it work every time? Sometimes, though, after you began working there I could tell you were more tired than I ever was. It's more than making people better with your touch, isn't it? You feel it, somehow."

Ted concentrated on the slow rise and fall of his chest as he lay warm in the church. Others were here; he sensed the presence of more members of the village quietly moving into the dark recesses of the old church. He was not as freaked out as he thought he should have been. Although he trusted Grace, he did not know the rest of these people and the scene smacked of a horror story of human sacrifice. The tension mounted while they waited. Ted tried to wiggle his hands and toes. He was not tied to the bed or restrained in any way, but he knew he was quickly losing the battle of mobility. Then he wouldn't be able to breathe either. Would it hurt? Would he feel like he was drowning or choking?

Once he understood what Grace's gift would do to her, he tried to make her stop. If he could, he would get up and leave. Even if she believed she could help him, there was no way he would be the instrument of her pain. It no longer mattered what happened to him in this earthly life. Now he finally understood death was only the beginning, he longed for something better.

Grace had explained more about her gift on the drive. "It's not magic. Although I think after a while I treated it that way myself. Jonathan tried to study the phenomenon at school. He went to the philosophy department and then the experimental psychology people. Poor Jonathan. How do you convince people something so strange is real, without being able to offer proof? He watched it happen constantly. He researched any shred of evidence of reports certain people, never clinically studied or proved, of course—only rumors—had the ability to transfer hurts and certain diseases through themselves away from a patient so they both recovered. He called it empathy—not the imaginative form, but an empirical form."

He let her talk on, trying to picture her as a child and as a young woman. Had she always had to try to explain herself? And what had been the gift of her husband, if he couldn't do the same thing, yet was a doctor?

"We went to school together, you know," she said. "I earned my degree as a Physician's Assistant while he got his MD. It somehow gave a sense of reality to what I could do, at least to Jonathan. He could accept my gift a little better. But it never changed the fact it was—is—a miracle. There is nothing that will change that. And I didn't regret the learning of course. The knowledge of why God made our bodies work the way they do didn't lessen the awe."

Grace pulled off the road into a turn-around to a view of a great wildlife refuge. She stopped the engine and went on with her tale. "My grandmother had the gift. It started when she was young. But it really came out during World War Two. Captured Japanese were brought into the POW camp set up for Germans right outside town. The army doctor was somewhat reluctant to treat the prisoners who killed his only sister at Pearl Harbor. There were too few medics to help and no one cared much about how the prisoners were treated. Members of the Town Council, Grandmother included, went to visit to see if anything could be done for the men there. Once she saw medical treatment was, oh—less than satisfactory, she stepped in." Grace shoved her hair back and opened the window. The air was damp.

"One and one-half years since you came into my life," Ted mused. "I never understood you and I'm sorry. It pains me to know only now I am learning these things about your life. I shouldn't believe your story, but I love you and can't picture this as anything less than truth. I've been so selfish."

"These are things I didn't want anyone to know," she reminded him, taking his hand, laying it against her cheek. His breathing calmed.

"Grandmother touched the prisoners. Their wounds went away. Twenty years later she healed a little girl with leukemia. Grandmother died. But I lived. Afterward I went to church with my parents to offer thanks and while praying, I bled from my hands and feet"—she touched his forehead— "and here, where the crown of thorns lay on his head." She touched his ribcage under his heart. "And where he was speared in the side. It was the sign of my gift—my gift of healing. I never questioned it. I was proud. Maybe too proud. Maybe I began to wonder who was worthy to receive the results of this gift."

"The wounds don't just go away," Ted said. "Something happens to you, like when you helped Jimmy."

"Not always, but yes, it does."

"And when someone is so sick, has something so wrong, like when you had leukemia, you could die if you touch him?"

"Yes. Jonathan was in so much pain," she whispered.

Ted could hardly lift his arms but forced himself to tug her shoulder, to pull her against his chest. He awkwardly soothed her hair with a hand gone numb. "Grace, you tried. I can't believe Jonathan wanted you to risk yourself like that, or that he would have blamed you."

"Maybe I didn't want to badly enough."

"I don't accept that! And you don't, either."

"When I first saw you, I knew it must be…it must be—right—for me to be here. I thought I just had to touch you and I would be forgiven."

She sat up. "But I was resentful for a long time God would want that of me—to try to heal you when I couldn't help Jonathan. I didn't know you, I wasn't even sure I wanted to help you, or that it would be worth it for me to try. You got better, and I thought I wouldn't need to, need to…"

She looked up at him, tears rolling down her cheeks. "It had been so long since I'd felt anything like love, even for Jonathan at the end. I felt sorry for him and especially for myself. After I got to know you, I couldn't help it. I fell in love with you. I felt more guilty for not being able to remember the kind of love Jonathan and I had." She looked down at her fingers. "That should not have happened. I don't know if I can help you. God seems to have deserted me, took the gift away. What if I can't help you? I don't know that I could go on…if anything, if it didn't…if God didn't let me go with you."

Go with him? But she was taking him to her home.

He knew then she did not mean Woodside. He tried to tell her to turn around. She had not listened, of course.

And now he was here in her home church, in some insane ritual that should have frightened him much more than it did. Where was she, anyway?

So be it. He blinked. There she was, at last.

Ted looked up at her, focused on the halo of the hair that escaped her pins. When he saw the blood in her hair, he began to struggle.

* * * *

Grace leaned over him. "Shh, Ted, peace. Be still. It's all right. I'm here. I'm all right."

She watched him close his eyes. "This isn't as much for you as it is necessary for me," she said to quiet him further. "I love you," she whispered. And she knew everything would be all right, that love was really what Paul had said to his church in Corinth, "the greatest" of the three foundations of faith. Not only love for this man. It was the love that Christ showed; this love he asked his followers to pass on.

Jonathan never really believed in miracles, even if he did accept salvation. That was why he studied the gift at school, trying to explain and rationalize it, when all he needed was faith and hope. But Ted did have that kind of faith.

Grace looked at Reverend Edwards and Lena. The Reverend nodded. Lena's eyes filled with tears.

"This is for always," she whispered to Ted. His chest heaved. She continued, "Therefore, I urge you, brothers, in view of God's mercy, to offer your bodies as living sacrifices, holy and pleasing to God…"

Pushing back her sleeves above her elbows, she leaned over Ted's still, washed-out form. She eased down to his left side, she touched her chest to his, forehead to forehead, nose to nose and lips to lips. After a moment she saw blinking stars in a black background as she realized she no longer had breath. She collapsed fully against him.

Ted's chest began to lift and fall in a terrible slow rhythm again and Grace eventually heaved a breath of her own, shaking. The murmuring prayers from the gathering church flowed softly over her and she could sit upright again. She stood and took his hands in her own, so cold, yet oddly large and strong, the tendons and muscles still firm. She prayed, "When I consider the work of your fingers…"

Gradually, color returned to Ted's hands and wrists. She took them and placed the palms on her collarbones above her breasts and his fingers around her neck, turning into him to do so. She leaned one hip against the gurney to reach above his wrists to his elbows and shoulders.

Grace shuddered as wave upon wave of tingly pain coursed along each nerve ending. She gasped for air. Her hands could not entirely encircle his biceps and she bent forward to feel all around his arms and shoulders. Straining backward, she needed to keep his hands in contact with her shoulders. It was so cold, yet great drops of sweat slid down her temples. Ted's skin began to take on a healthy definition.

She struggled to keep going. Her fingertips were on fire, melting the identifying whorls.

Reaching for his head, feeling his scalp with her fingers, she convulsed and swallowed the shriek as the pain of his hurt traced across her own skull. Her skin tore; she felt it open and dampness tickled her cheek on its way into her ear and then her eye. With a groan she tipped forward onto Ted's bare chest.

She couldn't move. What was wrong? Something was wrong. The pain was blinding, suffocating, and she breathed shallowly, trying not to vomit.

* * * *

Ted opened and shut his eyes rapidly. He saw Lena clearly. What was so heavy on his chest? Grace? She was so still. Please…

He reached up and took her shoulders, surprised he had feeling, that the strength had come back to his shoulders and hands. There. Had she fallen and hurt her head? Rusty-colored patches of blood flaked from her hair.

No. She must have touched him. This wound on his head was an old, old hurt. Why was she feeling it now? Something was wrong. He clutched her again, determined to break contact, to push her away and end her suffering. He wouldn't let her be hurt any worse.

Lena appeared. Why would they let this happen? Did they hate her, after all?

Grace writhed. She resisted his grip and pulled back. He felt her fingers on his cheeks. She shuddered deeply and moved on down his throat, the back of his neck. His skin was so warm it hurt where her touch lingered.

A noise like dried corn shocks in the field whispered from the dark.

"We are gathered in this place," singing voices echoed along the high ceilings and walls.

He could turn his head. He looked at the altar and saw people kneeling. Tears streamed into his ears and hair as he lay helpless, yet accepting Grace's gift. He moved his right forefinger to touch her jaw and prayed with all the strength and spirit he knew.

At his touch, mildly shocking prickles tingled down his palm. She seemed to draw strength from him and moved on down his body, feeling along his spine as she reached underneath him in a mortal hold. Ted's hands slipped from her shoulders to grip the side of the bed. Lena, Joshua, and Mark were ready to catch her.

The four of them completed the task, each of the other three accepting some of the damage the lesions had made on his nerves and the wasted muscles into themselves, helping Grace bear it.

Music, but not music, shimmied along the rafters. "Sorrow and love flow mingled down."

Ted recognized the quiet hymn from the dark womb of the church. An Easter song, he thought, but so appropriate here and now, where the love of Christ was being acted upon in the most intimate way he could have never imagined before. This was worship, but nothing like he knew back home.

Then he was alone and cold. What had happened?

They took her away. She looked so still and white. He panicked and swung his feet over the edge of the makeshift bed. Someone gripped his arm.

"No! Don't keep me from her now!"

"Hush!" The big man, Jeremiah Edwards, commanded. "No one is trying to stop you, son."

Jeremiah's look of deep sorrow and pain frightened Ted into trembling again. He willed himself to look over at the huddled forms on the floor of the sanctuary outside the circle of the spotlight. The congregation was quiet as death.

Jeremiah helped him to his feet and draped a sheet around him.

He stumbled crazily, not yet fully in command of the long-unused muscles. Plush carpet squished through his bare toes. Coolness rushed against his legs as he left the warmth of the gurney to drop heavily on the step to the altar next to her.

Grace.

"Please, God," he whispered and took her motionless and blood-spattered head on to his lap. He heaved a sob. "Please."

She moved, clutching his knee and turning her head to retch. He soothed her temple, which now bore only the red skin of a healed-over wound—his wound—and stroked her hair. Her shoulders shook and she took great, heaving breaths.

"Grace Runyon." Jeremiah Edwards spoke from above them, raising his arms. "You have faithfully and sacrificially, whole-heartedly and selflessly, used the gift you have been given. The saints stand as witness and agree with this."

"Amen!" the congregation replied.

Jeremiah dismissed them. "Go, filled with peace and the grace of God."

Chapter Thirty

Ted Marshall stood without aid and in peaceful reverence on the grave of Moira Eames, Grace's grandmother. He squinted in the chill November sunshine, huddled into his coat and repeated, "No greater love…" He hung the willow cane over the stone and folded his hands in front of him.

Something bright flickered nearby. He watched Grace walk across the churchyard toward him, smiling in a way that sent a surge of heat throughout his body. Eddy wandered along a nearby row, followed by Randy.

It was nearly Thanksgiving and he had a lot to be thankful for.

"I thought I might find you here." Grace tucked her hand with his inside his coat pocket and burrowed against his side. He pulled her against his heart and rested his chin on the top of her head. It felt so good to be strong again, to feel his feet and to take a deep breath without pain. To walk without help. To swing Eddy high and hear him giggle.

"Oh, you think? Well, I was paying my respects," he said.

Her nose was cold. He felt it through his shirt. There was a question he had to ask before he could leave this place. "It wasn't just for me, was it?" He recognized his need to know as both a plea for forgiveness and for understanding.

"Would it matter if you were the only person ever to receive healing? Is that what you're really asking?" She pulled back. He drank in her expression. "In the here and now this miracle was for me, too, and for all the others we will meet in the future. We aren't supposed to go around shouting about what we don't really understand and appreciate." She cocked her head at him. "And I think we both have a much better appreciation of love."

That answer he could accept. "I agree."

He jerked his head and nodded in a direction over her shoulder. "I actually started out over there."

She didn't turn her head to see which grave he meant, stiffened in a defensive posture. He regretted his comment when she tugged her hand from his.

"Had a good conversation, then?" she asked.

He wasn't going to back down now. "As a matter of fact, yes. Yes we did." Ted kept hold of her hand and gave her a little shake. She had to understand him, too. He had been given the gift of another chance to make something of himself. This time, he would get it right. He would not let her down.

She widened her eyes in mock surprise and touched his cheek. "Hmm, maybe you got too much healing."

Ted pulled her around closer, nuzzling her ear. "It's not a joke. I told him I was sorry. And I am! I also asked him, um, you know." Ted looked up and away, searching for Eddy.

"Go on," she demanded.

"Um, yeah, well, I asked if it was all right with him." He grimaced. She had already agreed to marry him and Eddy. He did not understand why he was nervous about this conversation.

"If what was all right?"

She wasn't going to make this easy. Okay. "Grace! You know."

"All right, then." She let him off the hook. "So what did he say?" She pulled his head back around to her and kissed him softly.

Ted deepened the pressure of the kiss, enjoying the freedom to love her. He lifted his mouth to brush the faint scar at her temple, the new one that matched his. It was the only remaining outward sign of her sacrifice. No jealousy in heaven, she had once told him. He believed it at last. Ted hugged her tightly.

"He said he understood. And it's okay." He tugged at her hand. "Come on, let's go home."

Discussion Guide

1. What kind of a person was Grace? How well did you get to know her? How did she feel about and use her gifts?

2. How did the personalities of Grace, Ted, and Randy support their actions?

3. How did Greg Evans and Matty van Ooyen fit into Grace's life?

4. To what did Shelby credit her successful pregnancy? Do you think Grace agreed?

5. Have you ever faced a traumatic situation like Grace's, where you just wanted to run away? Why do you think she took all the blame for her husband's death?

6. In what ways did the people of East Bay need Grace? Did she meet their needs? How or how not?

7. How did Grace need the people of East Bay? In what ways did they support her or not support her? Is your community similar or different to East Bay?

8. How did you feel when Grace finally let the past catch up with her?

Was her reaction a surprise? Did she need to go through that experience in order to reach out to Ted?

9. What were the main issues in the story? How do they compare to other books you or your group has read?

10. How was the Petoskey stone significant to the story?

11. Did the setting work to frame the scope of the story?

12. How easy or difficult was it to follow the course of the story?

13. How did the title serve the book's theme?

About the Author

Lisa Lickel lives with her husband in an old house built by a Great Lakes ship captain, collects dragons and enjoys travel. Besides novels, she writes short stories, magazine articles and radio theater. Lisa is an avid book reviewer, a freelance editor, a writing mentor, blogger and reviewer. She belongs to the Chicago Writers Association, is vice president of Novel-in-Progress Bookcamp & Writers Retreat, loves to visit with book clubs, and to encourage new writers. Find more on www.LisaLickel.com.

Follow her on twitter, @lisajlickel,

Facebook.com/lisalickelauthor, and

Goodreads.com/lisalickel

Books by Lisa J. Lickel

Available at MuseItUp Publishing and all reputable retailers

The Buried Treasure Series
The Last Bequest
The Map Quilt
The Newspaper Code

Centrifugal Force

Others:
Meander Scar – Grace Award winner
A Summer in Oakville
Brave New Century
The Last Detail
UnderStory

First Children of Farmington early reader series
The Potawatomi Boy
The German Girl
The Saxon Boy – Jade Ring winner
The German Girl
The Yankee Boy
The French Girl

Did you enjoy *Healing Grace*? If so, please help us spread the word about Lisa J. Lickel and MuseItUp Publishing.

It's as easy as:

•Recommend the book to your family and friends
•Post a review
•Tweet and Facebook about the book and author

Thank you
MuseItUp Publishing